Praise for *Stories from Suffragette City*

"As we approach the one hundredth anniversary of the first time women voted in a presidential race, how fitting it is to read short stories that illuminate one event that helped women achieve that right: a historic women's march in New York City in 1915. This book's collection includes authors whose work I devour—from Dolen Perkins-Valdez to Chris Bohjalian to Christina Baker Kline—and here they are, all in one place."

—Tori Whitaker for *Parade*

"A landmark 1915 protest for women's suffrage is the setting for the dozen short stories in this rousing anthology. . . . A diverse range of vivid characters brings human faces to a historical protest march."

—*Kirkus Reviews*

"[*Stories from Suffragette City*] gives assured voice and intriguing dimension to the actors of a pivotal era."

—*Publishers Weekly*

Stories from
Suffragette City

Stories from Suffragette City

Edited by

M. J. Rose and Fiona Davis

A HOLT PAPERBACK
HENRY HOLT AND COMPANY
NEW YORK

Holt Paperbacks
Henry Holt and Company
Publishers since 1866
120 Broadway
New York, New York 10271
www.henryholt.com

Distributed in Canada by Raincoast Book Distribution Limited

The Library of Congress has cataloged the hardcover edition as follows:

Names: Rose, M. J., 1953– editor. | Davis, Fiona, 1966– editor.
Title: Stories from suffragette city / edited by M. J. Rose and Fiona Davis.
Description: First edition. | New York : Henry Holt and Company, 2020.
Identifiers: LCCN 2020005019 (print) | LCCN 2020005020 (ebook) |
    ISBN 9781250241320 (hardback) | ISBN 9781250241337 (ebook)
Subjects: LCSH: Women—Suffrage—United States—Fiction. | Women—New York
    (State)—New York—Fiction. | Suffragists—Fiction. | Short stories, American.
Classification: LCC PS648.W6 S86 2020 (print) | LCC PS648.W6 (ebook) |
    DDC 813/.01083522—dc23
LC record available at https://lccn.loc.gov/2020005019
LC ebook record available at https://lccn.loc.gov/2020005020

ISBN: 9781250241344

Our books may be purchased in bulk for promotional, educational, or business use.
Please contact your local bookseller or the Macmillan Corporate and Premium
Sales Department at (800) 221-7945, extension 5442, or by e-mail at
MacmillanSpecialMarkets@macmillan.com.

Originally published in hardcover in 2020 by Henry Holt and Company

First Holt Paperbacks Edition 2022

Designed by Meryl Sussman Levavi

Map by Laura Hartman Maestro

Printed in the United States of America

1   3   5   7   9   10   8   6   4   2

For the women of the past who fought so hard for the Nineteenth Amendment, and those who continue fighting today to secure voting rights for all.

The best protection any woman can have . . . courage.
—ELIZABETH CADY STANTON

Contents

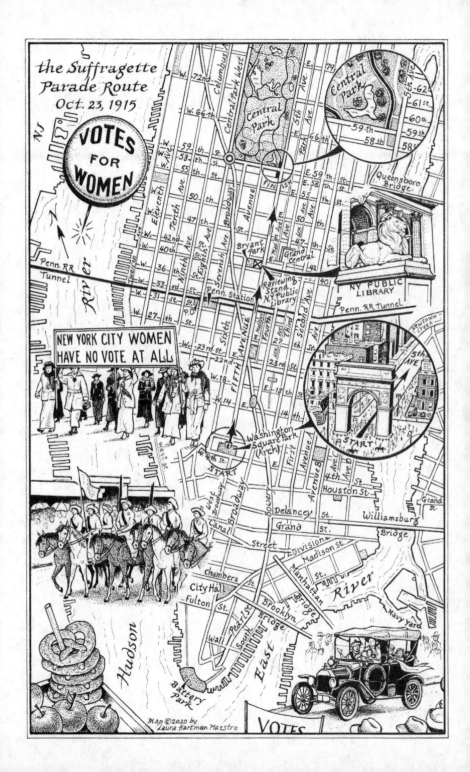

Introduction

✠

Kristin Hannah

I still remember the first time I voted for the president of the United States. It's such a crucial rite of passage, a pivotal pause on the road to adulthood. I remember reading newspaper articles in detail, listening to speeches, asking opinions of everyone I respected. I wanted desperately to be informed. I was in college at the time, at a large public university, and the upcoming election was big news. We painted posters and canvassed neighborhoods and put politics first in the school newspaper. Groups gathered after class to galvanize voters and encourage others to get involved. And then there was the actual day: walking into the room, presenting my voter registration card, and—at last—casting my vote.

But did I think about *how* I came to be casting my vote? At that age, I doubt it (although I'm sure my mother tried to tell me). Now, so many years later, I know how important a moment that was, both for me personally and in the context of women's history in America.

This year marks the one hundredth anniversary of the passage of the Nineteenth Amendment to the United States Constitution, which states that, "The right of citizens of the United States to vote shall not be denied or abridged by the United States or by any State on account of sex." Like all movements of its kind, the push toward gender equality has been, and remains, a multifront challenge, but there is little doubt that the right to vote—and to have a voice in the democratic process—is fundamental for success. There can be no equality in a democratic society in which the government listens to only some of its citizens.

In the past one hundred years there has been so much change in lifestyle, in technology, in transportation that the "old days" can seem distant and a little unreal. It's all too easy to forget the battles fought along the way and take for granted the hard-won victories. That's why it's especially important to remember and celebrate the women who fought bravely and paid dearly for their cause, and to teach our sons and daughters about the past.

Change in any political system comes at a cost, and women's suffrage is no exception. Words weren't enough to change the status quo and upset the long-accepted tenets of the system. Many women chose the dangerous practice of civil disobedience: they put their lives and their freedom on the line for their beliefs. Women were arrested and thrown in jail. They were force-fed when they went on hunger strikes. In many parts of the country, the passage of the Nineteenth Amendment was only the beginning. It would take years before all women in America, especially women of color, had both the legal right to vote and the actual ability to cast ballots in every state. The ability to vote, and to access the polls, are fights we still face. But the passage of the amendment allowed women to have a voice in the democratic process for the first time and caused a seismic shift in the political landscape.

The difficulties women faced in gaining the vote, like much of women's history, are often overlooked or forgotten or marginalized. Many younger women do not even know the story of the movement. It behooves us all to make a concerted effort to commemorate the triumphs of women and to tell their stories to the next generation. Victories cannot be taken for granted. There are still battles to be fought for the advancement of women's rights, and in remembering the women who came before, and how far we've come, we find the strength to continue.

Legislation is an important first step. The opening of the gate, so to speak. But in times like these, when the country is deeply divided, more is required of people. It is not enough to have the vote. We must exercise that right with conviction and keep in mind the great power that lies within the right to vote. Simply, we must honor the women who fought for this right by voting in our elections and continuing the fight for equal rights.

This collection, written by some of the most celebrated authors writing today, commemorates and celebrates the battles women faced in fighting for the Nineteenth Amendment. The stories focus on women of different ages, different backgrounds, different ethnicities, as well as on the contributions made by men who supported the cause. These talented authors bring the powerful, important, emotional tales of the suffrage movement alive. In reading these stories as a collection, I was struck by the importance of the message. We are often reminded that those who forget the past are doomed to repeat it, and I believe deeply in the truth of that sentiment. Few things are as vital as remembering and passing on history to future generations.

History is not a set of dry facts in a dusty old book. We keep the past alive by remembering the people who lived it, who fought for a more equal world and who paid for their convictions. This short story collection celebrates the women who fought for our voices to be heard. By voting, we join the ghosts of the women who came before us in the fight to make the world a better place for our children and grandchildren.

Stories from
Suffragette City

Apple Season

Lisa Wingate

It is, at least, apple season. That one thing might save them. Although whether it can is yet uncertain. The orchard Grandmother planted long ago on the mountain's craggy slopes has gone wild and spindly, without enough hands to tend it for three seasons now.

Still, the hardy little trees have done their part. As September slipped into October and New York's Berkshire foothills donned their scarves of fog, the ragged orchard came in heavy-laden. Branches bowed to the ground, sometimes split at the forks under the weight of the ripening fruit. The trees once again proved themselves to be the kind of scrappy, determined things able to survive on the rough-hewn hillsides high above the Hudson Valley, hidden away to themselves, never having much need of outsiders.

Except this season, there is need. Little else *but* need.

Outsiders won't come to the apples. That was what Ashmea had told herself weeks ago when the apples began bursting with color. *Something's got to be done before the crop goes to waste.*

She knew, without anyone telling her, that not one apple can be lost when apples are all you have to get by until . . .

Until . . .

Until always ended in a question she couldn't answer, and so she had tried not to ask it, even to herself, as she'd taken out the tattered baskets and prepared for the harvest.

The question had nibbled at her even before that, as summer waned and inched toward autumn, and there'd been no sign of her pa's usual homecoming. And so with no one else to take charge of the harvest, she'd done so herself. She'd prodded her stepma, Clarey, from the bed and dressed the seven-year-old twins who were neither Clarey's blood nor, in general, Clarey's concern. In Clarey's defense, she hadn't come to the mountain expecting or prepared to be a stepmother. She was only double the age of the seven-year-old twins, Dabine and Blue, and just three years past Ashmea's eleven.

Only fourteen, and already Clarey had birthed a baby that now lay buried out past the orchard, where Ash's mother rested under a marking stone that Ash and the twins had rolled there themselves. They'd selected a pretty one with flecks that glimmered russet in the sun like apple skins. Like Ma's hair. Her *real* ma, who'd fed the children, and stitched together clothes from scraps gathered or traded for, and had taught Ash, Dab, and Blue about the orchard . . . and had sent them there to hide anytime hiding was needed.

It'd been hard to say, when Clarey's baby was lost, whether Clarey would've done the same for her tiny daughter if it had survived. There'd been no way of knowing whether Clarey had mourned or thought ahead about how she'd slip the baby away to some safe place when Pa took to the bottle and the leaning board-and-batten house turned into a bad place.

Clarey spoke in some strange language none of them understood. What little English she did know was poor enough that she couldn't have possibly explained where Pa had gotten her from or if there was a home or a family out there, or anybody she missed. Clarey had the raven hair and dark eyes and high bones of the Indians who'd claimed these mountains before getting chased off to Ohio or married in with white farmers and timbermen. Her strange looks had been Ash's only clue to who, or what, she might be. Pa had just led her in the door one day last spring and said, "This is your new stepma. Name's Clarey. You show her where things are."

The girl had stood there stoop-shouldered and trembling a little, her gaze darting uncertainly toward the twins and Ash, as if she was more than surprised to end up in a two-room house with three half-grown kids in it.

And that was that. Pa had doted on Clarey like a new prize for a while. It'd given Ash the feeling that if things got too crowded and somebody had to go, it'd be Ash and Dab, and maybe Blue, too, though Pa would be more likely to hang on to Blue for work, since he was a boy. Ash might've gone to the woods and figured out how to get by on her own—she could hunt and she could fish and forage—but with Dab and Blue being just seven, and Blue having a foot that'd healed lame after getting caught in the wagon spokes, there wasn't much way.

Things *had* gone better for a month or two, with a new stepma around. Clarey could cook and she hadn't turned out to be lazy. But then Clarey's thin body had started thickening and rounding. Pa had gone off timbering and left them all there to sort things out on their own. Then the baby had come early and died, and Clarey had taken to the bed.

The last of the buckwheat flour had played out first, and later the cellar goods. All there'd been for a while was whatever Ash and the twins could trap or gather or catch in the streams . . . and the apples working their way toward ripe, promising better times ahead.

They'd started picking as soon as they could, a harvest crew of four, fighting off the birds and squirrels and the other creatures that would steal the bounty. Black bears had come at night and roared and grunted, bouncing their weight against the cellar doors, while the twins cried and huddled in their bunk. Ash had sat up in the rocking chair, the old rifle propped in her lap, but the long days and

fitful nights had proven worthwhile, as had the trouble of hitching
the rawboned bay mule and driving him slow and easy down the
mountain to find just the right places.

The sorts of places where there were people with money and a
taste for apples.

Places where a wagon with three little hill kids and a strange,
solemn, dark-eyed girl wouldn't be chased off by people who throw
rocks and wave their fists and stab their fingers through the air,
pointing away from their houses and storefronts and shade trees.

"Hillbillies! White trash! Go on. Get away!"

It's not that Ash hadn't heard the words before. In the far back
of her memories was the time she went off to school one fall, riding double on the mule with the brother who was just a year older.
The children there called them names and pulled her hair, but the
teacher was kindly.

She said Ash was a very pretty little girl, with her chestnut hair
and green eyes. And she said that Ash was smart. The teacher sent
home books and fat pencils and pads of paper with big lines to
write on. Magazines for Ma, too. And even a sewing pattern one
time, neatly traced onto butcher paper, ready for Ma to cut out.

But by early spring, Brother had caught a fever and died, and
nothing was the same after. Not with Pa, or with Ma, or with
school. The books stayed, though. The teacher never came up the
mountain to get those. If Pa wasn't around to yank the books away
and tear them up, Ma and Ash leafed through the pages together.
That was how Ash learned letters and words and saw pictures of
places far away from the mountain, like the factory towns and mills
along the Hudson, and the big city where Grandma and Grandpa
got off the ship from the Old Country before they came north to
the Berkshire foothills.

Those strange places, seen only in pictures, tease Ash's mind
now as she guides the mule past farmsteads with tall red barns
and through villages where all sorts of treasures wink from store

windows. The twins lean over the sides of the wagon, their hands clutching the worn siderails, their thin bottoms balanced on boards propped up over the apple bushels.

"My tummy wants somethin'," Blue complains, and rubs his middle with a hand that's cleaner than usual after being scrubbed with the horsehair brush. Before they left home in the barely dawn hours of morning, Ash had made sure they were all washed up and their hair was combed. *Nobody wants to buy apples from dirty children*, Ma used to say in the before-time, when they'd do this very thing—go down the mountain to find the sort of people who had money to trade for apples.

"Get some walnuts from the lunch bucket, Blue, but just six," Ash tells him. "And six for Dab, and six for Clarey." She's been teaching the twins to count when she has the chance, and this'll keep them busy awhile. Other than apples, the walnuts and a few persimmons are all they could find that'd carry well on today's trip. "Once we sell all these apples, we'll buy something better."

Ash feels Clarey look over with her slow-moving, careful eyes, hears her say something in that odd, thick-sounding language. Puckering her lips, Clarey presses all five fingertips against them.

"She says you oughta get six walnuts, too," Dabine pipes up. Since they started the apple harvest and Clarey found her voice again, Little Sister has taken to talking for their strange stepma.

"You don't know *what* she said," Ash snaps.

"I do *so*." Dab rises up a little and locks her bony arms over her chest, then sits back down hard. It's troublesome, the way Dab has clung close to Clarey lately, like Dab was just waiting for their stepmother to rise from the bed and take over being Ma.

Ash snorts. "Dabine Wolters, you better stop that lying or I'll pop you across the mouth. That's what dirty, rotten liars get." It's what Pa would say, if he were the one driving the wagon. Ash hears him in the words, and even though it's her own voice saying it, she feels her chin tuck and her head cower between her shoulders, like a big hand is sure to come out of the air and smack her hard enough that her ears ring. "Besides, Clarey can't tell me when to eat. She's not our ma. Only your ma can tell you that." Ash adds this, a little more quietly, as they pass by a farmhouse, where a woman hanging wash shades her eyes to watch.

"You want some apples to buy?" Ash calls out. "Golden Russets, Kingston Blacks, Ashmeads, Dabinettes, Blue Pearmains. Good for eating or baking!" Those were the words Ma would yell when they'd go down the mountain to sell apples, back in the times before Big Brother died and things went bad.

"Finest apples in three counties!" Dabine adds, and Ash's throat prickles and tears well up in her eyes. She didn't even know Dab had learned those words from Ma. Seems like Dab would've been too young to remember Ma used to say that of the apples. "'Specially the Dabinettes!" Dab tosses in.

Blue throws back his head, his red-brown hair catching the sun. "And the Blue Pearmains!" They've played this game a hundred times in the orchard. Each of them has a special love for the trees Ma picked to be their particular namesakes.

The farm wife waits until they're almost past the yard fence before she cups a hand to her mouth and answers, "Well . . . maybe a few."

Ash pulls the reins, but as usual, the mule responds in his own time. They're halfway down the farm field before the wagon finally comes to a stop.

The woman buys apples, anyway. They each hand her some, except Clarey, who sits stiffly in the wagon seat and holds the reins, keeping her eyes forward, like she's afraid she might spoil things by watching.

"Your sister all right?" the woman asks, and slides a glance Clarey's way.

"She's our stepma," Dabine blurts.

Ash snaps, "Hush up, Dab."

The woman widens her eyes and shakes her head, and Ash is quick to tell her, "Our pa, he's busy in the orchard, of course. Once we get all these apples sold—which ought not to take us long—we'll go back and help pick some more. Awful fine season for apples this year."

"Oh, my. I hope—" Whatever else the woman says is lost in the noise as an automobile roars around the corner and startles the mule. It's all Clarey and the wagon brake can do to hold him in place. A man in a leather bonnet and eye goggles sits at the wheel, and in the back ride three women young enough to wear their hair loose over their shoulders. White ribbons stream from their white hats, floating like tail feathers on the breeze.

The twins cover their ears and stand with their mouths open, their faces catching a fine spray of mud. They've hardly ever seen an automobile, except in magazine drawings, where fancy-looking men in tall hats and tailcoats hold the gloved hands of beautiful women in long, pretty gowns and lovely hats.

The women in the automobile are like the ones in those pictures, like butterflies and birds, something too fleeting and beautiful to be seen fully before it takes wing again and sweeps away.

Ash wheels about and sprints after them, dodging mudholes and ruts, keeping a view as long as she can. A yellow blanket, tied across the back of the auto, puffs in the breeze. Big, black words are painted on, but she can't read them before the rumbling beast rounds a curve and is gone, its polished skin flicking back splinters of sunlight.

When she returns to the wagon, Blue's mouth is still hanging open, and his eyes are as big as tin dinnerplates. "Woweee! A oh-doough-mobile."

"*Auto*mobile," Ash corrects. She reads to the twins, when they can find the time to play pretend. In their games, she's the pretty teacher and they're the little hill kids who've come down to her school to learn things that can't be known up on the mountain.

"Ffff," the farm wife spits under her breath. "Suffragettes."
Brushing the mud-spatter from her dress as she clutches an apple-
filled apron, she scowls at the now-quiet road, her face narrow and
red. The angry sweat breaking out over her cheeks doesn't match
the coolness of the day.

Ash fidgets uncomfortably, wondering if the woman might
change her mind about the apples. Having grown up always watching for the signs of Pa's mood going sour, Ash *knows* how to read the
clues. Fists clenching, hands slapping, tools banging, red skin, eyes
that scrunch up and turn hard.

Time to run for the orchard, if you can get away with it.

"We best settle up and be on our way, I expect." Ash holds her
arms stiff at her sides, fingers clenched over wads of her threadbare
dress.

"*Votes for women*," the farm wife grumbles, staring off down the
road yet. "A travesty, that's what *that* is. What in heaven's name
would a woman want with a vote? She'll only have to do what her
husband pleases with it."

Ash sends the twins to the wagon with only the slightest twitch
of her head. They have their signs, the three of them. Things no one
else can see. Ways of warning each other that there might be trouble.

"Well, *won't* she?" the woman demands, crooking her head to
regard Ash.

"I guess so," Ash says, and hopes it's the right answer. The one
that won't upend the apple sale.

"Shamefulness, I tell you. No decent woman would go about in
such a way." Cradling her apron load like a pregnant belly, the farm
wife sweeps off toward the house. "Come along!" she snaps when
Ash doesn't follow.

Ash trots after her into the yard, then hurries ahead to hold open
the door, hoping that might sweeten the farm wife's bad mood.
Ash's stomach grumbles and knots up as she gently lets the door
close, then waits on the porch, crossing her fingers behind her back,

praying the woman's apple money is enough to provide something better than walnuts and persimmons to eat tonight. Maybe they can buy some buckwheat flour, even. Fried buckwheat flour cakes would taste as good as cream straight off the milk right now. Better, even.

When the woman comes back, she offers Ash a small muslin bundle, tied up with a piece of string. "Here's four slices of bread and a bit of cheese. You share it with the others," the farm wife says. When Ash tucks the gift in one elbow and holds out her hands, the woman drops in three silver nickels, as well. "Now, you won't get five cents a pound from *most* other people you meet, but don't take less than four. Those are fine apples. You'd do well to go on south toward the crossroads to Patterson and Quaker Hill. It's early in the day yet, and fools will be traipsing off to catch the train to New York City, I suppose . . . so as to see *those suffragette women* make a spectacle of themselves this afternoon in their silly parade."

Fastening her gaze to the bundle and the coins, Ash nods, swallows the water in her mouth and the prickly swelling in her throat. The food smells good, and kindness is a thing so far back in her memory that its sudden presence makes her feel dizzy and uncertain.

"And take care you don't end up like that girl in the wagon with you. There's no good to come from marrying so young." Propping her fists on her hips, the farm wife towers over Ash. "You hill girls. Honestly. You can't help it, I suppose."

The sweet taste in Ash's mouth turns sour.

"Well, get on with your troubles, now," the woman commands. "I have wash to hang. If you hurry down the road, you'll likely catch some business yet."

Ash does as she's told, tucking the coins safely in her pocket and returning to the wagon. Giving the food bundle to the twins to divide, she prods the mule into a trot, hurrying on toward the crossroads, where, if the farm wife is right, they might find people who have money and need apples.

Real bread and bites of cheese improve everyone's mood, except the mule's, and help to make short work of the trip downcountry to the junction.

When they arrive, there's a woman in the road. Tall, and thin, and straight, she seems at first like a strange, wandering spirit, standing there in her white dress and hat. Her arms stretch skyward, hands extended all the way through the fingertips, as if she means to grab on to a cloud and float away.

The mule slows, unsure, or perhaps Ash pulls him up as she tries to make sense of the woman. *Maybe she bounced out of the automobile and it drove on without her?* The white dress is smudged and mud-spattered, and her hat hangs off-center in a way that says something's gone wrong with her day. Her long yellow silk scarf has fallen from one shoulder, its tip trailing in the mud.

The wagon is almost upon her before the rattle and squeal cause her to lower her arms and shuffle in a slow, unsteady turn that shows she can't be one of the young women who raced by earlier. Even before strands of gray hair come into view beneath the crooked hat, this woman's age is clear.

Not one of those from the automobile, Ash is relieved to realize. *Not one of the terrible kind the farm wife didn't like.*

"Praise be! You've come!" The stranger staggers impatiently over the muddy ground to meet them as Ash pulls on the mule. "I am the Reverend Octavia Rose, and I must have your help."

"We don't know you," Ash answers, but her throat is dry and the words come out weak and small. Pa never trusts strangers, and the few times one ever came up the mountain, he didn't take it well. Twice after Brother died, somebody named "Reverend" rode up and Pa turned that man away with a gun. Said nobody calling themselves "Reverend" was welcome. Ever.

"We just came to sell our apples here. To folks passing by," Ash lets her know. "You have need of some good apples? If not, we'd best get on with our work. Blue, Dab, hold some apples up so she can see."

The old woman doesn't even wait for the twins to scramble around and uncover the baskets. "I'll buy all of them," she says. "If you will kindly bring them to my automobile and assist me in righting it on the road. I've had an accident, but only a slight one. Even so, the poor thing can't seem to make its way out of the ditch. It's most important that I continue on my way as quickly as possible. I must be in the city by three o'clock for the parade."

Ash's heart upticks a bit. This *is* the sort of person the farm wife warned about.

But, if she might buy the whole load of apples . . .

"You one of them sufferin' women?" Blue pipes up, leaning around the wagon seat.

"Hush, Blue," Ash tells him, then turns back to business. "Now . . . we get four . . . I mean *five* cents a pound for our apples, and—"

"Yes, yes," the woman answers impatiently. "You may estimate the total pounds and we will settle on a price once the work is done. Is that a good, strong mule? And have you a length of chain or rope we might use to pull my automobile free? I don't believe much will be needed to set her right again. She's a good, sturdy Model T. There was a time, not so long ago, when I would have dug her out myself."

"Haven't you got nobody with you?" Blue asks, and this time Clarey and Dab shush him together.

The Reverend Octavia Rose raises her chin and straightens her hat. "Young man, I have not, and I *need* not," she tells him. "I've traveled the length and width of a dozen states in my day. Served as one of the first ordained female ministers in this vast country and campaigned in the cause of justice for the female sex. I've not required the help of man or woman to make my way, and I won't begin now." Moving to the rear of the wagon, she braces her hands against the rough wooden bottom. Her breath comes in tattered gasps as she attempts to gain a seat there. "And . . . while . . . some . . . some well-meaning persons in the family may attempt to question . . . my competence . . . at this . . . this juncture, I will not be dissuaded . . . in today's mission. Not by *anyone*. Boy, find something I might stand on to hoist myself into this wagon, or gather your sisters and help me in. We haven't time to waste."

"Her and her are my sisters. That one's my stepma, Clarey," Blue offers up, then scampers off the wagon.

The woman studies the three of them, then sighs. "Merciful heavens!" Her eyes roll upward. "I am reminded of why we must fight this battle until we can stand on the field no longer." With a sudden rush of strength, she drags and wriggles herself sideways into the wagon bed. Her lacy dress catches on rough boards and loose nails as Blue rushes around to help and Dabine crawls over.

"No fussing over me," the reverend admonishes, as Dab recovers a bit of dislodged lace and tries to hand it over. "We must hurry to free my Tin Lizzie from the mud. With a bit of good fortune, I will still arrive at East Eleventh Street in time to be in line with the autos and join the parade."

But luck, as it turns out, isn't with them. The Model T is heavier and more thoroughly stuck than the woman said, and the traffic coming down the road from Quaker Hill isn't what the farm wife predicted. An hour passes as they dig around the tires, and try with the mule, and dig and try. As the last great pull wrenches the automobile free, and it roars onto the road, its tires spitting out a fan-shaped spray of mud, the mule's dry, worn harness snaps at the uptug strap.

The reverend inspects the damage with Ash and Clarey, while the twins circle the Model T, peeking over and under, surveying its untold wonders. "These harness leathers are on the verge of disaster throughout. You're fortunate to have made it this far with such an ill-kept rig." Drumming her fingers on the mule's collar, the reverend eyes the road impatiently. "I can't send you off in this condition."

"If you'd just pay us for the apples, we'll be on our way," Ash prods nervously. "We can load them in your car? *All* the apples, like you said?"

But the reverend won't look her way. "It will be on my soul if the lot of you should perish in a wreck."

"If we head back upcountry now, we'll make it home before dark."

"I *do* know my way around a harness." The reverend turns from the road, her blue eyes gauging each of the twins, then Clarey, and finally Ash. "I was a farm girl . . . once upon a time, long ago. Worked to the bone caring for eight brothers and sisters and a mother who'd long since broken down under the strain. I know my way around a rig, and a mule, and the sort of toil that is heaped on a girl much too young to withstand it."

A chill travels Ash's body, but it's not the nippy fall wind at fault; it's the way the woman seems to look not at her, but *through* her. Into things Ash knows better than to tell.

Their eyes lock and hold.

Ash shakes her head a little to break the tie. Why is the woman watching her that way? What's the thing Ash should say? The words that will finish up their bargain?

"I simply *must* continue on to the parade," the woman mutters, tapping a knuckle to her chin. "I signed the participation pledge, and aside from that, it is the culmination of my life's work, this one final push in the fight to free women from their bondage, to give them the dignity of a voice in public affairs and the power of the vote."

"What would a woman want with a vote?" Ash echoes the farm wife's words in hopes of showing that she's not some little child. Not a *baby* like the twins. She *knows* things. "She just has to do what her husband tells her with it, anyway." As soon as it's in the air, Ash wishes she could take it back. The reverend's eyes go wide and fiery. Ash tucks her chin and ducks away. There's no mistaking *that* kind of look and what it means.

But the reverend doesn't strike. She doesn't slap, or grab hair by the handful, or clutch a skinny arm and twist it until it burns and stabs and goes numb. She only looks at Ash for a very long time.

"Transfer the apples to my automobile. Fill the splash apron in the back seat with as many as can possibly fit," she says finally, in a way that leaves no room for argument. "But leave the seats for yourselves. You will accompany me to the parade, in case I should need further assistance along the way. When we have completed our mission, I will pay you for the apples, as well as the day's work, and we will return to see about your wagon . . . and then we will see about *you*."

It's that last part that worries Ash. *We will see about you.* Those words cast a shadow over how exciting it'd be to get a ride in an automobile for the first time ever. "But . . . we've got our mule."

"There was a farm up the way I came, not more than a half mile." The reverend squints over her shoulder toward Quaker Hill. "No one was around the place when I tried for help there. We'll put your mule in the corral and leave a note on the fence explaining. We will manage the rest upon our return. Sometimes, my dear, we must do whatever is needed to seize the day while it is *yet* the day."

Within the hour, they've followed the orders of Reverend Octavia Rose, parked the wagon, secured the mule, and left a note signed by the reverend herself.

"Now, you children needn't worry about a thing," the old woman promises, as the twins, and then Clarey, scramble eagerly into the rear seat of the automobile and Ash slides uncertainly into the front. The reverend offers quilts to keep them warm. "Despite my slight miscalculation earlier, I am fully competent in the operation of a Tin Lizzie. In New York it may be uncommon for women to drive, but in Detroit where I am from, even the most common working families are now in possession of automobiles, thanks to Mr. Ford's affordable products, and the women operate them as well as the men. Even women of *an age*. I am a bit . . . out of practice, since a bout with pneumonia last winter brought me here to convalesce at my niece's home in Quaker Hill, that is all. But I believe the Lizzie and I are finding our stride, even as we speak." She adjusts various buttons and levers, places one foot on a floor pedal, and the Model T lurches forward.

"*Verbluffend!*" Clarey's squeal rises above the noise. "*Ik kan dit niet geloven!*"

The twins turn her way in surprise and the reverend lifts a brow, pausing to glance over her shoulder. "*Ben je Nederlands*, Clarey?"

"*Ja,*" Clarey answers shyly, her downcast gaze lifting and fastening to the woman. "*Mijn grootouders zijn Nederlands.*"

"Well, I'll be," the reverend remarks. "Your stepmother is a Dutch girl."

"She is?" Ash turns to study the stepma she has put up with for almost a year now, but barely known. "I thought she was a Indian. She looks like one."

"Ah," says the reverend. "More likely Black Dutch. Which only goes to show that gauging the truth of a person merely by looking is a fool's habit."

Ash sinks back in her seat as they start off down the road. The car's odd rumble tickling her feet and legs and its thrilling speed barely tug at her attention. She watches and listens, instead, as the reverend continues questioning Clarey, their loud conversing carrying on the cold breeze in that strange-sounding language Clarey long ago quit using on the farm, because nobody understood it, anyway. Now that someone hears her, Clarey has come to life. She pours out a story of some sort, her hands whirling and her face lengthening as tears pool in in her dark eyes and drip onto the quilt. Clarey has never cried before, not that Ash knows of, anyhow—not even when the too-small baby came into the world and never drew a breath.

The reverend listens, answering in soothing tones, until finally Clarey sighs and presses herself back into her seat, looking intently at the passing fields and wiping her moisture-stained face.

"That poor child," the reverend says, shaking her head. "That poor, poor child."

"What'd she tell you?" Ash can't help but ask, and wonder. And worry.

Shaking her head, the reverend considers the story for a bit, seeming to decide how much to repeat. "When Clarey was barely eleven—about your age, I'm guessing—a man came to her grandparents' farm promising that he had good factory work for her in the city. He told her grandparents she would be permitted to come back to visit on holidays, as well as to send money home to help the family save for her parents' passage over from the Old Country. But the man who took Clarey away was not a good man. He was the *worst* sort of man. Terrible fates have befallen this dear girl, and that is how she came to meet your father, whom she believed would help her escape and return to her grandparents, but indeed did not. He took her to the mountains and kept her for himself. I have, I can see now, been given a mission to see that she, as well as you and your brother and sister, are left in different and better circumstances before this is through."

Different and better circumstances. Ash tries to decide what that might mean. *Given a mission . . .*

Sniffling, the reverend moves her mouth as if she's working on a bite of gristle. "You asked me," she says finally, "a question some time ago as we started off on this journey." She turns Ash's way as they slow at a bend in the road, where the automobile splashes through a shallow pool of water and the wind quiets. "You asked *why* a woman would want a vote. What she might *do* with it. This girl, my dear—your stepmother by no choice of her own—is the reason. She and thousands more like her. *They* are the reason we fight. The reason we persist in our cause, though the way be rough and rocky. Until women and girls are given a voice, they will have no rights. It will continue to be the case that the young ones are bought and sold, forced into marriages when they are but children themselves, and that the old ones are robbed of their property and their independence. Those of us who can protest it, who can insist on fairness and justice, simply must. That is all. We must make a nuisance of ourselves when it matters. *That* is why we march."

"I . . . I guess . . ." Ash stammers, and tries to imagine all that has been hidden behind Clarey's silence, but she can't. Finally, she looks into the back seat at her stepma, who really isn't that at all, but just a girl taken so far from her home that she had no hope of finding her way back.

Ash can't help but worry as they travel on, the countryside flattening and becoming less familiar, the farms crowding closer together, then disappearing into town after town. Each time, the town is larger, the buildings taller, until finally the buildings don't end. They tower over the road on both sides like the tall rock walls of a canyon. And there are people. So many people! Wagons and harnessed teams, and cars, and pushcarts loaded with fruits, loaves of bread, fish, hams, sausages. Everywhere, there is noise. Voices and horses, bells ringing and wheels clattering, men yelling and dogs barking, engines chugging out smoke and trains whistling by on high bridges, with caves underneath for wagons and autos to pass through. Traffic clogs the roads and slows the way, and the reverend sounds the Model T's horn, adding its voice to all the rest as they pass into the city.

"Move along! Move out of the way!" she shouts. "Make haste! Make haste!" Over and over, she checks the pretty gold watch she wears on a chain around her neck. She grumbles and murmurs about the late hour of the day. "We'll miss it. We'll miss it." She complains, her face anxious and moist, "They'll be starting soon."

And then later, "Oh, by now they've begun. We've still so far to go."

And as even more time passes, the light dims between the buildings, and the evening sharpens the icy edges of cold autumn wind,

"They've been under way for over an hour now. Oh! It's too long," the reverend frets. "Surely, it's too long. We are so very late."

Rising onto her knees, Ash leans over the car door. "Out of the way!" she calls. "Move along!"

In the back, the twins echo her chorus. "Move 'long! Move 'long!"

Clarey takes up the call in her own language, as well.

Their efforts are of no help. Dusk presses in as the Tin Lizzie inches onward, working its way over bridges and through streets, each more congested than the last.

"Look! The crowds!" The reverend points down an alley when finally they've reached the heart of the city. "There are spectators in place yet!"

"I hear somethin'!" Dab rises in the back seat and leans out, and Clarey grabs the little girl's dress to pull her down.

"I hear it, too!" Blue agrees. "Somebody's singin' someplace."

"It's a band," the reverend corrects, turning an ear toward the rhythmic sound. "Oh, a band playing. In the parade. They *are* still here! We might make our way, after all. Hold tight, children. The autos are last in the parade."

Inch by inch, foot by foot, they count down the distance together, as the music of one band fades and another strikes up. Voices echo along alleys and bounce off walls, the shouts from countless mouths they cannot see.

"Votes for women!"

"A vote for suffrage is a vote for justice!"

"Women suffrage in New York now!"

"Women suffrage in New Jersey now!"

When finally they reach East Eleventh Street, moving only as fast as any one of them could have walked, the old woman releases the steering wheel and throws her hands up, then grips the wheel again.

"Glory be! There they are!" she cheers. Ahead, dozens of automobiles sit parked and ready, their metal skins adorned with yellow flags and banners, their occupants milling about in coats and blankets, struggling to keep warm as the moon crests the tall buildings, and electric lights flicker to life overhead. "We have arrived, after all," the reverend cries out, seizing Ash's hand and lifting it triumphantly into the air. "My dears, we have arrived. I couldn't have made it without you. Thank you for helping an old woman accomplish one more mission."

Ash takes in the cold, weary-looking yet determined crowd as a woman guides the reverend's automobile into place at the rear of the line. For a time, the five of them sit quietly, catching their breath and gazing down the long row of automobiles, dozens upon dozens. More than Ash would have imagined there were in the entire world. Drivers and passengers cluster around the cars impatiently, rubbing their hands and jumping up and down to stay warm.

"I'll bet they're hungry," Ash muses. "Maybe they might like some apples."

"Smart girl. I believe that is a fine idea," the reverend agrees. "A very fine idea. But you children stay near. If you hear a whistle or see engines being cranked, hurry back to the Lizzie."

Slipping from the Model T, Ash, Dab, Clarey, and Blue hurry among the crowds, distributing the crimson and yellow Dabinettes, the Blue Pearmains good for eating or baking. The lemony, sweet, golden Ashmeads are passed from hand to hand, the bounty of the orchard Grandmother started and Ma tended to the last of her days, high on the mountain. The moment is joyous in some new way. Ash can't help thinking that her mother would be filled with happiness at seeing them here, in this strange place that feels like something from a dream.

In return for the apples, other paraders offer sweets and pocket pies and breads and tiny jars of jam from their baskets. The children return with so much that they feast in the Model T together as the moon rises higher overhead, pushing its glow into the sharp, square canyons between buildings.

And then, finally, the time arrives. A group of men marching in support of women's suffrage troops through the intersection ahead. They carry banners and sing in loud, raucous voices.

When the end of their procession passes, the whistles blow, and the autos follow, taking to the parade route in formation, line after line, until finally the very last turns onto Fifth Avenue.

Ash gapes at the rows of spectators flanking the street, men and women of all shapes and sizes. Children propped on their fathers' shoulders, wrapped in scarves and hats and blankets. Thousands upon thousands of people, braving the cold October night to witness the last of the parade.

"Sit tall and wave, children," the reverend Octavia Rose commands, as she unwraps her mud-spattered scarf and hands it to Ash. "Now is the time to go forth and show the powers that be that until women's voices are heard, we will persist in making of ourselves a fine and proper nuisance!"

Scrambling onto her knees, Ash leans over the door to hold up the square of silk, yellow-gold like autumn leaves on the mountain, like the apples for which Ash was named. Laughing, she watches as the fabric unfurls, straining against its tethers as it rises into the night sky and takes flight.

A First Step

✣

M. J. ROSE

GRACE WAS ALREADY DRESSED FOR THE DAY AHEAD IN A WHITE pinafore, black stockings, shoes, and her lovely white coat. Draped diagonally across her chest was the sash that Katrina and Grace had sewn and embroidered together. White satin, edged with amethyst ribbon, the green letters spelling out *Miss Suffragette City*. An appliqué of the Statue of Liberty finished the piece.

"I'm all ready for our parade. Look!" Grace sang out, as she ran into the dining room and pirouetted in front of her aunt Katrina.

Grace had been followed by Ginger, the cocker spaniel who never left the seven-year-old's side, and who now, sensing the child's excitement, was wagging her tail as fast as a propeller.

Katrina, who had been standing at the sideboard, spooning eggs onto her plate, did as the tiny terror demanded and regarded her niece. The morning light shone through the stained glass windows, casting lovely blue and green watercolor reflections on Grace's coat. The dining room windows, like all the windows in the Thirty-Sixth Street apartment, had been designed by her father-in-law, Louis Comfort Tiffany. Not only the windows, but the vases, silverware, glassware, accoutrements on the desktops—everything including her own engagement and wedding rings—were all from the family-owned emporium on Fifth Avenue, Tiffany & Co. Sometimes Katrina looked around at all the beauty thinking that she was plainer than everything in her own house. It wasn't that she was unhappy with her looks, but she was realistic about them. Her husband, Charles, the only surviving son of the owner of Tiffany's, had chosen his bride for her brains, not her beauty. Back then, that had been what was important to him.

"Aunt Katrina?"

The little girl was waiting for a reaction.

"You're the very spirit of the day, darling," Katrina said with a wide smile. "But"—she glanced over at Grace's nanny, Tribly—"it's too early to be all dressed and ready to go. The parade isn't till this afternoon. Let's take off the sash and coat, and put on an apron so you can have breakfast with me."

"Ready to go where?" Charles Tiffany asked, as he strode into the dining room.

Ginger went to greet her master, tail wagging, knowing that she was soon going to get some eggs.

Katrina gave her husband one of her wide smiles and, instead of answering him right away, greeted him. "Good morning, dear. Breakfast looks especially good this morning. Can I make you a plate?"

Charles came over and inspected the silver salvers.

Katrina watched him, judging his mood. He seemed pleased enough as he kissed her on the forehead and told her that, yes, he'd appreciate a plate. She'd always enjoyed listening to his voice. It resonated with his fine education. He'd gone to the best prep school and then on to Yale. Like his father, Charles was a tall man with thick chestnut hair and brilliant blue eyes. But unlike Louis Comfort Tiffany, Charles didn't take in everything around him. He didn't notice beauty with the same appreciation that his father did. After all, he didn't create exquisite objects like his father did; he only sold them. She often wondered if that's why there was a joy in the father's eyes that was missing in the son's. Katrina hadn't been aware of it when she'd first met Charles. She hadn't even realized it the first few years they'd been together. One day, she'd broken an iridescent vase that her father-in-law had given her and been distraught over it. Charles had called in the maid to sweep up the pieces, and then, as if it had been an ordinary white china cup, told Katrina not to be so concerned, that he'd bring another home from the store. As if they were all interchangeable. She was certain that he had to know better, with a father who noticed every feather and pebble and shaft of light, that no two vases were alike. That each had a patina and sweep of color unique to itself, and that the one she'd broken was especially beautiful. But he hadn't seemed to. As the years passed and Katrina continued to study the dynamic between father and son, and listened to the nuances of Charles's stories about growing up, she came to better understand her husband's reactions. Too many times, Louis Comfort Tiffany had adored his glass, ceramic, and jeweled creations and often made more of a fuss over them than over his family, which created resentments among his children.

Katrina added more eggs, bacon, and tomatoes onto the plate she was holding and took it over to Charles. Returning to the sideboard, she prepared another for herself as she addressed Grace's companion, Tribly.

"Nanny, help Grace change so she can have breakfast with us."

The two of them left, and Katrina watched the little girl skip out of the room holding Tribly's hand.

When Grace had come to live with her aunt and uncle while her parents spent the year in India, Tribly had come with her. That, as it turned out, had been a very good thing. As much as both Katrina and Charles loved their nieces, nephews, and godchildren, without children of their own, they were a bit lost when it came to day-to-day caretaking.

Grace was a highly intelligent and sensitive little girl. But being an only child meant she was something of a loner, possibly too attached to her mother and father. She hadn't handled the transition as well as Katrina had hoped. Tribly's presence, though, had helped both emotionally and practically. Almost as much as Ginger, Katrina and Charles's spaniel.

Katrina had taken to teaching Grace sewing and embroidery. Katrina's stepmother had taught her, and she was enjoying passing the hobby on. She and Grace practiced by creating a wardrobe for Ginger, who patiently put up with the fittings. Katrina wasn't sure who was more proud of the clothes when they went out for walks: Ginger wearing the concoctions, or Grace showing off her prowess with the needle.

"So where is it that Grace is going today?" Charles asked his wife.

Katrina put her plate down next to him and took her seat.

Before she could answer, Wilson, the butler, emerged with a silver pot and proceeded to pour wonderfully fragrant coffee into Minton Somerset Green china cups, made exclusively for Tiffany & Co.

"I thought I'd bring her to the march," Katrina said, as she splashed cream into hers.

Charles took a sip of his black coffee too quickly and grimaced.

Katrina silently cursed, knowing from the louder-than-usual clink of porcelain what was coming.

"We discussed all this and agreed Grace would stay home today," he said.

"We did. Yes. But I changed my mind. Grace should be exposed to what is going on in our world. Today is going to be historic. I know it. And I want her to experience it. This fight for the vote is nearly seventy years old."

"Yes, but we agreed," he repeated.

"This is Grace's future. I want her to see women marching, with the men who support them—" She paused to take a sip of her coffee, surprised that despite the scent and the cream it was a bit bitter. "Oh, Charles," she pleaded. "What harm is there?"

"The harm is the child's safety. Why do I have to remind you? My responsibility is to take care of Grace. And of you, my dear. Of everyone who lives under my roof. These suffrage events can turn ugly, Katrina, you know that. If it were up to me you wouldn't even be marching. But there's nothing I can do about that, is there?"

Ignoring the question, Katrina continued. "How many protests have I attended and how many parades did I march in in college? I'm hardly one of the precious vases or lamps from the store, Charles. I haven't gotten chipped, smashed, or dropped in any of them. And I won't today."

"You can't know that. You've had luck on your side. These marches are not safe. We both know there have been women badly hurt both here and in England. Imprisoned! And you are much more precious to me than any one of our vases or lamps. I couldn't bear it if anything was to happen to you. Or to Grace."

His sentiment was heartfelt, and Katrina knew it. She sighed. Navigating a marriage was no easy thing, and she was the first to admit she didn't always get it right. It was like the new car that her father-in-law had just purchased, that she had borrowed to practice driving at Laurelton. Turning the wheel required a lot of strength, and even when you managed it smoothly, there was no controlling the road beneath the chassis.

Grace came running back into the room.

"I don't believe I got my morning hello," Charles said to the little girl.

She skipped over to him and kissed him good morning. Gently, he reached out and brushed an errant curl off her forehead. And for what felt like the millionth time, Katrina felt a pull deep inside her.

At first she'd thought that she had been the one unable to conceive, because it seemed impossible that her strong, capable husband would be sterile. Katrina's grandfather had been a doctor. She herself had been in the 1897 graduating class of Bryn Mawr with a double major in chemistry and biology and understood more than most women about the goings on inside the womb. When after two years she still had not fallen pregnant, Katrina and Charles sought advice from physicians, none of whom discovered any reason for it, other than the mumps that Charles had contracted during childhood. The illness must have made him sterile.

Once the two of them accepted the situation, Katrina brought up the idea of adopting a foundling. She was a secretary of the executive committee of the Infirmary for Indigent Women and Children and treasurer of the Sunnyside Day Nursery. She saw children in need who broke her heart, whom she and Charles could do so much for. But her proud, stubborn husband hadn't been able to embrace the idea.

She had forgiven him for his sterility, but Charles had not forgiven himself. He had learned to cope with the fact that unlike his father, he was neither artist, nor jeweler, nor inventor of a unique style of stained glass. Charles could accept that there were many things Louis Comfort Tiffany had done that he would never do. But there was one thing the elder Tiffany had done a half-dozen times that Charles could not accept. And that was his ability to father a child.

Now here they were. Married fourteen years. And suddenly a child had come to live with them, bringing with her so much joy. And yet at the same time reminding Katrina, and she assumed her husband, all too often of what they didn't have.

Before Grace had moved in for the year, Katrina and Charles had settled into their routine. They were eminently busy between the work they both did—he at the family-owned concern, and she with the suffrage movement and various charities and garden clubs—plus their social engagements, family obligations, and weekends in Long Island. They frequented the opera and the theater. They shared a love of tennis, golf, and sailing. They seemed to have worked out a life that even without children was rich and fulfilling.

Then Grace had arrived. It was different than having dinner with their extended family that included many nieces and nephews. Different than spending weekends with friends who had children.

Day after day, this feisty little creature who cried and laughed and learned and gave affection with abandon reminded Katrina of what she'd never had. And, she imagined, reminded Charles of what he could not give his wife.

She'd thought she'd come to terms with their childlessness but now she saw she'd only buried her feelings under a pile of good works. What had her husband done with his?

"Uncle Charles, I'm going to march in the parade with Aunt Katrina!" Grace told him as she scooped eggs onto her fork.

"I think we need to discuss that, Grace," he said in all earnestness.

"What do you mean?" She put down the fork. She was suddenly on high alert, hearing something in her uncle's voice that made her very nervous.

Katrina watched the little girl start to worry her thumbnail with the pad of her forefinger, her tell when she sensed trouble.

"I think it would be much more fun for you and Nanny to come to my office instead of getting all tired and dirty at the march. We can sit in the window seat and watch it all as it goes by."

Grace's lips quivered. She looked over at her aunt. Katrina could see the little girl was about to cry. And she couldn't have that. It made Katrina remember when she'd been a bit younger than Grace and her mother had died. Her aunt had come to Katrina's bedroom and sat down on the edge of the bed and told Katrina she had some bad news and was going to need her to be a big girl and not cry. But Katrina hadn't been able to swallow her grief.

"I think your uncle has come up with a grand idea. You can have a party at his office with Tribly. Hot chocolate and cakes. And you can stand at the window and wave at me and all the grown-ups and . . ." She was trying as hard as she could to come up with more, and then she hit on it. The perfect idea. "And if you promise to be careful with it, I will give you my Brownie camera! And you can be the parade's official photographer, which is much more important than marching. Would you like that?"

"Your Brownie?" Grace asked in astonishment.

Katrina nodded with all the solemnity the moment allowed.

Grace was obsessed with the camera. When she first arrived and saw it, she'd begged Katrina to teach her how to use it. She'd broken it the second time she'd tried and had been inconsolable. Katrina had bought a new one and had been giving her lessons ever since.

As good as Grace was at sewing, she was even better at photography. Even at her young age, she had shown a very sophisticated eye for framing.

Now Katrina watched her niece's expression go from sorrow to elation. "The official photographer for the parade?" Then she scrunched up her forehead. "What does that mean?"

"Sit down and while we eat, I can explain."

Grace did as she was told, and Katrina described what "official photographer" meant and what Grace's obligations would be if she accepted the job. Which the child did with delight. Over her cup, Katrina glanced at Charles, who was reading the morning paper, having divorced himself from the conversation now that he had gotten his way. He always expected to win and was petulant when he didn't.

Theirs wasn't the ideal marriage she'd envisioned when at twenty-five she had fallen in love with a man three years her junior who'd been more taken with her for her accomplishments than her looks. It had been quite the scandal that she was older and involved in the suffrage movement. She'd expected the gossip to bother him more. But if anything he'd seemed to enjoy the shock of it all. As had she. She'd loved that they were flaunting propriety a bit. When he introduced her to friends and family, he always mentioned how much he admired Katrina's gumption to go to college—his sisters had as well—and to have graduated with a double major. And to be taking up causes. But it seemed as if all that pride had turned to anger over what she was fighting for now. Was it his resentment that she had something she loved so much outside of their home? That she was fulfilled by the movement in a way he wasn't by his work? And if it was, then he was being a spoiled child.

She chided herself. It was unfair of her to judge him harshly. Charles was generous, thoughtful, and very kind. Like Katrina, he had lost his mother when he was very young. She at age five, he at six. They shared that heartache. Charles had grown up with six sisters and liked women in a way that not all men did. That endeared him to Katrina. It was part of his attraction. Unlike other men, he had never ignored what she had to say or thought less of an idea just because it had come from a woman.

Charles also had to accept that he'd been the replacement to the firstborn Charles Lewis Tiffany, who had died as a baby.

Katrina thought it cruel that her father-in-law had named his second son after his first. What a burden for a child to have. Katrina saw its ramifications. Charles wasn't quite the son Louis had wanted. Not creative. Not an artist. Not capable of giving the Tiffany name an heir. Not someone who would change the world the way Louis had, or his father before him.

All that frustration and the sense of being less than came out in ways that over time Katrina had come to dislike. She knew from her close friends that no marriage was immune to feelings of anger and even hatred. It was typical for a couple to get on each other's nerves. But if you were lucky, as she was, respect and abiding love would get you through. Except for the last few years, his refusal to embrace the movement that she was devoting her life to was becoming a real obstacle in their union. He confounded her. Here was a man who adored women and cherished them and trusted them and looked to them for advice and yet clung to old-fashioned notions of protecting her.

"So it's settled, then," Katrina said to Grace. "I'll wave up at you in the window of Tiffany's, and you'll take my picture along with pictures of all the other women and men marching. It's a very important job, but I'm convinced you're going to do us proud. And maybe we can use one of your photographs in our next pamphlet."

Grace beamed, and Charles looked on, amused.

"Well done, dear," he said. Then he squinted and leaned closer to her. "Katrina, what is that pin on your lapel?"

She reached up and touched the amethyst, peridot, and diamond butterfly pin she'd attached to her white shirtwaist. She could have waited to put it on at the march and prevented Charles from noticing it. But she prized honesty above all other virtues, even if it meant another row with her husband.

Katrina had a few pieces of jewelry she'd been given as a young woman that had come from other stores. Upon her graduation from high school her stepmother and father had given her pearls from Bailey Banks & Biddle. When she'd graduated from college they'd presented her with a diamond watch from the same shop. But except for a few odds and ends she had inherited, all her pieces came from the Fifth Avenue store started in 1837 by her husband's grandfather. And Charles didn't recognize this one.

"It's a suffrage pin. Dr. Kunz helped us get them made. A dozen of us have them, and we're all wearing them today."

"Dr. Kunz? Our Dr. Kunz? The head of the gemology department at Tiffany's?"

"Of course. Who else would we ask?"

Charles shook his head. "This is really going too far, Katrina. Did you go behind my back and ask Dr. Kunz to do this for your group?"

"As a matter of fact, no. I wouldn't do that, Charles. Would I?"

He looked almost sheepish except that was an attitude he never adopted. He wasn't very good at admitting he was wrong, or apologizing. Something he'd clearly inherited, along with blue eyes and a strong, handsome face, from his father.

"George Kunz is a member of the Men's League for Women's Suffrage—"

"Don't remind me," Charles interrupted.

Katrina frowned. This was old ground and tiresome. "And among the members are the husbands of many women with whom I work, of which you are aware. Mrs. Belmont went to Dr. Kunz and asked him, and he was only too happy to help her create something symbolic. And what better than a butterfly—a symbol of metamorphosis and endurance. Butterflies prove that change is a beautiful thing."

"I love butterflies," Grace chimed in. "There are so many at

Laurelton. Grandpa planted all those butterfly bushes to make sure they'd come visit, didn't he?"

"Yes," Katrina said. "They're called *Buddleia* bushes."

Uninterested in the Latin name for the plant, Grace continued talking. "Grampa once told me a butterfly was a garden with wings. So is your pin a garden with wings, too?"

Katrina nodded. That was so like her father-in-law to say. He lived to create beauty and revered it. He'd used the symbol himself, in lamps as well as in freestanding stained glass butterflies and dragonflies that he hung from the windows and would give as small gifts, delighting everyone who received one.

"I don't know if I approve of Dr. Kunz creating Tiffany jewelry that is going to be associated with this radical movement."

"It's too late, darling. Just like it's too late for antiquated views about suffrage." Harsh words but communicated softly, as was her style. "You know, you really are a complicated man. You met me—already a total radical, already committed to the movement, a college graduate scandalously three years your senior—and you married me. I told you I wasn't going to change. And yet you've spent the last few years shaking your head as if you suddenly woke up and discovered I was a political creature determined to get women the vote. And we are going to get it, Charles, despite you and your friends who for God knows what reason are scared of us entering the voting booth."

"The reason is that there are spheres in which feelings should be paramount and kingdoms in which the heart should reign supreme and those belong to women—"

"Charles, don't go quoting that ridiculous anti-suffrage nonsense suggesting men are the only ones capable of understanding politics. What is that phrase I keep hearing? Oh, yes, 'politics degrades women more than women purify politics.' Please, that's not true any more than any of those other platitudes men keep circulating."

"Are you two fighting?" Grace asked in a very serious tone of voice. Katrina laughed and then Charles joined in.

"Actually, yes, dear," Katrina said. "But that doesn't mean we don't love each other. Like when you and I fight over you not behaving."

"That's what Mama says about her and Papa fighting, too."

"Because it's true," Katrina said.

Beside her, Charles sighed. "I did know whom I was marrying, my dear. But I didn't think that you'd devote yourself to this quite the way you have. Getting even more involved in it. I thought . . ." He broke off.

Katrina put her hand over his, covering his wedding ring with her palm. They both had their disappointments. Of course he hadn't expected her to get even more involved. They'd expected to start a family. Expected she'd have babies and become the mother she had been so desperate to become.

At eleven o'clock, before Katrina left to go downtown and start helping prepare for the march, she stopped in on Grace and her nanny. Giving Tribly the Brownie camera, she instructed her on the plans for the rest of the day.

She was to bring Grace and the camera to Mr. Tiffany's office at three and remain there for at least an hour until Katrina and her group had walked under the window and Grace was able to take her photograph.

"And I think since you have the camera, you should leave the dog at home," Katrina said to Grace, who agreed.

In the front hall of the brownstone on Thirty-Sixth Street, Katrina put on her hat and jacket, checked her reflection in the mirror, and went outside to the car and driver she'd ordered. Her destination, she told Miller, the chauffeur, was Washington Square West. But he might not be able to get all the way there due to certain streets being closed off because of the parade.

Katrina had a good feeling about today. The excitement had been palpable for weeks. There had been dozens of marches in New

York, Philadelphia, Boston, and other big cities since the movement had really taken off in the States in 1909. But the rumors were that this was going to be the biggest. As one of the organizers, she was anxious that everything go well. The mayor would be at the main reviewing stand, along with state officials. There would be other reviewing stands on the parade route for more dignitaries. There would be hecklers, too—angry men and even some angry women— who, much like her own husband, didn't want things to change. Thousands of police would help control the crowds and keep the peace if in fact any altercations broke out. She hoped there would be no arrests and no one got hurt.

In England, the movement had been much more violent. But Katrina, along with her fellow activists in America, had chosen to pursue a more peaceful path. So far it had mostly worked, but women were getting tired. Tired of the fact that since Susan B. Anthony and Elizabeth Cady Stanton had begun this movement in 1852, it was still ongoing. Here they were in 1915, and they still had to protest and fight and explain and cajole. They still had to put up with archaic notions that women were second-class citizens, incapable of figuring out for whom to cast their vote. Or as Charles had said at breakfast, they were fragile and needed protecting. *Fragile, my foot*, Katrina thought, and gave a deep sigh.

"Is everything all right, ma'am?"

"Yes, Miller. I'm thinking about today."

"The missus is marching. She's got all her gear. I helped her with her banner."

Katrina grinned. Miller's wife was the family's seamstress and a delightful woman. The couple had three young daughters, and Katrina spoiled them.

"Thank you for being so supportive of our effort, Miller."

"Well, the way I look at it, I don't want my little girls to grow up in an unfair world."

"You're one of the enlightened ones," she said, not voicing the rest of what she was thinking. That she didn't know how her Yale-educated husband, who ran one of the most important stores in the country, where women made up the greatest number of customers, who had six sisters, who loved his wife with passion and devotion, couldn't manage to open his mind the way their chauffeur had.

Miller took several detours, but as Katrina had predicted, the closest he could get her to her destination was Ninth Street and Sixth Avenue. She didn't mind walking, she told him, and thanked him as she got out and merged into the crowd.

Katrina knew the map of where they were all to meet by heart. She'd helped organize it. Businesswomen were to congregate on West Thirteenth Street. Letter carriers' wives on East Ninth. On West Eleventh near Fifth were the artists and actresses and dancers, architects, other occupational groups. Some meeting places were organized by profession, others by the clubs the women belonged to.

Everywhere she looked women were dressed in white, carrying yellow or purple, green, and white banners. Some wore celluloid buttons. Others had pinned white feathers onto their hats. The feeling in the air was jovial, excited, and portentous.

After ten minutes, Katrina joined the other members of the Woman Suffrage Party of New York. Almost everyone was there, many of them wearing George Kunz's pins, the peridot and amethyst wings glittering in the sunlight.

The march finally started with a surge at three in the afternoon. A lively brass band began playing, filling the air with the exciting sounds of trombones and trumpets. Katrina felt the drumbeat through the soles of her shoes, making its way up inside her until it reached the tips of her fingers. Her heart pounded to the rhythm.

She felt her eyes fill up with tears as she passed underneath the arch at the north end of Washington Square Park and, arm in arm with her sisters, trekked up Fifth Avenue. She had been devoted to the cause her entire adult life. This was the moment she had been waiting for, and it was already spectacular. They had expected crowds, but what she was seeing heartened her. These were much bigger and grander than any she'd imagined. She couldn't see the fronts of the buildings anymore. In some places, it looked like the spectators were eight or nine rows deep.

Yes, there was something different about today. Maybe 1915 would be their year. Thirteen other states had already ratified and given the vote to women. Maybe this march, two weeks before the ballots were to be cast, would be what finally made the difference in her own beloved city.

※

At noon, Charles Tiffany's secretary, Inez Goddard, knocked on his door. Because the store was open on Saturdays, Charles often came in for half a day and his secretary did as well. There were always jewelers on the premises, too, in case an important client had an emergency. Tiffany's was known for its customer service. Charles's grandfather had prided himself on being available and satisfying every customer's needs. Charles and his father knew that philosophy had helped build the store's stellar reputation.

"Dr. Kunz is here to see you, sir," Inez said.

When he'd arrived that morning, Charles had asked Inez to see if the chief gemologist was in the building. And if not, to put a call in to his home. It appeared she'd located him.

"Please send him in."

George Kunz walked into the room. Right away Charles noticed the orange-and-black celluloid pin on the gemologist's lapel. The words "Men's League for Women's Suffrage" encircled a three-petaled flower. Charles swallowed his sigh and greeted Dr. Kunz. At age fifty-nine, Dr. Kunz was a leader in his field and had been for more than twenty years.

"Have a seat, George. Would you like some coffee?"

"Thank you, yes." The white-bearded, white-haired man sat down easily. He exuded energy and curiosity.

Charles had always liked him and felt a bit awkward about this encounter. Rising, he walked over to the bar in the corner of his office where Inez refreshed a silver urn with coffee several times each day. He filled two cups, splashed cream in both, and walked back to his desk, where he handed the gemologist a cup. Charles sat down across from one of the most revered members of the Tiffany's firm and hesitated for a moment. He didn't want to antagonize Dr. Kunz. Having worked side by side with Charles's grandfather and then his father, Kunz was a part of the Tiffany's legend. By the time he was a teenager, he had collected more than four thousand mineral specimens. He had even discovered a new gem in 1902, a lavender-pink gemstone that had been named after him, kunzite.

"So, Charles, how can I help you?"

"I'm . . . I was glad I caught you in."

"I'm only here for a few hours. I'm marching in the parade."

"Yes, yes. It's about that, actually, that I wanted to talk to you. About this brooch you've made for some of the ladies in the movement." He paused. Charles thought of Dr. Kunz as a member of his family, an uncle even. He'd known him his whole life. Dr. Kunz had been to his wedding. Charles had attended the gemologist's wife's funeral, as well as his granddaughter's christening. They'd traveled together and argued politics before. But this conversation was sure to be more difficult.

"I happened to see my wife wearing her brooch this morning."

Kunz smiled. "Yes, I'm quite fond of it. We created more than a dozen butterflies with some lovely amethysts and peridots. The insect is a perfect symbol for these strong women and this brave fight."

The store's elder statesman had traveled all over the world, dug for gems, discovered new minerals, staved off robbers and thugs. He'd carried a gun hunting amethysts in Siberia. He'd written the definitive book on the folklore and magic of gems, of Shakespeare's use of precious stones, on the history of talismans. And he was a sentimentalist. Just a few months ago, Charles had been to the Riverside Park ceremony where a twenty-foot-tall equestrian statue of Joan of Arc had been unveiled. Along with five other men, Dr. Kunz had been responsible for raising twenty thousand dollars to have the piece sculpted, cast, and installed. The artist they chose was a woman, no less, Anna Vaughan Hyatt. An avant-garde decision. But then, Dr. Kunz was a liberal progressive. He believed mightily in democracy and equality. He often spoke about how poorly the African diamond miners were treated, of the squalor and illness he encountered in China during his searches for jade, of the terrible poverty he witnessed in India. He'd become a staunch advocate for labor and women's rights. So when Joan of Arc had come back into popularity in France and been named a saint, Dr. Kunz, along with steel fortune heir J. Sanford Saltus, decided to adopt her as a symbol of what women could accomplish.

To honor Saint Joan, Dr. Kunz had traveled to France to collect stones to include in the statue's granite base. In Rouen, he'd picked up pebbles from the castle where Joan of Arc had been imprisoned. From Reims Cathedral, he'd obtained masonry fragments from the room where she'd watched Charles VII's coronation. He'd collected rocks from Domrémy, where she was born, and some from Orléans, where she so valiantly led the troops.

Kunz had also buried a time capsule inside the base: a box made of copper that held souvenirs from her recent canonization—commemorative medals, copies of the speeches, and some American and French coins. But of all the things Charles had taken note of, the staurolite crystal that Kunz had included was the most moving. Fairy stone, as it was called, was meant to symbolize the tears shed for the saint.

"The butterfly brooches are lovely, but I'd prefer to keep politics out of the store," Charles said.

"They were not put on display for exactly that reason. They were a private transaction between me and several of the leading ladies of the movement." He cleared his throat. "Including your wife."

"Yes, yes . . . as I mentioned, she's wearing it today for the march."

"What is it that bothers you, Charles? That Katrina is wearing the pin, or that she's marching?"

Charles felt that same frustration he'd experienced at breakfast, that he'd felt for the last few years whenever he and Katrina butted heads over suffrage.

"Damn it, it all bothers me. It bothers me that I can't convince her to give up this fight."

"But, Charles, it's not you or me that they're fighting. They are standing up to be treated as equals. We trust women with our love, our health and happiness, to take care of our home, to raise our children. We ask them to work with us in our factories and offices and often do the same jobs we do. Why shouldn't they be equal and vote for the politicians who will make decisions about their lives?"

"I imagine your daughter is marching?"

"Ruby is a grown woman with a daughter of her own. She doesn't clear her activities with me. But, yes, of course she is. And with her daughter."

"And I imagine Ruby has one of these pins, too?"

"Charles, this conversation is—"

"I know, I know," he interrupted. "I'm being old-fashioned. I don't like all this uproar and change. I worry about Katrina."

Dr. Kunz nodded. "You know what is one of the most wonderful things about gemstones? In this world that is constantly changing, you can count on a sapphire always being royal blue and a ruby always being bloodred. We appreciate the permanence of jewelry, you and I, and your father and grandfather. How a stone is passed down from generation to generation, enduring through time. But you can't apply that to people and customs and desires and politics. They will never be as constant as a hundred-thousand-year-old diamond. Life is what our thoughts make it, Charles. Joy is born of gratified desire. Be it a woman putting on a bracelet adorned with precious emeralds, or standing up and fighting to be treated as an equal. Both make her heart beat faster. As will the heart of the man who gives her the bracelet or stands by her side in the fight."

"Is there nothing I can say that would cause you to at least consider my way of thinking?" Charles asked.

"Consider this. Stop thinking of women as objets d'art made of glass, son. Think of them instead as gems. Yes, the diamond is king, but the pearl is queen—with that touch of feminine frailty that is part of a woman's charm. Yes, the pearl is slightly less impermeable. Yet, like a woman, it has endurance. Every bit as much as the masculine gems. You see that, yes?"

No, Charles didn't see it. Nothing was as hard as a diamond. A pearl could be smashed with a hammer. The gemologist was romanticizing. Charles drained his coffee cup.

"I wanted to ask you to please not sell any more of those butterflies, even privately."

"I can't agree to that. They're not stamped with the Tiffany and Co. seal. I used my own gem stock and paid the jewelers out of my own pocket. You'll never see them in the store, that I can guarantee. But never create more of them?" He shook his head. "I'm sorry, Charles, but I cannot give you my word on that."

※

A few hours later, Charles's office door burst open, and with impish delight, Grace came skipping in, Tribly a few steps behind her.

"There are so many people in the street!" Grace said breathlessly.

She was wearing her white coat, her *Miss Suffragette City* sash, and holding the Brownie camera like her little life depended on it. Tribly had done up her hair in perfect ringlets, with purple and green intertwined ribbons, and had pinned a suffrage ribbon on her own coat.

Mr. Tiffany frowned at it, but Tribly seemed to ignore him.

The nanny didn't work for him, after all, but for Grace's parents. It wasn't his place, but he wanted to ask her to remove it. He was sick of the whole thing. It seemed everyone around him had fallen victim to the madness of this movement. He even suspected Inez Goddard had one of those ribbons tucked underneath her collar, but he was too much of a gentleman to ask.

"Yes, yes, it's going to be a very grand parade," Charles said to Grace. "Now come see your perch." He stood and took her hand.

He smiled as he felt the small, warm fingers curl into his. Of his six sisters, five were younger. Grace reminded him of them—especially the youngest, Dorothy, who had married the year before. There was a time when she used to put her little hand in his, the way Grace was doing now, whenever he took her down to the beach at Laurelton for a swim or a sailboat ride.

Charles indicated the navy-blue cushioned window seat. "Now, if you sit here, you can look out and take pictures of the people as they pass by. I've figured out that your aunt Katrina will be passing by in about thirty to forty-five minutes if the parade is on time."

It was, in fact, precisely forty minutes later when Charles, who'd gotten up to watch the marchers with his niece, saw his wife. She was at the head of the parade carrying a large American flag, marching to the sound of the big brass band. As they watched her come closer, the wind whipped up, and the flag wrapped around Katrina's face, obstructing her from view.

"Oh, no, I can't see Aunt Katrina to take her picture!" said Grace with a note of panic.

Grace had been snapping photos for the last half hour, taking so many, Charles had had to change her film twice.

"Just wait, sweetheart, the flag will blow off in a second."

"But I can't take her picture if I can't see her face!" Grace was distraught.

"Any minute the wind will die down," Charles reassured her as he watched the scene. The wind held the flag to his wife like an embrace. How fitting that was, he thought. She was as married to her causes as much as she was married to him. But that's exactly why he'd found her so fascinating when he met her. Her determination and her enthusiasm, along with her ready smile and spirit of adventure, defined her.

How he wished they could see eye to eye on this one subject, though. That they didn't have to argue about it so often.

Charles continued watching the flag. Finally, it blew open for a moment, and he caught a glimpse of Katrina laughing as she struggled against the folds of fabric.

"Now, Grace," he said. Then the wind whipped up again, and Katrina was gone once more.

Behind him he heard the child's nanny call out in a concerned voice: "Grace?"

Charles looked away from the parade and down at his side. His niece wasn't there.

"Grace?" Charles called as he spun around and looked over at Tribly. "Where is she?"

"She must have run out," Tribly said, heading to the door. "I was reading. I didn't see . . ."

Charles outran Tribly and raced out of his office. He sprinted down the hall and took the stairs, Tribly barely keeping up.

They reached the first-floor landing.

The store was crowded with patrons who'd been watching the parade and then had come inside for a look around. He and Tribly stood surveying the crowd.

"Where could she be?" Charles asked. "Where would she go?"

"She was so concerned about not getting a photograph of her aunt marching. Maybe she went outside to see if she could get one that way?" Tribly suggested.

"Into that mob? Oh, no!" Charles shouted as he pushed his way through the shoppers in the aisles of his store, panicked at the thought of the tiny child caught in the throng of people outside.

Charles hurried to reach the doors to the street. For the first time in his life he forgot about where he was. He'd been taught since he was a little boy that he had to be careful in the store. There were precious objects in every cabinet, on every shelf. One always had to be mindful so as to avoid bumping into someone or knocking against a cabinet. But not today. Every second that he slowed down to let a woman pass or dodge a glass corner was a second that Grace was venturing deeper into the crowd.

Had Katrina seen her? He hoped so. He prayed the little girl had run right up to her aunt. He imagined Katrina being surprised to see her, picking Grace up and laughing that she could walk with her after all. He pictured his wife taking Grace's hand, as he had not an hour ago, and the two of them marching the rest of the way together to Fifty-Ninth Street.

"Ouch!" a woman shouted, as Charles accidentally stepped on her foot. He mumbled an apology as he swerved to miss her and felt his shoulder hit something.

He'd lived in dread of hearing the sound, that terrible sound, that meant he'd been careless and broken some precious object his father had made or collected. The sound that told him he'd be getting punished for his infraction.

He'd never broken a lamp—not even as a boy playing hide-and-seek with his sisters in the house that was filled with dozens of stained glass lamps. Not even while throwing a ball on the lawn at Laurelton, outside the estate that boasted more than a hundred stained glass windows.

Now he heard that sound. For one second he looked down. A table lamp—red tulips, emerald leaves, and orange butterflies—broken, ruined, in pieces, scattered on the floor and on the countertop. But Charles couldn't waste any more time. He ran out of the store and into the street, looking for Grace. It appeared she had indeed been swallowed up by the damnable parade.

For a moment he was swallowed up also. He turned around and

around. He tried to shout over the sound of the marching band, but after the third time he'd hollered, "Grace—Grace—Grace . . ." he knew that it was fruitless. The band played on as more and more women marched by carrying their flags and banners.

He turned around and around once more.

And there she was. Grace, standing off to the side, petting the nose of a white horse. And Katrina, still holding her flag, by her side.

Charles took a deep breath. He hadn't lost her after all.

He pushed through the crowd, making his way over to his wife and niece, both of whom were surprised to see him.

"Grace!" he said, kneeling down in front of the little girl, taking her by the shoulders, wanting to hug her and shake her at the same time. "You can't go running out like that. I couldn't find you. You have to mind when someone tells you what to do."

Grace's face threatened tears. Katrina looked at Charles and said, "She's sorry." Then she looked back at Grace. "You are, aren't you, Grace? Apologize to your uncle."

"I am sorry."

"Why did you run off?" Charles asked.

"I wanted to take a better picture of Aunt Katrina. I told you."

"Yes, you did." Charles stood. " Let's take the picture now, and then I'll take you back upstairs." He looked at his wife. "All right?"

"Yes, absolutely."

Charles watched as Katrina posed and Grace lifted the Brownie to her eye and positioned the camera exactly how she wanted it.

"You look like a soldier, Aunt Katrina," she said. "A soldier in the parade."

Taken with the child's description, Charles looked from Grace back to Katrina. She did look like a soldier. A soldier with a smile on her face.

Grace took another photograph and then lowered the camera.

"Thank you," Katrina said to Grace.

"For what?"

"For saying I look like a soldier. For seeing me the way I want to be seen," Katrina said.

Charles saw the light shining in his wife's eyes. What she'd said echoed in his mind. He repeated it to himself. Thought about it. He forgot about his niece for the moment. And the parade and the music. Charles closed the gap between them.

"I haven't changed my mind about the parade, Katrina, but . . ."

Katrina was surprised by the softness in his eyes. "What is it, Charles?"

"I haven't been seeing you the way you want to be seen, have I?"

She shook her head. "Not for a long while."

"I'm sorry about that."

She bowed her head for a moment, so he couldn't see the tears in her eyes. So he wouldn't know how much that mattered to her. She didn't want to be weak like that, not here, not now.

"Thank you for that. We'll talk about this later. I need to get back to the parade."

Charles nodded. "I'll get Grace and—"

He looked from Katrina to his left, where Grace had been a moment ago.

"Grace?" he yelled.

She'd just been there. And now she was lost again.

"Grace!" he called out again.

"You look back that way," Katrina said. "I'll start looking ahead."

"She can't have gotten far. We'll find her," he said.

"Of course we will," said Katrina.

And they both ran off in opposite directions.

Deeds Not Words

※

STEVE BERRY

RANDALL WILSON KNEW HE SHOULD HAVE REFUSED DOING the favor. Everything signaled that it was a bad idea. Nonetheless, he'd agreed.

And he was, if nothing else, a man of his word.

So he rolled out of bed at 4:45 a.m., a solid hour and fifteen minutes before his usual rising time. He'd barely slept, trying to figure out what he should do and, more important, in what order. Go to the police first? Maybe. Or go to the office and listen to the phonograph again to try to figure out just exactly what he'd stumbled upon. Spying on a fellow member of the Men's League for Women's Suffrage seemed, if not unethical, at least unchivalrous. Yet that was exactly what he'd done. And if what John Charles Stuart had told him was true, then Timothy Brisbane deserved to be spied upon.

Brisbane owned a prosperous insurance company that had, of late, been facing hard times. The fraud cases were mounting in the courts, and Brisbane's name had been splashed across the newspapers, each story raising serious questions about his business practices and ethics.

But that wasn't why Stuart wanted Brisbane spied upon.

"You know he's my sister's husband?" Stuart asked. "She's pregnant with their fourth child and I think the scoundrel is seeing someone on the side. Not just that, but I think he's planning on leaving her or doing something drastic. Before I confront him, I need proof. He's reserved the lounge for a private six p.m. meeting. Please, can you help me?"

Sure. Why not? What were friends for?

But he was more than a friend.

He was Randall C. Wilson, Esquire. A respectable lawyer with a thriving practice specializing in criminal defense. He had a reputation for honesty and integrity that he worked hard to maintain.

And spying on other people didn't seem consistent with either one of those.

As a lawyer, he'd had the good luck of several times using a Dictograph machine, the absolute latest in covert surveillance. Sold by the General Acoustic Company of New York City. Lightweight. Compact. And quite useful. Police and private detectives had come to swear by it. Some lawyers, too, himself included. The device came packed in a simple wooden suitcase lined with leatherette. Inside were microphones, headphones, volume control, and a set of connecting wires with lugs, all able to accommodate different lengths and varied destinations. Everything needed to secretly record what other people were saying. He'd used it enough to know its quirks and, more important, how to maximize its advantages. So yesterday afternoon he'd set it up in a room below the men's lounge of the Men's League for Woman Suffrage. He ran the wires out the window and up to the lounge, secreting the microphone behind the curtains. Then, at 5:45 p.m., he'd sat down in the lounge, with a cigar and newspaper, and waited until Timothy Brisbane arrived.

Which wasn't long.

Once his target had settled into a comfortable chair, he'd left, hurrying downstairs to ensure the Dictograph was operating properly. For all its wonder, the thing could be finicky. And a bit frustrating, because usually a stenographer had to be on the receiving end, listening through an earpiece, writing down everything being said. But recent changes had been made to the technology so that now it could be hooked to a phonograph and the words electronically recorded.

Which was marvelous.

The idea had been to memorialize Brisbane's private meeting, his extramarital dalliances proven through his own words.

The Men's League for Woman Suffrage had come about in 1910 with the idea of openly supporting women in their quest for the right to vote. A noble cause, with some of New York City's most politically enfranchised men being a part of it. Men whose support would be needed to win the vote. Which made a lot of sense as only men would ultimately vote on the question of whether women should be allowed to do the same.

The Men's League would meet from time to time and decide how best to aid the suffragettes. Being involved was risky, since many members had been subjected to public ridicule and condemnation. But hundreds had joined to lend their support. The lounge was where they relaxed. Where men were men and the talk many times turned away from politics to more personal concerns. Apparently, his friend, John Charles Stuart, was hoping that Timothy Brisbane would brag about his extramarital exploits, as men would sometimes do.

Instead, the Dictograph recorded the planning of a crime.

No question. The plot clear.

Somebody was intent on bombing the suffrage march scheduled for later today.

The event had been planned for weeks. The goal simple. Turn New York City into Suffragette City. Have tens of thousands of socialites, doctors, lawyers, journalists, schoolgirls, nannies, scrubwomen, secretaries, factory workers, you name it, all dressed in white, march down Fifth Avenue demanding a woman's right to vote. All ages would participate. From the elderly with canes to children, teenagers, and mothers cradling babies. They'd carry yellow pennants proclaiming VOTES FOR WOMEN, which would dance in the sure-to-be-brisk October air, creating a dazzling mass of rippling color in the streets. Hundreds of thousands more people would line the way. Sure, many would come to heckle—that was to be expected. But many more would come in support. To explode a bomb in such a gathering would be to invite carnage and disaster. But that was precisely what he'd heard being discussed.

One problem, though.

There'd been several voices, and the Dictograph, for all its ingenuity, was short on clarity, so it was impossible to know who was speaking. When he'd hurried back upstairs to the lounge thirty-five minutes into the conversation to see who might be there, it wasn't Timothy Brisbane but Samuel Morrison and another man—lean, hard-looking, with a thin black mustache, his identity unknown—who walked out. Where was Brisbane? When had he left? When had Morrison entered? He had no idea of the answers to any of those questions.

But he did have the recording.

Samuel Morrison owned a group of gossip magazines and tabloid newspapers that made money off other people's troubles. He was, though, one of the original founders of the Men's League, but not among their most genteel members. Randall always felt unclean when around him and tried to keep his distance, as Morrison's publications exploited anyone and anything to sell more copies.

"Decency be damned" was their motto.

And damned it was.

Why Morrison felt the need to be part of the suffrage movement could probably be explained as a public relations move to the women who routinely bought and read his publications. It simply looked good for him to be with them. Randall found the portly little man offensive in every way. Ethics were something more than words on paper. They were a mantra by which he lived his life. For him, there was the law of God and the law of man, neither of which could be ignored.

But from what he'd heard—

Samuel Morrison may be doing just that.

On both counts.

Randall resolved his quandary by deciding to go to the police first. It seemed the fastest way to inspire action. So he dressed in his best dark-navy suit, loose-fitting in the newest style. He preferred the double-breasted, two-vent jackets, as they shaped his slim frame better. A white shirt with a round collar, a maroon tie, and black patent Oxfords finished off the ensemble that screamed "respected professional."

He walked into the 18th Police Precinct promptly at 8 a.m. It was located in a newly built five-story building at 230 West Twentieth Street. He'd worked with its captain, a man named Donnelly, before and trusted him. So he seemed the perfect person to bring into his confidence. But Donnelly was out of the building, at a meeting. His assistant, an officer named Figaro, a small man with a thick mustache and wavy black hair, was temporarily in charge. Not the best choice, but the only one available.

"Randall Wilson," he said, extending his hand and removing his dark-gray bowler. "I'm a lawyer."

Figaro stood up from his desk and they shook hands. The man was short and bulky, and as they met, Randall noticed the pointed look given to his lapel pin. The round metal badge was provided to every member in the Men's League and showed the organization's name, surrounding a stylized black flower on an orange background. Distinctive. Different. Every member sported the button, which signaled not only moral support for the cause, but also a sign to any suffragette that its wearer could help her.

"I have evidence that there's a plot to set off a bomb during the suffrage parade today," he said.

Figaro's right eyebrow raised in skepticism. "That's a serious accusation. What kind of evidence?"

Randall carefully laid the phonograph on the man's desk and removed the recording he'd brought with him. "It is on this disk, which you can listen to. Is there a place to plug this machine in?"

The policeman took the cord. But its length was a little short to meet the wall socket, and instead of carefully moving the unit, Figaro tugged. The machine jerked sideways, and before Randall could prevent it, everything crashed to the floor. He was fast enough to catch the machine, but not the disk, which shattered into three pieces.

"Damn it," he cursed.

"I'm so sorry," Figaro said. "Can't you just glue it back together?"

He stared at the idiot with an incredulous glare. "No, you can't. The recording is ruined. My evidence is gone."

"Can't you just tell me what was on it?" the officer asked.

He knew he should have written it all down the old-fashioned way. But the whole point of the machine's new iteration was to eliminate that chore. Besides, an actual recording was far better than a stenographer's interpretation.

He stared at the broken pieces in his hands. "It's not the same. This had the actual voices on it."

"How about you start at the beginning?" Figaro suggested. "Where was this conversation you wanted me to hear recorded?"

"At the Men's League for Woman Suffrage, last evening."

"And what precisely was said?"

"It was a conversation between two men about how a bomb thrown from a window during the parade could create major havoc."

"That doesn't sound to me like a criminal plan to act. More just a conversation about what might happen if something like that occurred."

Randall kept his temper in check. "I assure you, the conversation was much more than that, which you could have heard for yourself if you had not broken the recording."

"Who are these two men?"

Randall knew his answer wasn't going to be received well. "I'm not sure."

"Not sure? Yet you're here making accusations. You're theorizing that someone's going to do mischief at the parade, but you don't know why, and you don't know who, and you want us to investigate? How many men are members of the league?"

"Over five hundred," Randall said. "But I saw who went in the room and who came out."

"Over what period of time?"

"About thirty-five minutes."

"And you were watching the room the whole time?"

The officer's barrage of questions unnerved him.

"I was not in the room during the conversation," he said. "It had been reserved by a man named Timothy Brisbane for a private meeting. I was downstairs, below the lounge, where the Dictograph machine was located. I couldn't get it to work right at first. It took a while. But eventually it started recording."

"Why were you doing such a thing?"

"A favor for a friend that did not turn out as planned."

He caught the disapproving look on the policeman's face.

Which he did not disagree with.

"I made my way upstairs, but was waylaid by several members having a conversation in the hall. But eventually, two men came out of the lounge, neither one of whom was Timothy Brisbane."

"So during that time, this Brisbane exited the room and others entered? And then that might have even happened again. If you were gone for over a half hour there might have been two or three or more people go in and out, without you seeing them. Is that right?"

Reluctantly, he nodded.

He wanted to suggest that Figaro missed his calling and should have been a lawyer. Throwing doubt on a situation was exactly what he did every day in court.

"I know for a fact that at least one of the men I suspect of having this conversation isn't ethical."

He described Samuel Morrison and how he misrepresented and exaggerated the news to sell magazines and tabloids.

"I am aware of Mr. Morrison," Figaro said. "His publications are some of the most popular in the city. Forgive me, Mr. Randall, but it sounds like you are the one with the active imagination. Maybe you should be writing for one of Mr. Morrison's magazines."

He resented the barb. "I know what I heard."

"And I know what you are telling me. A conversation between two men about a hypothetical situation is hardly evidence. Not to mention why on earth would these men, who belong to an organization that is helping women get the vote, want to disrupt the biggest parade this city might ever have seen, all in support of that effort?"

After twenty years as a lawyer he'd developed certain instincts, and every one of them was telling him that something bad was coming. Unfortunately, he simply did not have the right answers that this skeptic would accept.

"Is that all you have?" Figaro finally asked.

He nodded. "I did have a recording."

Figaro ignored the jab. "We have a busy day ahead of us monitoring the parade and keeping the peace, which is never easy during events like this. They are expecting ten thousand marchers and maybe that many or more onlookers lining the route. At the end of the suffrage parade last year we had every cell full, with both men and women. Tempers run high over this issue."

Randall ignored the observation.

Instead, he gathered up his machine and left.

Back on the street he checked his watch.

9:05 a.m.

Six hours until the parade.

The weather had turned chilly, with a bitter wind whipping between the buildings and knifing through his clothes. He had to get to Florence's and try to convince her, yet again, to stay away from the parade. His girlfriend was a staunch suffragist, determined to be part of the cause.

But first he had another stop.

He found Samuel Morrison's town house on East Sixty-First Street, a three-story affair with a brick front. A manservant answered the door and advised that Morrison was at his office, but the obstinate employee refused to provide an address. That forced a visit to a nearby newsstand and a quick glance at the latest *City Herald* in order to learn the publishing office's location from the masthead. It took another ten minutes for him to find a carriage for hire, then twenty minutes to reach the Flatiron Building.

Which had garnered quite a reputation.

Built in 1902, it stood at twenty stories, one of the tallest in the city, filling a triangular block formed by Fifth Avenue, Broadway, and East Twenty-Second Street. The name came from its clear resemblance to a clothes iron. Inside, he boarded a crowded elevator up. Morrison's offices were abuzz with activity, surprising for a Saturday. But, in addition to weeklies, the company printed both a morning and evening tabloid seven days a week. Tonight's edition would surely be all about the parade.

A receptionist announced him to Morrison, who agreed to see him, so he was shown into the publisher's office. They knew of one another, but did not *know* each other. There'd been a few conversations in the lounge, but always with others around. So it was no surprise when the older man looked puzzled by his visitor's presence.

"This is a first," Morrison said. "How can I help you, Randall? It's a bit busy around here today, what with the parade starting in a few hours."

"It's the parade I came to talk to you about."

Morrison was short and squat, like a tree stump. His long nose overhung a grizzly mustache, but his scalp gleamed nearly bald. A leather armchair was offered, and Randall sat before a large desk

awash with paper and piles of magazines and newspapers. He settled into the chair, noticing a map on top of one of the piles with a
crayon red circle around a section of Fifth Avenue, along with the
time *4:15 p.m.* scrawled beside it. It was along the announced parade
route, which was also denoted by a red line drawn down a section
of Fifth Avenue. Randall had lived in the city all his life and knew
every nook and cranny. The circle was not far from here, north on
Fifth near East Thirty-Fourth Street.

Morrison caught his interest and slid the pile, with the map,
away, dropping the bundle on the floor. "Just more junk. I have a
bad habit of keeping an untidy desk."

"I know the feeling. Mine is not much better. Are you marching
today?" he asked, not sure where he was headed with his questioning.

Morrison shook his head. "I have to be here to get out the evening edition. But I wish them all the best."

"I'm embarrassed to admit, but I don't read the *City Scope*. I
assume, like you, it's pro-suffrage?"

"What kind of hypocrite would I be if it was anything but?
Only an ignorant fool would be anti-suffrage."

The words sounded sincere. He'd heard them many times at
the league. And why would a man who donated time and money
to the suffrage cause, a man married to one of the city's most vocal
suffragists, disrupt the parade?

"Forgive me, Randall, but what is it precisely you want?" Morrison asked.

"Do you know of anyone at the league who might not be in
sympathy with our goals?"

Morrison appeared puzzled. "A spy?"

He shrugged. "Maybe. Or just someone acting under false pre-
tenses, motivated by hate and bigotry. I heard a rumor that's made
me wonder if we have a traitor in our midst."

"What kind of rumor?'

He waved off the inquiry. "It would be unsavory of me to repeat, until it is verified as true."

His host appeared annoyed by the comment, which Randall had meant as a rebuke of what Morrison routinely published. "If we do have a spy, I wouldn't know who it is. I've heard nothing but positive support from all the members. It's downright inspiring, actually. What's this about?"

He could not voice the truth, so he opted for a lie. "Just something that has caused me concern. I saw you in the men's lounge last evening. I didn't recognize the other gentleman who was with you when you left."

Morrison's eyes narrowed. "Because he was a prospective new member."

The lawyer in him rose up. "Really? What is his name?"

"It would be unsavory of me to reveal that, until he decides whether to join the cause."

Touché. Score one for the opposing team.

"In fact," Morrison said, "there were several men there last night. All prospective members. We had a lively conversation on how we can be better auxiliaries to the brave women fighting the fight today."

That, Randall knew was a lie.

The conversation he'd heard was between only two and it had been far different.

"Now I'm sorry, Randall, but I have to get back to work and finish my editorial. I'm writing a glowing tribute to the march and its success. We have a vote to win in two weeks, and the movement needs every bit of support we can offer."

Out on Fifth Avenue, his bowler back on his head, Randall noticed that traffic was steady, but all that would change in five hours. The march would go from Washington Square to Fifty-Ninth Street, a distance of about three miles, which would take it right by here. He imagined what the scene would be once the parade started. People would line the route on both sides of the street. Officer Figaro mentioned thousands could be here. Recent suffrage parades in other cities had exceeded expectations for both marchers and crowds. The same could be true for today. So many people—who might all be in danger.

And now even more so considering Samuel Morrison's lies.

Damn that stupid policeman for his carelessness in breaking the recording.

But, at the moment, he needed to deal with Florence and convince her not to march in the parade. She was planning on participating along with her daughter, Margaret. Both were proud of their involvement with the movement and had been looking forward to the march for weeks. But even before the potential threat had manifested itself, he'd tried to talk them out of attending. He supported the movement. Absolutely. Women should have the right to vote. And he would fight with any legal means to achieve their goal.

But he was not a fan of public displays.

Perhaps he was stuck in the nineteenth century. To him, displays like today's demoralized women and associated them with common streetwalkers. Ridiculous? Probably. Blame it on his upbringing. The attitude seemed ingrained in his psyche, and he'd not been able to shake his revulsion. Florence and Margaret laughed each time he brought up his objections and teased him about being a puritan.

Maybe he was.

But they hadn't changed his mind. He remained adamant that it was beneath a decent, God-fearing woman to march on the streets. No matter that many of New York's socialites would be dressed in white and parading, too.

The Mink Brigade, they'd been dubbed.

For him, it was still unsavory.

He hustled toward the subway entrance and decided to give it one more try with Florence, particularly considering what he knew now. He took the train to Union Square, where he changed platforms for the 5 to Brooklyn. The time was approaching ten thirty. He knew she planned on lining up for the march at two thirty. It took thirty-eight minutes to arrive at the Flatbush Avenue station and another three minutes to walk to Florence's building.

He rang the buzzer and waited.

No answer.

He rang again.

Silence.

He checked his watch.

Eleven fifteen.

Four hours left.

The day was getting away from him. Maybe they'd gone out on an errand and would be coming right back? Or maybe they were already on their way to the parade, arriving early? He sat down on the stoop, deciding to give them fifteen minutes. But after less than thirty seconds, he started to pace, imagining horrible scenarios. How many people would be in the street at any given spot along that three-mile route? What kind of bomb were the agitators planning on exploding? How much damage could it do? How many would be hurt or killed?

At the fifteen-minute mark, he decided to give them another five minutes.

He was crazy in love with the widow, Florence Lennon, and had started to think of her and Margaret as his own family. He'd been married once, to his childhood sweetheart, who'd died of pneumonia early in their childless marriage. He'd never known pain like that before. Thank goodness for work—he'd thrown himself into becoming a successful criminal lawyer. He missed Helen and mourned her for the longest time. Eventually, he came to accept the loss and moved on. He'd never suffered for companionship. But none had tempted him to settle down a second time.

Until Florence.

She'd been a witness for the prosecution in one of his cases. Something about her had touched him in a way that no woman had in a long time. She was a hostess at the Suffrage Cafeteria, and he'd courted her at first by eating lunch there every day for two weeks. Thankfully, the food was excellent. But then he wouldn't have expected anything less from Alva Vanderbilt Belmont, the social denizen who'd taken up the suffrage cause as her raison d'être. Her dozen restaurants all over New York were advertisements for the cause. *Votes for Women* was painted on all the china plates and stamped into every piece of silverware. Suffrage posters plastered the walls. You could not leave one of her establishments without a full stomach and the message etched into your mind.

Meal by meal he fell in love with Florence.

But it took effort to get her to go out with him.

She was a hardworking single mother who didn't suffer fools gladly, and didn't have much time for socializing. What spare moments she did have were devoted to the suffrage cause. She desperately wanted to change things. And not for her, but more for her daughter. Eventually, he wore her down and convinced her to try just one night out with him.

She had.

They'd shared many nights since.

And while he'd grown to love Florence, he'd also grown close to Margaret, a freshman at Erasmus Hall High School, who was blossoming into a fine young woman. He felt protective of her, and enjoyed offering her help and guidance. Not becoming her father, who was dead. But more her friend. Someone she could count on.

Like with what had happened to her the previous week.

On the Flatbush Avenue trolley, a man sitting beside her had tried to flirt. Middle-aged. Wearing glasses. With a scholar-like appearance. Harmless? Hard to say. She'd felt uncomfortable with the unwanted attention and moved away. The gray-haired man, undeterred, came closer, smiling, endeavoring again to engage her. Then he placed his hand on her thigh, leaned close, and whispered obscenities. She'd fled in fright at the next stop and found a policeman, reporting the assault. The officer caught up with the trolley a block away and she identified the molester. The man protested, calling the accusation false, claiming outrage. But Margaret, true to her tough nature, insisted that he be arrested.

Good for you, he'd told her. *Well done. You might have saved a lot of other girls from harm.*

And he'd meant it.

His own sister, at age twelve, had been brutally raped and traumatized. She was never the same after. He constantly worried that lapsing attitudes were encouraging men to go too far. Styles were changing. Morals loosening. Women had begun to smoke and drink in public and show their ankles, which, to him, seemed downright provocative. Worst of all, they marched. Add to that the rampant proliferation of pornography, and society was simply asking for trouble.

And it wasn't that he was a prude.

Actually, he fancied himself quite the romantic. But men should be gentlemen, and women should be feminine and treated with respect. It was wrong for a man to abuse a woman. His revulsion was amplified when he accompanied Florence and Margaret to the courthouse for the trial and learned that the accused was Reverend Richard H. Keep. Forty-eight years old. A retired clergyman. Charged with the same crime three times before. But, being a man of the cloth, he'd not been prosecuted.

Outrageous.

The reverend had sat with his eyes closed, head bowed, hands clasped. The prosecutor called Margaret to the stand and she told the judge what had happened. Her voice stayed firm and steady, her demeanor one of an outraged victim. It would be hard not to believe every word she said. The defense lawyer stood to cross-examine her.

"Do you want to see this man of God go to jail?" Margaret was asked.

"If that is needed to stop him from doing this again."

"Are you sorry for him?"

"I am. He is a sick person."

"And are you sorry that you made this charge against him?"

"I am not," she said, loud and clear. "Why I would be sorry for the truth?"

Randall had been proud to hear her not retreat. That was another thing he found appalling. How women were always expected to back down and yield to a man. The judge found the ex-preacher guilty and sentenced him to sixty days in jail.

Which was precisely what he deserved.

"What are you doing here?" a voice asked, bringing his thoughts back to the present.

He glanced up to see Florence standing below on the sidewalk, staring up at him as he sat on the stoop.

"I need to speak with you. Can we go upstairs to your apartment for a moment?"

She led the way.

Inside, with the door closed, they sat on the settee in her parlor.

"Where's Margaret?" he asked.

"At a friend's house. I'll get her when I leave for the march."

He noticed paraphernalia for the parade all around. Two banners they would each be carrying. Sashes they would wear. Celluloid buttons and feathers for their hats. Everything encouraging support for the suffrage movement.

"I am going to make one more plea that you and Margaret stay home today."

She looked at him incredulously. "We've been over this. Repeatedly. You know I value your opinion. I truly do. But this street-walker worry is ridiculous. Tens of thousands of women are going to be marching today. No one is going to associate us with women of the night." She shook her head. "This is important to me, Randall. Especially after what Margaret went through last week. That scoundrel wanted to blame her for his indecency. That lawyer wanted her to be sorry she brought the charges. What an insult. Today's march is important for her—"

"It's not about that anymore," he said, interrupting. "I have reason to believe there is a bomb threat on the parade. It's not safe for you and Margaret to be there."

"A bomb threat? You can't be serious. That's how desperate you are to stop us from going?"

"I'm not making it up. It's real."

She shook her head. "For such a dear, liberal man, you are incredibly old-fashioned. No. The answer is no. We are going."

He wasn't surprised by how she was reacting. Over the past two weeks he'd overplayed his hand to stop her from marching, allowing his social conservatism to get the better of him. Pursuing this any further seemed pointless. She wasn't going to believe him. But he had to say again, "I'm not making this up. There is a credible threat."

She glared at him. "Do you have proof?"

"I heard two men talking—"

"Do you have proof?"

"You sound like opposing counsel, cross-examining."

She gently touched his arm. "Randall, I love you dearly. But this preoccupation doesn't become you."

"I overheard two men talking. One might have been Samuel Morrison—"

"The publisher? Isn't he part of the league? Why would he do such a horrible thing?"

He had no answer. "Florence, this has nothing to do with me caring how it will look for you and Margaret to be there. You convinced me that I was being ridiculous and completely prudish about that. I understand. This is different. I swear to you."

"So Samuel Morrison, a successful publisher, is going to bomb the suffrage march? Randall, you missed your calling. O. Henry has nothing on you."

He shook his head. How could he get her to believe him? Then something caught his eye. On the coffee table among the suffrage papers. A map of the parade route with circles on it. He pointed. "What is that?"

"Places along the way where members of the city council and government will be in viewing stands. We need to be mindful of them when we pass."

"I am begging you—"

She stood, leaned forward, and kissed him. "I have to get ready to leave. They're saying the parade will be over by six thirty. Mrs. Belmont is throwing a party at her restaurant. Will you meet us there?"

With no choice, he nodded.

"I'll be there."

※

He left the apartment and decided to head back to Manhattan and see if Captain Donnelly had returned to the 18th Precinct. Maybe he would have a more sympathetic ear. At the Flatbush Avenue station he hurried down the steps but missed the train as it headed off. He stood alone on the empty platform, annoyed, but there was nothing he could do but wait for the next one.

Suddenly, he was grabbed from behind and yanked backward.

The violation shocked him.

"What is the meaning of this?" he shouted at the two men, trying to twist away from their grasp.

They were both bigger and stronger and dragged him off the platform into the shadows. One of their hands covered his mouth and prevented him from calling out. He'd yet to see their faces. He ducked his head down, wrenched his mouth free, and managed to bite one of his attackers' hands, tasting blood. Amazingly, the man didn't scream, or let go, or even flinch. Another hand was clasped over his mouth. Firmer. Tighter. They kept tugging him along until they had him in what looked like an abandoned tunnel.

He was shoved to the ground.

The sole of a shoe was planted against his spine, pinning him down, keeping him still while the other man bound his hands and feet with rope. He wanted to cry out, but the foot pressed harder, taking his breath away.

They rolled him over.

He saw the faces. "I know—"

A big, bloody fist whirled through the air, straight at him.

Then blackness.

He struggled to open his eyes.

The right side of his head pounded. He reached up and felt a bump the size of a walnut, crusty with blood.

"Can you hear me?" a male voice asked.

He could, but his eyes had yet to focus. Everything was blurred and swirling, like he was in a fog on a rolling boat deck.

The man sounded far away.

His body was turned over, and he felt the pressure at his wrists and ankles being released. Then he remembered. The two attackers had bound him, before slamming a fist into his head.

"Don't struggle," the man said. "I'm untying you."

His arms and legs were freed. He rubbed his sore wrists as his eyes began to focus. A man in a uniform leaned over him. One of the ticket agents. Randall tested his arms and legs. Everything seemed okay, but his head really hurt.

"What happened to you?"

"Two thugs attacked me."

"After your money, were they? Hope you didn't have much. Why, look at that. They left your watch. Wonder why they didn't take it?"

Randall glanced at his left wrist and noticed the time.

2:47 p.m.

"It's nearly three o'clock?" he asked.

The march was about to start. He'd been out awhile. He felt for his wallet. There, too. Then he remembered what he'd seen right before being punched—a face he recognized. One of his attackers was the man with the thin mustache who'd been with Morrison the previous night at the men's lounge.

The ticket agent helped him up and into a small office out of the chill, where he accepted some coffee and aspirin. He used a wet towel to clean up the cut on his forehead, then bandaged it.

"How did you find me?" he asked.

"I was just takin' a break to have a smoke and walking, as I do. Sitting in this office selling tickets for hours at a time isn't good for my back or legs. Gotta get up during my breaks. I try to do a mile of track for every break. Sometimes I find things. A toy. A scarf. A book. Never found a man before."

Randall fished a five-dollar bill from his pocket and gave it to the man, thanking him for the assistance.

"They didn't steal that from you either?" Randall was asked.

He heard the train approaching the station. Time to go. "Thank you so much for everything."

And he shook the ticket agent's hand.

He then hurried to the platform and hopped onto the waiting train, crowded with men and women, many of whom carried banners and wore white. Not a seat to be had. His head still pounded, but he couldn't let that slow him down. He had to get to the parade.

"Would you like my seat?"

He glanced down and an older woman pointed to his bandage.

"Does it hurt?"

"Only when I laugh." He was trying to make light of her concern. He actually wanted to sit down but was worried he might not get back up. "I appreciate the gesture. But I'll stand."

The woman was holding a copy of *City Scope*, the same edition he'd consulted earlier. But he'd only studied its front page. She had it open and was reading an article whose headline caught his attention.

SUFFRAGETTES TAKE DIFFERENT PATHS
TO MAKE THEIR POINT

"Could I see that article?" he asked.

She smiled. "Of course. I've finished reading it. Quite enlightening, I might say. I never knew."

He stood, holding on to the leather strap, and scanned the page. The story dealt with the vast difference between the British and American movements. The fight for suffrage started in England in 1872 but had not gained strength until 1906.

Currently, it was going strong, just like in America.

The big difference between the two was the violence.

In England, some suffragettes had resorted to extreme tactics to gain attention. Communication networks were disrupted by cutting telephone and telegraph lines. Postboxes destroyed. Four postmen had been injured by phosphorus left in different boxes. Cultural objects had been attacked. Paintings, statues, and even the Jewel House at the Tower of London had fallen victim. Sarcophagi were defaced in the British Museum, and at Kew Gardens, a tearoom was burned down. Arson attacks had occurred at theaters, sporting pavilions, and even the homes of members of Parliament. Three years earlier, four suffragists had tried to set fire to the Theatre Royal while the prime minister was there during a packed show. Then a suffragette threw herself in front of the king's horse and was killed. Two others, in retaliation, burned down the pavilion at Hurst Park Racecourse.

Physical attacks also seemed a regular occurrence.

One activist attacked Winston Churchill with a horsewhip. The prime minister's car was assaulted with catapults. A suffragette plot to kidnap the home secretary and several other cabinet ministers was foiled. Just the past year, a young suffragette leaped on the footboard of the king and queen's limousine in Scotland and tried to break its windows. The English press dubbed it perhaps the most daring act that had occurred in the history of the women's suffrage agitation.

But the most disturbing information was the bombings.

Detonated at banks, trains, churches, even Westminster Abbey. Two railway stations were leveled. One bomb exploded at the Royal Observatory in Edinburgh. Another was planted outside the Bank of England. A three-inch pipe bomb obliterated a greenhouse at a park in Manchester. Another bomb damaged the home of Chancellor David Lloyd George.

Shouting down speakers, throwing stones, smashing windows, and burning down unoccupied churches and country houses seemed commonplace. The rallying cry of these militants was simple.

Deeds not words.

Once jailed, hunger strikes became a way to garner further sympathy and make their point. But Parliament passed what had come to be called the Cat and Mouse Act to prevent suffragettes from becoming martyrs in prison. The law allowed the release of those whose hunger strikes and being force-fed had made them seriously ill. But it also provided for their reimprisonment once they recovered. The move had backfired, though, and only resulted in more publicity for the suffragettes' cause.

In the article, several commentators weighed in on the terroristic tactics.

One said the militancy clearly damaged the cause and set back the movement. Even worse, a large portion of the movement had started to give priority to militancy rather than obtaining the vote. One observer noted that it had become a kind of holy war, so important that it could not be called off, even if continuing it prevented suffrage reform.

Which seemed, as the article noted, the big difference between there and here. The American movement had not succumbed to violence. The focus remained on obtaining the right to vote through peaceful and civil means.

He'd never known that about the Brits.

Another story on the page caught his attention.

It dealt with the National Association Opposed to Woman Suffrage. Founded by a woman in 1911, its members strongly opposed the suffrage movement. A quote from its mission purpose seemed to say it all. The great advance of women in the last century—moral, intellectual, and economic—had been made without the vote, which proved that suffrage was not needed for their further advancement. Incredibly, quotes in the article alleged that the majority of women did not want the right to vote. They believed that the men in their lives accurately represented the political will of women around the country.

Not any of the women he knew.

For NAOWS, true womanhood was quiet, dignified, and regal. Supposedly, political equality would deprive women of special privileges now afforded them by law.

He wondered what those were.

The quotes also made the incredible assertion that doubling the vote with women would increase the undesirable and corrupt vote. And, lest anyone forget, a woman's present duties filled up the whole measure of her time and ability. There was little room for more.

He had a hard time fathoming that anyone with a brain actually believed that. But, apparently, there were some who did. The group was headquartered in Manhattan and there was a picture of their storefront establishment with the article. Located on East Thirty-Fourth Street, just down from the Fifth Avenue intersection.

His fogged brain cleared.

And he visualized the map that had been on Samuel Morrison's desk. The red crayon circle had been around that intersection, along with a notation for 4:15 p.m. Was it possible? Had he found the target? Was that why he'd been attacked?

He had to get to East Thirty-Fourth Street and find out, so he worked through the math and geography, as any New Yorker could. The train he was on to Union Square stopped at seventeen stations and would take at least forty minutes. It was a long way from there to Thirty-Fourth Street, especially with the crowds. Surely there would be another train from Union Square to the Thirty-Fourth Street station, but that would take ten minutes with at least two stops. That was fifty minutes, plus another five for getting to the other platform and up the steps.

The whole trip? Right at an hour.

He'd have just enough time, with a few minutes to spare.

The train pulled into Union Square.

He rushed across the platforms and barely caught a train north to Herald Square. There, he fled the car and ran up the steps, wincing with the effort, and came face-to-face with a mass of people, all facing toward Fifth Avenue. Was every person in New York at the parade? He elbowed his way through the crowd and was just about clear of them when he heard a child cry out.

He looked down.

A little girl of about six or seven lay at his feet, on her knees. Crying.

Had he knocked her over?

"I'm so sorry," he said, as he reached out and picked up the child.

She had long, reddish hair and the greenest of eyes. She wore a white coat, dirty in places, with a sash across her chest that read *Miss Suffragette City*. In her hands she clutched a box camera.

"Are you hurt?" he asked.

She shook her head, her eyes still brimming with tears.

"Where's your mama?"

Every second he delayed could mean disaster.

"In India," the child said.

Had he heard right? "Who are you here with?"

"My aunt Katrina."

"Point her out and I'll get you to her."

"I don't see her. Not anywhere."

She gave a renewed sob. He could not waste another moment and spied a young woman a foot away who looked sympathetic.

He approached her. "Miss?"

The woman turned.

"This little girl—" He looked down. "What's your name?"

"Grace." She sobbed again.

"Grace is lost and can't find her aunt. I have—an urgent appointment. Might you please help her?"

He didn't wait for the woman to agree. He just handed the child over to the young woman, who set down the art case she was carrying and took the little girl from him.

He hurried down East Thirty-Fourth Street and could hear a band's big booming drum and brass horns blasting in the distance.

The parade was drawing nearer.

The throbbing in his head threatened to slow him down, but he refused to concede to the pain. Was this a fool's quest? Was Samuel Morrison really planning on bombing the anti-suffrage headquarters? Perhaps as a way to bring the violence of the Brits to their shores? A way to discredit the movement? Or further it? Hard to say. It all sounded so preposterous.

Until he saw the man with the pencil mustache.

The same man who'd been with Morrison last evening and the same one who'd attacked him a few hours ago. Headed down the sidewalk, carrying a small suitcase, the hand holding the case bandaged where it had been bitten.

In all the excitement, no one paid the man any attention. The focus was behind him, at the Fifth Avenue intersection, on the rapidly approach parade. It seemed that whatever was about to happen had been coordinated with the parade's arrival. Greater drama? More impact? More carnage?

Ahead he spotted the storefront and the makeshift banner above it that read HEADQUARTERS NATIONAL ASSOCIATION OPPOSED TO WOMAN SUFFRAGE. Affixed to its window were various posters and leaflets. Men in suits and hats were stopped reading them. More people wandered in and out of the open front door. Apparently, the organizers were taking advantage of the crowd to spread their anti-suffrage message. A sign above the front entrance proclaimed PLEASE COME IN.

His attacker was a hundred feet ahead, approaching the anti-suffrage headquarters. People milled back and forth on the sidewalk, many headed toward the parade, others away from it. Lots of activity. Movement. Plenty of distractions for no one noticed a small suitcase laid down near a pile of trash at the curb. Then Pencil Mustache scattered some of the trash over the suitcase to cover its presence and turned, heading back toward him.

Randall decided enough was enough.

At the next trash pile, he grabbed a short length of wood, about the size of a baseball bat and equally stout. There were so many people on the sidewalk that it would be difficult to isolate him from the crowd, and he used the bodies ahead of him for cover.

His target approached.

Twenty feet.

Ten.

He cocked the board back and stopped, allowing people to flow around him like a boulder in a stream.

The man saw him too late.

Randall swung and the board caught Pencil Mustache solidly in the gut, doubling the man over. Randall recocked his arms and crashed the board down onto the man's spine, sending him to the sidewalk.

People reacted to the assault with fright and raised voices.

"Get out of here," he yelled. "There's a bomb."

Some began to flee; others seemed paralyzed.

"Go. Now. There's a bomb here."

He tossed the board aside and rushed ahead, pushing his way around people running in both directions. At the trash pile he found the suitcase and grabbed its handle. He had no idea of the time but it had to be close to, if not after, four fifteen. He kept moving, conscious of the fact that he might well be carrying an explosive device.

An alley. That's what he needed. Anything off the street.

Just ahead, he spotted one.

He came to its end and stared down a narrow corridor between two tall buildings. Nobody there. He launched the suitcase into the air.

"Get away," he screamed to the people around him. "Now. Get away from here."

They all began to scatter.

He took cover against the building at the alley's entrance, out of any line of fire.

And waited.

He kept motioning for people to stay away from the opening.

Two policemen appeared and ran his way.

"There's a bomb in the alley," he called out.

They both stopped, not yet to the point where the alley opened to the sidewalk, and drew their weapons.

"Do not move," one of them said, as both guns were aimed his way.

⁂

He sat, alone, in the cell, where he'd been for the past three hours.

The two city cops had arrested and handcuffed him, then transported him to the precinct. He'd tried to explain, mentioning the man he'd cold-cocked, Samuel Morrison and Officer Figaro, but no one was listening. Finally, he did what he told his clients to do when confronted with the police and went silent. No one he'd defended had ever talked themselves out of jail, but nearly all of them had talked themselves into it.

No bomb had exploded, either.

At least not while he was on East Thirty-Fourth Street.

What happened after?

Who knows.

Quite a mess he'd gotten himself into. And all from trying to help out a friend whose daughter was married to a cheating husband. Of course, he'd never uncovered a single shred of evidence on that allegation.

A door opened and someone approached the cell.

Captain Donnelly.

With Officer Figaro.

Donnelly opened the barred door and looked at Figaro. "Do you have something to say to Mr. Wilson?"

The younger man looked embarrassed. "I apologize for not taking you more seriously earlier today. It was a grave oversight on my part."

He stared at them both, tired and still a little dazed from the earlier head blow. "Yes, it was. But it's over now. Forget it."

Donnelly dismissed his subordinate, stepped inside, and sat on the metal bench. "You did good today."

He waited.

"That suitcase contained a bomb, along with screws and nails that would have caused a lot of carnage. When you tossed it into the alley, you damaged the detonator and it failed to explode."

He could sense there was more.

"We arrested the man you attacked. You gave him quite a beating."

"Which he deserved."

Donnelly smiled. "Remind me not to rile you up."

"Is he okay?"

"You broke a couple of his ribs. Otherwise, he'll survive. But he did give up Samuel Morrison and told us about the whole plot. It seems Morrison is not really a supporter of women's suffrage. He joined the Men's League as a way to keep abreast of what was happening. His intent all along was to cause mayhem and mischief and implicate the movement in violence. With it happening in Britain, where it's all but ruined the message of an equal vote, he thought the same could be made to happen here. The suffragettes would deny any link to the bomb. But no one would have believed them. He saw it as the fastest way to end the whole thing."

"And he could not have cared less how many people he hurt or killed?"

"It didn't seem so. What you did was extremely brave. The witnesses said you grabbed the case and flung it into that alley. That bomb could have exploded at any moment."

"Don't remind me."

"We went to arrest Morrison, but he fled his office to the roof and leaped off the Flatiron Building to his death."

Coward. But Randall would have expected no less. "That's no great loss."

"I agree." Donnelly slapped his hand on Randall's knee. "You did a great thing, my friend. We'll be charging the man you attacked with the assault on you and attempted murder for the bomb. Of course, you're free to go."

❉

He left the precinct and stepped out into a chilly evening. The wind continued to whip through the buildings. It was nearly eight p.m. and he recalled what Florence had said earlier. *Mrs. Belmont is throwing a party at her restaurant. Will you meet us there?*

So he headed that way.

Inside, he found a large group of suffragettes celebrating after the march, everyone's spirits high.

He spotted Florence and Margaret.

Thank goodness they, and everyone else, were safe.

No telling how far Morrison would have gone if he'd been able to bomb that building. He might have thrown the whole movement into jeopardy. And disparaged the work of so many brave women in both England and America who never resorted to violence. Who instead mustered courage and used civil disobedience to make the point that they deserved the same voice in government as men. They'd endured ridicule, arrest, imprisonment, hunger strikes, being force-fed, and so many other indignities.

But they'd persevered.

And would continue to do so.

Truly placing a whole new light on the negative mantra of deeds not words.

Florence hugged him, a smile filling her face. Then she pointed at his head. "What happened?"

"Nothing. I fell down. Stupid me."

"It was glorious," Margaret said. "Wonderful. What a great day."

He was thrilled at the joy on the young girl's face.

"And, see," Florence said, "nothing happened. It all worked out perfectly."

Yes, it did.

Thylacine

※

Paula McLain

Lucy Cuthbert woke from a dream of fire to the feeling of—all too real—being burned alive. The heat came with terrible pressure, radiating in molten waves from her stomach up through her chest and neck, flaming into her face, which pulsed and vibrated unbearably. She threw off the duvet, feeling sure she wouldn't be able to stand it, not this time. Her heart was beating so violently she could feel it thrashing everywhere. She was a kettle on the boil, a lobster pot. A kiln. Her nightgown was a wet glove, pasted to her torso. She couldn't breathe. This was the end. It had to be. She would incinerate and be nothing but ash and regret and insufficiency.

But wait. *There.* Something had shifted. The fire had reached the top of her skull and climbed *through* somehow, into the wall, to the inner workings of the house, and been absorbed materially. Or perhaps that wasn't it at all. Perhaps the heat had simply collapsed in on itself, retreating to wherever it had originated from. Either way, she was empty now, wrung out and trembling, and all too awake. This would be the worst part, she knew. There were hours ahead of her with nothing but her restless mind, her worries and her fears, for company. Whatever time it was—she didn't want to look—it was already tomorrow. Through this dark would come the dawn, then morning, then an anxious lunch—she couldn't imagine an alternative—and finally, at three p.m. exactly, the banner parade would begin at Washington Square Park, tens of thousands marching, and Lucy in their midst. If she didn't lose her nerve first.

Tugging her nightgown after her like damp netting, Lucy turned toward the wall and worked to solidify the speech in her head, the one she'd been fretting over since she'd filled out the pledge card three weeks ago. Edwin hated spectacle, hated ostentation of any sort. Parades and theatrical pageants, open-air meetings in parks and town squares, hunger strikes, picket lines—all connoted hysteria in Edwin's opinion, an unseemly urgency. His was a scientific mind, a temple of right order. Evolutions had their own pace, he insisted, and shouldn't be bullied this way, so unnaturally.

Lucy still remembered their exchange the morning after the first official suffrage parade, in May 1910, when Harriot Stanton Blatch had led four hundred women and a single supporting man up Fifth Avenue to Union Park with banners and horses and a marching band, of all things. Edwin had flicked away *The New York Times* as if it exuded an embarrassing miasma and then walked away, into his study, putting an end to the matter, dismissing it, while Lucy had sat frozen, afraid to respond, uncertain of her own mind. Did she think that women were equal in every way to men? Did she truly believe that a woman was sovereign to herself, whole, able to govern her own life and mind? *Did* she, or only wish she did?

The parade had been a radical act, to be sure. Women didn't march; soldiers did. Women didn't stand on wooden scaffolds berating the New York state legislature for failing to advance the suffrage measure. They didn't demand; they yielded. She, Lucy, had yielded all of her adult life, not daring to question her role. Her *self*. But the newspaper still lay there. Lucy picked up the *Times* where Edwin had dropped it and felt a rising tide of contradictory emotions. The photographs of the parade formation passing along Fifth Avenue didn't look hysterical or unseemly, but somber, almost funereal: dark-suited bodies surrounded by dark buildings, a heavy sky, pressing afternoon fog. One image showed a contingent of women who'd traveled all the way from Colorado, which had passed the voting referendum in 1893. The sign above their smart hats, very smart for Colorado, actually, declared: WE HAVE VOTED FOR PRESI-DENT. Was that pride in their eyes? Triumph? Another photograph caught Dr. Anna Howard Shaw, National American Woman Suffrage Association president, mid-speech, her mouth cupped around some assertion or demand. One gloved hand gripped the scaffolding. Her shoulders were broad and immovable-looking in her black dress and doctoral robes—the whole of her appearing less like a gentlewoman than a human bulwark of sorts. What was she shouting? *No? Now?* Or was it the word *you*, perhaps? *You*, as in: *You, Lucy Eileen Cuthbert. I see you there, hiding.*

That first parade had taken place five and a half years ago. And though she had said nothing that day to Edwin, not a single word to either agree with him or stake a small claim in the other direction, something had begun to stir in Lucy, a dark thing, nebulous and unformed, incredibly new and yet as old as she was. She was afraid to look at it, afraid to give it air or space or even a drop of water, but it had grown all the same. It prodded her now in the dark of her room, accosting her. Ready or not, tomorrow had become today. She'd run out of time to waffle or avoid the issue. Edwin had no engagements, this being a Saturday. He would be there in the house as she dressed in her white jacket and long white skirt and put on the pale straw boater she'd had since the year they met, when she was eighteen and utterly in awe of him and his keen analytical mind, his deliberateness.

Sometimes she missed the simplicity of that early time. How easy it had been to let Edwin lead the way into their lives. Before they were married, even, he'd shared his plan with her, that he'd teach zoology at Columbia if they'd have him, or at Fordham or Barnard if not. That they'd live downtown as newlyweds, on Varick

Street, perhaps, visiting his parents in Stamford and her parents in Tenafly on alternating weekends; that once they were more established, they'd move to the Upper West Side, to an apartment near Riverside Park, with a view of the Hudson.

How persuasive it had all sounded to Lucy then. In Tenafly, she'd spent her childhood looking east to the river, but Edwin was promising the opposite view, a journey not of distance but of perspective. How symbolic that had felt at eighteen, how like true arrival. But there had been more as well. When Edwin had proposed in 1889, he had shown her the roll of parchment paper where he'd scheduled everything, right down to how many children they'd have—four— and at what intervals—every three years, so as to really linger over and enjoy their infancy before rushing on to the next. She wouldn't have to think of anything. It was all there in writing; she only had to agree and give away her name and then she'd be there, be *that* Lucy instead of this one.

She'd had other suitors, of course, the most memorable being a classmate of hers in school in Tenafly, Lars Pederson. He was the second son of a Dutch immigrant farmer, and he and Lucy had grown up together without her really seeing him, somehow. Then, just after her seventeenth birthday, she had noticed him all at once. How blue Lars's eyes were, the color of cornflowers. How he carried a little copy of William Blake's poems wherever he went and had memorized many of them, as a personal manifesto, a metaphysical path that seemed wonderfully outrageous to her, as if Lars spoke a foreign language in his heart.

One summer day when they had taken a walk along the Hudson, Lars had stopped and looked across the river. Yonkers lay on the other bank, but Lars seemed unbound by such ordinariness. He was imagining distant lands and vistas, the world. He told Lucy that he wanted to be a pianist or a poet or a gypsy or all three, living in a colorful caravan and traveling everywhere. Didn't that sound fine, he wanted to know? "Oh, yes," Lucy had told him. And she'd meant it. She also knew he wasn't simply dreaming. Lars would get to that place. She could hear it in the tenor of his voice: he'd already sent his longing on ahead, like a bright lantern, and only needed to follow it now.

Not long after that walk, they'd taken another, through the woods near his family's farm. They had stopped near an egg-shaped pond, where Lars had bent to place a baby frog in Lucy's hand, yellow-green with dewy, shimmering skin, and she'd been struck by how alive it was, how full of possibility. Lars had said nothing at all, only kissed her very lightly, for the first time, and in the same moment, the little animal had stirred in Lucy's hand. Twenty-seven years later, she had not forgotten that. How she had felt herself shimmer with a kind of permeability—as if, like the frog, she could take in life itself through her skin. Whatever had happened to that feeling, Lucy sometimes wondered now. How could such a moment present itself with such force and not change you altogether? It didn't seem possible to her, and yet it was. The proof was here, in the still middle of the night, in the middle of her life, and she could do nothing but let it come—like the hot flash—and feast on her.

⁂

A few hours later, Lucy woke again, without ever being aware that she had fallen asleep. Her shoulders ached and her neck was impossibly stiff, as if her head—there on the pillow—had alchemized into concrete and back again in the last of the early morning hours. Through the far wall, the door that led past her dressing room into Edwin's dressing room, and then his bedroom, Lucy heard her husband rise from bed, the creaking of the polished maple floorboards as he found his slippers and went to wash and relieve himself. She sat up, reaching for her dressing gown just as a light rapping came at her door.

"Are you awake, pussycat?" Edwin called.

Pussycat. Lucy stiffened automatically. When had she come to hate that nickname? It had been sweet once, even tender. "Yes," she finally called back, feeling terrified that he might open the door, just as he had every right to.

"Meet me downstairs, then?"

Relief flooded her. A reprieve. "Yes, dear. Soon."

When he was gone, Lucy rose, avoiding her mirror, pinned up her long hair, now the color of gunmetal at her temples, and dressed in a blue muslin skirt and shirtwaist. It was far too early to put on her white skirt and jacket. There were hours and hours to fill between now and the parade, and besides, Edwin would be confused to see her costumed this way and expect an answer immediately. She *was* going to tell him, though. At breakfast, she would find a way to conjure the words that retreated from her now, in terror and self-doubt. Somehow, she would have to find the strength to bear Edwin's derision or disbelief—whatever his response might be. Would he laugh? Mock her decision? Forbid her? Or would he simply close the door of himself, the way he often did when he didn't approve of or understand Lucy, shutting off his emotions, his reassurance. His love.

If she were really being honest with herself, this was what Lucy dreaded most. Why else had she remained immobilized on the matter for years now, pulled toward the precipice, while simultaneously resisting it? Annually, since 1910, the woman suffrage parade in Manhattan had doubled and tripled in size, growing in force and dimension. This year's event had already been presaged in Philadelphia and Boston, where the Votes for Women campaign was making a last brave push, just as New York was, for the referendum that would take place on November second. New Jersey had already defeated the measure, though Woodrow Wilson had publicly endorsed it, and though all of the west now, save Texas, had reached liberation.

The east was still bafflingly resistant, entrenched, which was why

Lucy felt this was her moment to act. Signing the pledge card had forced the matter, and yet Lucy was all too aware that this upcoming conversation at breakfast, one woman trying to explain to her husband just what she believed in and why, would mean not just acknowledging the vast emotional and intellectual divide between herself and Edwin, but plunging right into it, into nothingness. Of course Lucy was trembling. In the smallest possible way, in her home, the world was teetering on a knife's edge. Today, October twenty-third, was either the end of days, or the end of Lucy's ability to live with herself, and didn't they amount to the same thing?

Half an hour later, when Lucy finally stilled the palsy in her hands enough to button up her shirtwaist and descend the stairs from her room, she found Edwin in the dining room, cheerfully drinking coffee and reading the newspaper. He was humming under his breath. She couldn't even remember the last time she'd heard a snatch of song in him. It was unsettling at best.

"You look awfully pretty," Edwin said as Lucy took her chair.

Even more off balance, she felt her mouth swing open in surprise, and then recover, rearrange itself. "Do I?" Lucy's voice came breathily. "Thank you."

"That color favors you," Edwin went on, still looking at her.

"Thank you," Lucy said again, feeling dizzy and out of place, as if she'd somehow stumbled into someone else's dining room by mistake. She reached for the ivory linen napkin and opened it on her lap as her heart rattled and rasped inside her chest. Marta had already put out warm rolls and glasses of juice. The smell of bacon on the fry drifted through the closed kitchen door. The Chippendale table shone with care. *Now,* her mind whispered fiercely. *Speak.*

"Did you sleep well?" Edwin asked genially, setting aside his paper altogether.

"Hardly," she allowed.

"Poor pussycat. I know what will cheer you up. I have a wonderful idea for today."

Lucy stopped breathing then. Time iced over. Whole eons passed, the rise and fall of species, of continents. "Oh?"

"Why don't we go to the Bronx Zoo? The weather's supposed to be beautiful all day and we haven't been in ages. There's a male thylacine I've wanted to see. The other zoologist in my department says it's a fine specimen."

"What's a thylacine?" Lucy managed to ask, while her inner workings continued to tumble and gyrate in the wildest of storms.

"*Thylacinus cynocephalus*," he replied professorially. "A carnivorous marsupial from Tasmania. They don't do well in captivity. Two before this one have died, and I don't want to miss my opportunity."

"Died? How?"

"General illness, I suppose, an inability to adapt. The weather here isn't anything like in Tasmania. Nothing to be done about that, I suppose."

Nothing? Lucy thought to herself. *Couldn't they leave the poor animal alone?*

"Shall we go, then?"

This was Lucy's moment. Her true feelings welled up, insisting on themselves. No was the only answer. She was already committed elsewhere today. She should have been committed years ago, actually. There wasn't a single cell in her being that wanted to see a sickly animal at the zoo. And what were they *doing*, she and Edwin, pretending all was fine and well, pantomiming agreement and affection, when really there was a hollowness between them, a dark and yawning lack?

Lucy gripped the table, steeling herself to speak her mind, just as Marta came through the door with their breakfast plates, agreeable as ever. In the many years she'd worked for Lucy, Marta had never once been out of sorts or raised her voice. She'd never burned a meal or scalded the pudding, or if she had, Lucy hadn't ever suspected it. It all went off without a hitch. The eggs were beautiful, creamy and pale yellow. Marta had placed two strawberries side by side on the plate so that they leaned on each other. It was the loveliest possible meal, utterly without reproach, and yet Lucy suddenly couldn't bear any of it. Before she quite knew what was happening, she was sobbing into her napkin, crying out as if she were suffering. And wasn't she?

"Oh, missus," Marta said, blanching. "What's happened?"

"Everything's fine," Edwin said to Marta, her clear cue to leave them. She did, in a flustered way, while Edwin kept his chair. He pushed up his round wire-rimmed spectacles with one finger, his face seeming to soften with the gesture. Then, with a gentleness Lucy rarely heard from him, Edwin said, "I'm sorry you're out of sorts." He paused and drew his hands together professorially. "It's the change, isn't it? I know this time can be difficult for a woman."

Lucy found herself blinking at her husband. How *could* he know what raged in her? He wasn't a woman, after all. But it was also true that Edwin had seldom spoken to her with even this much empathy. It *was* hard, she wanted to say—and not just the change, either, but everything. Their entire lives together, from the very beginning. That roll of parchment paper had failed them both, but he couldn't see it. Edwin was still safely inside the life he'd built for them, while she'd been marooned along the way.

"I'll tell you what," Edwin went on, ever so calmly. "Let's forget breakfast. You go upstairs and collect yourself. I'll have Marta pack a lunch for us, and we'll take it to the zoo. You've been under strain lately. It's all right to admit that. A day away will be just the thing. You'll see."

Lucy closed her eyes, her lashes spiked with tears, and felt very small' suddenly. What had she thought, signing the pledge card? She'd been playacting at bravery and progress. She was a silly woman; it was embarrassingly obvious. Sighing resignedly from a deep and awful place, Lucy opened her eyes again, knowing that she was now less than she'd been even moments before. "Yes. All right."

※

October was always a wonderful month in New York. How the auburn and crimson leaves tumbled in drifts along the avenues. The way the light tipped at a sharpening angle toward the buildings. If Lucy could only focus on these known things, she told herself as she and her husband passed through the Southern Boulevard gate of the Bronx Zoological Gardens a few minutes before noon, she just might make it through the day.

She'd washed her reddened face and put on a dark wool jacket over her shirtwaist and skirt, not at all what she thought she'd be wearing today, but the perfect weight for this sunny, cool day with its fresh gusts of breeze. Above their heads, just past the grand entrance, a single white cloud bobbed past like a carnival balloon. *You are this cloud,* Lucy tried to tell herself. *You are just this moment. Don't look further.*

The park was full of children calling out to their mothers, pointing with awe and delight; pairs of young women walking side by side under pretty parasols; handsome, contented-looking couples drinking lemonade on brightly painted benches. Lucy tried very hard to be happy for all of them as she and Edwin passed the Butterfly Garden, still surprisingly lush for the turning season, and made a wide circle through the main exhibits, pausing at the Rockefeller Fountain, where crystalline water droplets sent prisms bending and unfolding through the air.

"Wasn't this a good idea I had?" Edwin asked her then. "Do you feel better?"

"Much better," Lucy lied. "Thank you."

The Barbary lions had always been a favorite of Lucy's, and so she and Edwin stayed a long while watching their movements. Bedouin Maid, the female, was drowsing in a patch of dust, her fur the color of smoked gold. Sultan, her magnificent king, paced fluidly along the eastern wall of their enclosure, turning with grace, his tail flicking back and forth like a metronome. Long ago, Edwin had told her the lions had come from North Africa, from the Atlas Mountains, which bounded Morocco and the Sahara Desert. She'd always liked how well traveled the pair were, how much they'd seen of the world, but today, her shoulders tightened, thinking how unfair it was that they should be here at all, instead of free. Every animal should have freedom, she thought: the ungainly giraffes with their long black tongues; the elephants with the leathery folds beneath their eyes that seemed to hold sadness and regret, so much regret; and even the young women with their parasols. Freedom to do and be whatever and whomever they chose for themselves.

Past black wrought-iron posts, a mossy boulder of a tortoise moved glacially forward on ancient clawed feet toward its supper of lettuces and eucalyptus leaves. As the tortoise chewed with impossible slowness, Lucy felt in a stabbing way that this was her marriage, and she wanted to be eighteen again, to start her whole self over. She barely heard Edwin begin to give a speech about the life expectancy of giant tortoises and how resourceful they were, dispersing themselves to islands deep in the ocean by being able to float with their heads up out of the water and to survive for months and months without food or water. This was just like her husband, to praise not the animal's tenacity, its endurance, or even its will, but its ability to tolerate deprivation. Six months without food? Now there was heroism.

Lucy was still in a kind of trance when she and Edwin finally arrived at the exhibit they'd come for, the thylacine, one of a very few left in the world. As it trotted back and forth along an invisible line in its enclosure, the creature didn't look like anything Lucy had ever seen before. It was the size of a wolf or large dog, but shaped like something between a tiger and a giant rat, with a swath of dark stripes only on its rump, protruding claws, and a long, stiff tail like the branch of a tree.

Edwin began to chatter away to Lucy about the animal's significance, how the carnivorous marsupial had evolved millions of years ago. "It's a living fossil," he said, with a kind of awe, and went on elatedly. How the thylacine was pouched in both sexes, like the water opossum, and related to both the numbat and Tasmanian devil. As he spoke, Edwin looked neither at his wife nor at the animal, but at the air just above his nose, a tic of his. His zoology and paleontology students at Columbia probably laughed at him for it, but perhaps not. Perhaps they were persuaded or even in awe of him, as Lucy herself had been once. She'd been Edwin's wife for twenty-six years now, long enough for her to pass through dozens of doors of familiarity, intimacy, knowledge, and even love, yes, before arriving at this estrangement. If they'd had a child, would any of it have been different? Would she be different? Lucy would never have a chance to know. Each of her pregnancies (there'd been four; that number at least was in keeping with Edwin's plan) had ended in a stillbirth, an ocean of grief. Finally, they'd stopped trying, to spare her any further suffering. She'd turned forty-four in June. She should have been a grandmother, as many of her friends were. Instead, her body blazed and steamed in the night, seeming to mock her. This was "the change." She was changing, but from what into whom?

There in front of the enclosure, Edwin's voice drifted further and further away from Lucy as she took in the thylacine, trying to decide for herself what it most resembled. It's eyes were diamond-shaped and sharp, bright, consequential. *Don't try to name me*, the eyes seemed to be saying to Lucy with utter clarity and sovereignty. *I've seen everything. Millions and millions of years, the rearranging of continents, oceans retreating from the land. I am myself and nothing more.*

"Are you all right?" Edwin asked from the other side of a widening chasm. "Pussycat?"

It took great effort for Lucy to answer him. Her voice was dreamy. Had she been dreaming, or was she finally completely awake? "Yes."

"You seem winded. Shall we have lunch?"

"I have to go now," she said.

"What's that? Go where?"

Lucy shook her head. It was all so clear to her suddenly. "I should have lived in a gypsy caravan."

Edwin's expression was pained and fearful. "I don't understand anything you're saying."

Lucy felt great sympathy for him, suddenly, but even more for herself. "I've been so afraid. I see that now."

Before them, the thylacine made a noise in its throat that was so strange, so specific, Lucy couldn't have described it to anyone. She felt something turn in her, the great flaming wheel of her courage, or her soul.

"I'm going to be late," she said to Edwin.

"What?" His eyes had grown more and more bewildered, but there wasn't time to try to explain. There were miles and miles between the Bronx and Washington Square Park, where the marchers had already begun gathering. There were miles and miles to go for women. Suffrage was sixty-seven years old—an old woman, and yet an infant, too.

So many changes lay before and behind all women, for every living thing. There weren't words for any of it, and no time at all for anything but running, which is exactly what Lucy Cuthbert did that day, there at the end of one world and the beginning of the next. Through the park, past the laughing children, past the tortoise and the fountain, feeling breathless and new again. She ran until her feet failed her, and then she flew.

Siobhán

🦂

KATHERINE J. CHEN

I

In her free moments, she remembered home, as it had been. About five miles from the squat, one-room cottage she was never, in her youth, ashamed of, a grassy path fitted with wildflowers led to a stunted hill, and from the hill, a view of the horizon and the sea. She used to lie on her stomach in this place, bony knuckles propped under a pointed chin, and look out from gray eyes to the foaming crest of blue-green waves, rising, falling, tossing with the abandon of children splashing in a large puddle the smooth film of water that rippled and never ceased to move. A trick of the light, she knew, was why the sea on a sunny day could become a mine of glittering treasure, of winking sapphires and drifting diamonds, which blinded as much as beckoned to whoever looked upon its face. And when she'd had her fill of the view, when she felt dizzy from both the height and the smell of clean, solid earth packed tight beneath her, she would roll onto her back and lie motionless in that spot for close to an hour, eyes shut, listening.

Her mother had said to her, as a child, to bend her ear to the sea when there was trouble. Here or here, and she would indicate first her head and then her heart, as the source of one's difficulties. Later, in the years after her father's passing, when three meals became two, then finally one or none, her mother would add to this demonstration, from head to heart to stomach. It does wonders, the sea, she would tell her and her younger sisters, and she hadn't deceived them. The sound of this natural turbulence, a symphony of gurgling, roaring, and hissing chaos, as the spray flung itself and broke against a jutting point of rock, smoothed over whatever ache she happened to feel, occasionally for her father, sometimes, as was only natural, for a boy she thought herself in love with, but always for food, for bread and the taste, no, the memory of meat, of melted bacon fat in a coal-black pan held close over the fire.

The sea will save you, her mother told her, out of the hearing of her sisters one night as they slept. She remembered, too, her mother's face, not as clear as it was in the brightness of day but half-hidden, half-alive in the twitching flame of a solitary candle. A pouch of coins fell into her lap, and she knew, without meeting the eyes carefully watching her, that many a breakfast and supper had been missed for the realization of this moment; that it was a hard thing, perhaps the hardest thing, for a proud woman to have to borrow and to beg from neighbors and relations who had long ceased to visit in order to send away her eldest child. She weighed the coins in her hand in silence, and neither of them spoke, for they were craning their ears, listening to the deep-throated rumblings coming outside from an angry water. The scream of a migrant seagull caught in the storm chilled them, and she had felt a tremor in the hand that held the money.

II

Where she lived now—not her home—there was no trace of the sea, except in imitation. Nimble fingers, aided by machinery, had stitched the froth of waves into a delicate netting of lace that decorated sleeves and collars, or ran in neat, parallel fringes down the fronts of dresses from Worth and Doucet. Like water slipping across sand, the silken train of a lady's gown receded noiselessly over carpeted floors, leaving no sign it had ever disturbed the ground or even paid a visit. Birds abounded, though not in clouds. Their feathers reached skyward from the latest fashions pinned to a gathering of poised, exquisitely covered heads, and the stones—the emeralds, sapphires, and diamonds—these shone in their gilded settings and were none of them illusions dancing across the water.

In one of the many drawing rooms of Mrs. Alva Vanderbilt Belmont, at her Madison Avenue address, a meeting of this artificial sea had converged during the hour of luncheon. For the occasion, the chrysanthemum chairs with gold brocade had been uncovered, dusted, and arranged in four rows of five. A painting by Sargent, recently acquired, and which had hung in pride of place over the mantelpiece, was removed, out of consideration by the mistress of the house that the loveliness of the picture shouldn't distract from either the speakers or, more significantly, her own person when she stood to address her audience. Food was to be served buffet-style on the most forgettable set of Wedgwood plates. "Nothing flashy," Mrs. Belmont had instructed the chef, whom everyone, save the lady herself, addressed as "*Monsieur.*" "Let's keep it low-key. Ordinary, even. They're not here to gorge themselves." The next morning, she approved the menu sent up to her on gilt-edged ivory cards emblazoned with her monogram. Thirteen dishes, none over the top, most discreet, and all admirably suited for consumption on small plates that would easily fit in a lady's hand. There were the usual bluepoints and lynnhavens, Spanish olives, the chef's signature lobster salad and his less-well-known crabmeat salad, as well as smoked tongue and smoked salmon, bite-size cucumber sandwiches garnished with dill and a peppery mayonnaise, followed by assorted desserts on trays, butter-suffused custard pastries, and fresh slices of melon. It was decided the offerings of dessert would be served along with three varieties of tea, and that the guests would arrive before the speakers in order to have plenty of time to avail themselves of this everyday fare.

She was called Marjory now, which had been the name of her

predecessor, a perfectly suitable name, everyone agreed. It was easier this way, she was told, her real name being unconventional, even strange. No one could be expected to learn it, not even the scullery maid, who was Swedish. The thin line of the butler's mouth had curled into a grimace at the very sound.

"No, no," Mr. Riggs, the butler, tutted, which was his way of restoring order without raising his voice. "No, you'll be Marjory. If we're lucky, Mrs. Belmont won't notice the difference." And Mrs. Trevor, the housekeeper, had stifled a smile.

"Marjory," she repeated, as if it were a foreign word she was learning. "Marjory."

The luncheon being held that day was a private event with a social cause. Mr. Riggs called these social causes of his mistress "her parlor entertainments." Suffrage, he would count off on his fingers, being first and foremost, women's rights, then labor. And the last would send all of them, if they were collected together in the servants' dining room, into a fit of polite but amused laughter.

"She's invited a veritable carnival this time," Mr. Riggs said, stressing every syllable of the word *veritable*. "Monkeys, you know, from the factories, to tell their tragic tales to the ladies. That kind of thing."

"It's more parlor entertainments, Mr. Riggs," Mrs. Trevor said, using the language of her compatriot. "Just think of it that way."

"We're never going to be serving them?" the head footman, named Richard, asked from the doorway, while chewing a biscuit.

"What? The monkeys?" Mr. Riggs said in his most professionally stupefied tones, the same that could utter "Ma'am" while removing a bowl of cocktail sauce with a water bug in it, if the situation ever called for such an intervention. "You needn't worry yourself. *Monsieur* only cooks for the ladies, and I do mean ladies. He would be offended if word got back to him, and you know how the Morgans have been trying to poach him for the last year and a half." Shaking his head, he tutted.

There'd been more than one occasion when Marjory couldn't keep up with the discussion. She was still inclined to take references literally, and when Mr. Riggs mentioned the "monkeys from the factories," she had instantly pictured a chimpanzee wearing gloves and a cloth cap operating the bottling machine of a molasses refinery.

She had checked her disappointment at the back door when the "monkeys" turned out to be no more than an Irish shopgirl, a Polish seamstress, and an elderly Italian matron accompanied by her two granddaughters. She had been told to take their things and place them quite apart on separate wooden chairs, and while doing so, to hold whatever items she received, a coat perhaps, or a hat, at arm's length, in no way touching or brushing against the wallpaper, any other furniture, cushions, dishes, much less cookware and appliances, along the way.

By the time the speakers were led into the drawing room, the sea nymphs had already settled in the chrysanthemum chairs with their plates. Introductory remarks came after, and an encouraging round of applause succeeded only in making the faces of the honored guests, who stood at the front of the room, blaze redder than a basket of ripe cherries.

It was considered a step up that Mrs. Trevor had asked her to serve during the talks. Marjory held the tray, while another maid, named Janey, poured.

The Polish seamstress went first, talking in high-pitched, plaintive tones. She was fair-haired and tall, with well-built shoulders and long arms that stretched outward when she grew excited. It was somehow evident, without anyone remarking on the fact, that she had worn her best dress for the occasion and that in all likelihood she had labored in the morning over the immaculate polishing of her shoes. Her boots shone brighter than the small gold cross that glinted from her chest.

"I wish I could say more has changed since Triangle ..." she

began, alluding to the fire at a well-known shirtwaist factory that
had taken place over four years ago. "I wish . . ." she repeated, as the
light-blue pupils of her eyes moved dramatically over her audience.

At that moment, Marjory's own eyes settled on an image of
genteel loveliness. A single finger had made itself known to them at
the other end of a row, and they had hurried to oblige the call for
more tea.

Slowly, as she approached, the speech of the seamstress slipped
away from her. Slowly, and with relish, Marjory witnessed the last
tuft of crabmeat disappear between two pink lips, exposing a bottom line of endearingly crooked but pearly teeth and the moist
surface of a tongue. This, surely this, was what we all aspired to,
she thought to herself, and she marveled at the subtle working of the
jaw, which betrayed no hunger, no eagerness to consume. It was a
languid, subtle chewing, accustomed and therefore unimpressed by
the supply of tender, fresh meat from the sea. It was a beringed hand
of very white fingers that balanced, at its tips, the least impressive
of Wedgwood plates and the remains of what had been consumed:
three shrimp tails, two pieces of lettuce, the shells of oysters. She
counted two bluepoints and one lynnhaven, gracefully, even artfully,
set aside, like the border of a garden.

When tea was poured, she marveled at the ease of the hands
that lifted the steaming cup to the mouth. A large stone of vibrant
cerulean glinted from the right forefinger.

"The needle of the machine," the Polish seamstress said, "sliced
through my finger. It simply slipped. Blood everywhere."

And the eyes that had transfixed Marjory to the spot, which
made her breathless with an inexplicable wonder, raised themselves
and seemed to say, questioningly, *Oh, really? Did it?* before the neck
bent to sip again from the delicately flowered tea.

She knew of the suffrage and labor movements only what had
been told her by Mr. Riggs and Mrs. Trevor at the dining table.

"It doesn't involve us," Mr. Riggs, who had worked in the early part of his career for the Goulds, explained with his usual authority. "Even in labor, we're servants, you understand. It isn't considered labor to them, not to the unions or even the women. We're domestic and therefore off-limits, you see. But I don't mind that. Do you, Mrs. Trevor?"

"No, I can't say I do, Mr. Riggs," Mrs. Trevor replied. "We handle things our own way—privately. You won't ever find me in a ballot box."

"Oh, the thought of it, Mrs. Trevor!" Mr. Riggs said, turning red with laughter, before Mrs. Trevor herself joined in on the gaiety.

And Marjory, though she didn't laugh, had smiled, too, because it seemed right that she should. In the eight months she'd lived in New York, the household staff of Mrs. Alva Vanderbilt Belmont comprised her limited circle of acquaintances, and, to the extent permitted, persons she trusted. She recalled, even now, the first time she had set foot in Monsieur Arnault's kitchen, all the servants crowded around at the center table, and Mr. Riggs, flaunting his showmanship, theatrically offering her an orange.

"How would you eat this?" he'd asked, and then inclined his head to the table where dazzling lines of silverware awaited her.

She thought she would cry, but Mr. Riggs said gently, as her face showed the first signs of puckering, "You wouldn't begrudge us a bit of fun, would you, Marjory? Not on your first day?"

So, she took a knife, what later she realized had been a steak knife, and sliced the orange in half, then in quarters. With all eyes blinking at her, she took one of the quarters, put it in her mouth, and sucked. Noisily.

"Ha-ha-ha!" everyone had cried, clapping.

And what began, in that moment, as a vague feeling of inadequacy had, in the months since, evolved into certainty of her own ignorance. Her mind, at first resisting, in the end turned on her. Now she knew that she knew nothing, except what had been, at the address

of 477 Madison Avenue, explicitly taught her. She realized, initially
with a kind of horror, and afterward with resignation, that nothing
could be more terrible than to confuse the coffee and demitasse
spoons, to misname the patterns most common to flatware—
that is, names like Olympian and Winthrop—and, most deeply
ingrained in her soul, more than lines of memorized Scripture and
prayer, remained the memory of the orange. To correctly digest an
orange, she now understood, one must use a citrus spoon and apply
its serrated tip to the pulp.

It was the Irish shopgirl's turn to speak. Glancing toward the front
of the room, Marjory caught dark, girlish curls framing a flat and
sincere-looking face. She imagined that such a face would do well
behind the store counter, and her own cheeks colored with the
embarrassment that some, perhaps Janey or Mrs. Trevor, might
assume she was being indirectly represented by an individual who
was, after all, only a stranger to her. She hoped, if the stray eye of
one of Mrs. Belmont's guests caught sight of her that they would
guess she was native-born, perhaps a migrant from the South or
from a city called Philadelphia located in a state similarly named.

When she returned to the buffet table where Mrs. Trevor stood,
her flushed complexion attracted immediate attention from the
housekeeper.

"Ah, you did just fine, Marjory," she whispered, more gently
than was her custom. "I didn't have cause to notice you at all."

She was told to leave quietly and to go clean the servants' staircase.

"Richard trails in all kinds of dirt," Mrs. Trevor sniffed, refer-
ring to the head footman. But Marjory felt that Mrs. Trevor knew
the truth of the matter, and this was, in fact, a small mercy delib-
erately bestowed upon a grateful supplicant.

"I just want to be treated like a real person," the Irish shopgirl implored, as Marjory was leaving. "I want to be seen. I'm not a tool or a part of a machine to be used and thrown away."

These were the last words she caught as she hurried down the stairs to the familiar comforts of obscurity.

III

In bed, she reflected, as Janey snored across from her, that she hadn't behaved at all well on the steps of the servants' staircase earlier that afternoon.

The Italians were leaving. From above, the heavy tread of the grandmother descended, followed by the light, dancing step of her two wards. Their language, as they whispered, resembled the faint, muffled chatter of birds, who out of necessity must speak to one another but have no wish to draw attention to themselves in the trees.

As they passed the step where Marjory worked, the older woman coughed, and Marjory thought, with some distaste, that in addition to the usual scuff marks and dust to be found on the stairs, she must wash away an Italian's spit as well.

The younger child, who was no more than eleven or twelve, repeated in English, over her grandmother's coughing, "Ask her. Ask her."

"Ask her, why not?" she said again.

She had learned what to do on such occasions. In her first week, it was Janey who had enlightened her as to the steps that should be taken.

"If you're polishing something," she said in her easygoing way, "you must stop without making a fuss about it and simply leave the room, moving straight to the nearest door. You must look ahead of you, and pretend like you didn't know who had come in, and take away whatever things you brought with you to clean. I'm warning you now, don't forget. A girl lost her job here once because she was stupid enough to leave a dust cloth on Mrs. Belmont's marble table. The one shipped from *Par-ee*."

"What if I'm spoken to?" Marjory asked, thinking it an intelligent question.

"Well, then you have to answer," Janey said, and Marjory could tell from her expression that she had nearly rolled her eyes at her. "If they ask for something, you do it straight away. Or if you can't do it yourself, you find me or Mrs. Trevor."

"Now, it's more difficult to leave quietly," Janey continued, "when you're stooping or washing the floor. If that happens, all you have to remember is to stop and turn away. Stop and turn away."

"Stop and turn away," Marjory repeated, and Janey nodded.

"I wouldn't worry too much about it, though," Janey said cheerfully, as a conclusion to the day's lesson. "Mrs. Trevor is a wonder at timing all the errands. She's so good at arrangement and things like that. And it's like Mr. Riggs said. If we're lucky, Mrs. Belmont won't even realize the old Marjory's married and gone."

So, though she knew that they were all three of them staring at her on the steps, waiting, Marjory set aside her dustpan and looked in the opposite direction toward the servants' quarters. Her posture, as she folded her hands across her lap, suggested, she hoped, the discretion of the good servant who is patient but eager to resume her duties.

"Ask her," the girl repeated. "It is only water."

"No, no," her sister said, talking loudly. "You think it is only water to them? No." Her voice betrayed the frustration she felt. Embarrassment had moved her finally to anger. She broke into Italian, and a steady stream of foreign vitriol filled the hall.

By the time they reached the last stair, the grandmother's thick voice had taken turns admonishing first the one, then the other at her arm. The younger girl was sobbing. Their steps quickened, and with the alacrity of thieves, all three drew toward the door that led out onto the street, as if they couldn't bear a moment longer to stay inside the house.

She looked up too late. The door had shut, and seemingly on cue, Janey emerged from the kitchen.

"Oh, I would have given them a cup of tea before they left," she said, "if I saw them."

"I didn't know if that would have been the right thing to do," Marjory said, reddening. "I wanted to. I just didn't know."

Stop and turn away, she thought. *That's what you told me.*

Janey shrugged, leaning against the spindles of the staircase. "No harm done," she said. "And it saves us a cup, well, smashing three perfectly good cups, anyway. No knowing what diseases they might have in the factories. Not everything kills you instantly, I've heard, and it's better to be careful."

"Did you see?" Janey asked, before she moved off. "No, I think you'd left by then, so you wouldn't have. The old woman lost both her thumbs bookbinding. She showed all the ladies in the drawing room." Giggling maliciously, she looked over her shoulder at the door. "They think they're better than us anyway, those factory girls."

"Us?"

Janey gave her a look. "Servants. We're what's holding back the modern age, aren't we?"

IV

The next morning, Marjory unfolded a letter. The paper was a cheap, yellowing, and waxy type, as if it had been stored and archived for years before being mailed as an afterthought.

"Is that where you're from?" Janey asked, peering over her head. "How on earth do you pronounce that word?"

"There are all kinds of words like that where I'm from," Marjory said, trying hard to keep the edge out of her voice.

The letter, from a Father McKinnon, was only a few lines long.

Her mother was feeling poorly. Please send, if feasible, more funds in order to settle some outstanding debts and for a doctor to visit her at home.

"Is that how your name is spelled?" Janey inquired. "Your real name?"

Holding the letter in both hands, Marjory placed her right thumb over the word in question. Then she turned her thumb downward so the sweat of it would smear the ink and she wouldn't have to look at the word again. She collapsed the paper as it had been, into thirds, and slipped it under her pillow.

"So?" Janey hissed. "What are you going to do?"

She watched as her friend's eyes traveled to the end of her mattress. With a pocket knife, borrowed from the head footman one evening three weeks ago, they had cut out a small compartment after everyone had gone to bed. And inside that compartment, a bottle of dark glass still remained sealed.

"Did you or didn't you?" Janey asked, and Marjory, a numbness taking over, shook her head.

"Jesus," Janey cursed, a vein in her neck throbbing to the surface. She looked like she might be sick. "Jesus! What are you going to do?"

✳

She had begged before. At the crossroads of the village, she could always count on a passing cart to take her to town, and then she would stand on the busiest thoroughfare, before the more upscale shops, and wait and watch. The trick was to discriminate, to fix on a kindly face or a drinker emerging from one of the better pubs who might have change to spare in his stout-induced good humor.

But that wouldn't work, not here. She couldn't stand in front of Tiffany's with her hand outstretched, blocking the view of a pair of gold vases or a peridot necklace set in diamonds. In New York, everyone moved with a purpose. It was impossible to stay still.

In the way stray thoughts do, it had occurred to her without prompting one night that some exchange must have transpired in this city, which only the best families, perhaps that esteemed body of American gentility she heard tell of so frequently—the late Mrs. Astor's Four Hundred—secretly knew about and were in on together. It was a silly idea, to be sure, and she felt at once ashamed for letting her imagination run away with her. But she had wondered, even considered, for the few distracted minutes that she lingered beside a window after supper, whether a pact might have been made, signed, and sealed with blood early in the city's relatively short history. Before her eyes rose the interior of a Neoclassical ballroom, walls brushed with gold, a five-tiered chandelier removed from its protective bag for the occasion and painstakingly cleaned. The curly heads of putti decorated the cornices like victims of religious sacrifice, while a tangled mural of angels, trumpets, and lilies of the valley soared omnipotent overhead. Everywhere, installed above the Palladian windows and hidden alcoves where lovers stole kisses on divans, loomed carvings in solid gold. Here, an eagle about to take flight. There, a sylphlike Diana with two hounds baying at her feet. She saw all of this and the procession of couples who entered one by one into the room with a kind of photographic clarity. And, at the opposite end, beneath a window illuminated by a high and full moon, stood a desk with a long scroll of thick legal paper, a heavy black pen placed at its head, and a silver needle mounted on a crude wooden stand. A caped figure wearing a top hat sat behind the desk, beckoning, and the couples, forming a line, went up to sign their names and prick their thumbs, which they pressed next to each of their signatures. At the end of the party, when everyone had had a turn, the figure rose from his seat. He thanked his guests for coming and removed first his cape, his white gloves, then his shiny top hat, and everyone saw, without any semblance of amazement, that it was not a man at all who had entertained them that night but a creature with horns and a pointed tail.

"You will receive your wealth very soon," the Devil said, rolling up the scroll, and by the following morning, certain families had been made rich and their rivals bankrupted or steeped in scandal. From the depths of the earth, the Met Life building had sprung overnight like a newborn, and New York was transformed from a stick-and-mud settlement of dilapidated farmhouses into a metropolis of steel and skyscrapers, suspension bridges and automobiles. The windows of the mansions on Fifth Avenue gleamed, and the Devil waited, patiently grinning, for the collection of the souls promised to him.

How else, Marjory thought, could one account for all this finery? For Cartier clocks? For ivory-handled silk fans from Tiffany? Or vaults of Gorham silver, which made, every summer, a trip in chamois bags to mansions in Newport and then returned to sit in rooms finer than any Bayard Street tenement?

She had walked the Ladies' Mile and found the shops overwhelming. Everywhere, in the vicinity of where she lived, there was something pleasant to be spotted and taken note of: a woman's easy laugh, the *click-click* step of patent leather Oxfords on the pavement, a new window display to herald the changing of the seasons at B. Altman's. She felt sometimes, her heart stirred by a strange longing, that there could be no place more refined, more *ahead* in the world than New York. She had only to look upon the red awnings signaling the opening of a steakhouse on Fifth Avenue or the triumph of the sprawling Waldorf Astoria Hotel to feel that, in gaining these innovations, this supremacy over the known universe, something unspeakable had also been lost to the city's inhabitants forever. Beneath the veneer of agreeableness, as barely perceptible as a rising fog, there lay a stratum of unease and disquiet. The racing pulse of a criminal conscience rendered everything loud and fast. There was always the sound of construction, of engines screeching and steel rising or stone being blasted. Fresh finery was made, then purchased, and the cycle continued. Everyone talked a lot and spent a lot, and there existed no unhappiness or temporary spell of petulance that couldn't be eased and finally resolved by the purchase of an ermine muffler from Bergdorf Goodman or the digestion of a dish of roasted squab drowned in sauce at Sherry's.

You could not stand on a street corner and beg, like a clown.

*

She was aware, with a great sense of irony, that it was she in the end who had made a pact with the Devil. It was she who crept, concealed behind a sheet of rain, to the scratched red door of a four-story brownstone on her evening off. Her hand, slippery and cold, gripped a door knocker shaped in the curling horns of a ram's head. She pounded twice, then three more times before the door finally opened. From the threshold, a small woman, dark-haired, with an angular jaw, blinked at her.

"It is only natural that you should be nervous," the woman said, as they moved from the hall to a dimly lighted parlor. "Poor Francis," she added, and a finger casually indicated the direction of the entrance. "All my visitors abuse him terribly."

Money was counted, then counted again, before the woman asked, as if it were a question to be disputed, "This is just the first installment?"

Marjory nodded.

"I can be trusted. I'm employed," she began, but the woman shook her head.

"I don't need to know specifics," she said, secreting the first of what would be four payments into a pocket of her dress. From the same pocket, she produced a bottle of dark glass. "Here."

*

Afterward, Janey had said, sitting on her bed, "My friend told me she's a tiny woman. She thought she was the parlor maid when she answered the door. Is she small?"

"She's short," Marjory replied. "Frail-looking. Bony," she added, trying to think of how to describe her. "You couldn't really remember her face. She looked away from you most of the time."

"Probably being discreet," Janey said.

"Yes, that's likely."

It went quiet between them. Then Janey, smoothing a crease in the pillow, spoke. "Who was it that night? Was it the dark-haired one with the thick brows?"

"No, he had light hair. Yellowish. Green eyes." She almost smiled. "You had the dark one, remember?"

"Yes, but we only kissed a few times on the mouth. At least, that's how far I let it go."

The rebuke hit her like a slap.

"Was he the first?" Janey asked kindly, perhaps feeling she had been cruel.

She stuttered a little, shaking her head. "No," she finally said. "There were two others. Back home, that is."

Janey's eyes bulged. "Well!" she cried. "You can never tell!"

"I thought I would marry the second one," Marjory explained.

"Well!" Janey repeated. "Still, I shouldn't have taken you with me."

"It's not your fault."

"I didn't think you had it in you, though," Janey said, as if to discharge herself of any blame. "You were dancing so much. Spinning like a child's top all the time with your hair loose over your shoulders. What were you thinking?"

Marjory shook her head. "I don't know. Perhaps I wasn't thinking. Perhaps all I wanted was to be seen."

V

It was a few nights after the "monkeys from the factories" had given their talk that she had a dream.

In the one-room cottage back home, her sisters discovered a mouse in a pail. The youngest screamed, pulling in fright at the ends of her own hair.

"Ah, kill it!" they both shouted. "Kill it! Kill it quickly!"

All four of them—she, her mother, and her two sisters—stared down at the intruder. It was a brown, furry creature with patches of hair missing from its back and a thin, flesh-colored tail that twitched every now and then like a worm. Bits of blood stuck to the claws where they had been rubbed raw against the wood.

"How will we kill it?" her mother asked evenly.

"Wring its neck," one of her sisters said, without offering to do anything.

"No, don't touch it," her mother said. "It might bite you, and then we'll have more trouble on our hands."

"Beat it to death," her other sibling suggested.

"With?" their mother asked.

They looked to her for advice.

"It's such a small thing," she heard herself say in a shy voice. "Such a small, stupid thing. Look at it trying to get out." And they turned their eyes again to the creature, which was standing on its hind legs, scratching at the impenetrable sides.

"It's vermin," her mother said. "It needs to be killed."

"We could let it go," she said. "We could take the pail and just tip it over in a field. It would run away, and we wouldn't have to touch it, not once."

"And come back," they all said together. "It would come back."

"Mice always come back where there's food," her mother explained, and when she had said this, everyone looked down and away at the floor because they knew it wasn't true. They had each of them only a slice of black bread that morning.

It was her mother who decided, after considering, that a kettle of water should be heated, and when the water reached boiling, that she would pour the water into the pail. Her sisters thought this a good idea.

"I'll throw it out afterward," her mother said. "The water and the mouse together."

And as they waited for the kettle to warm, she felt sicker and sicker at heart. Her sisters sat across from each other at the table, the youngest one drumming her fingers or scratching her nose until it turned pink. Her mother bent over the stove, rubbing the end of her lower back where she felt pain.

As the first wisps of steam began to rise, she glanced again at the animal, and the sound of the scratching that they had all been forced to listen to, like the ticking of a clock, filled her with horror.

The kettle emitted its high-pitched whistling, and from her throat, a scream came out, like a shot. A chair was knocked over, and in both hands, she scooped up the pail. When she ran, it was as if the wind was at her back, pushing her in the direction of the fields.

She woke up, sweating, the sheets beneath her soaked through.

⁂

In the early hours of dawn, she sat on her bed, moving the bottle between her hands. With the nail of her left thumb, she unsealed the cap and peered inside the glass.

The letter from the priest lay unfolded next to her.

> Dear———,
>
> I am sorry to write with bad news, especially while you must still be adjusting to life far away. But I think you'll agree that some things one can't escape knowing even from foreign shores. Your mother is ill, and your sisters, though they try, have had a hard time coping on their own. I have given them what I can, but it isn't enough.
>
> Your mother and sisters say the money from you stopped a while ago, four weeks, to be precise. They don't understand why this is and hope you haven't caught any sickness from the air in New York.
>
> Please write when you can and send what you can feasi-

bly spare to the address enclosed. The doctor thinks your mother has a growth and that it is located somewhere in her spine. But he won't visit her again until she pays for the first consultation, and there are other debts to be resolved at the grocer's and chemist's shops, to name just a few.

Yours Sincerely,
Father McKinnon

It was many hours later, upstairs, that she felt a small tug at her stomach. From a crate, she had lifted the latest of a series of ancient bronzes ordered expressly from a dealer in Rome. She had clutched to her chest the bust of a bearded deity, metal curls brushing the bottom of her chin, as the first wetness touched the inside of her leg and slid down her ankle.

VI

The tray that Marjory carried into the drawing room was unusually heavy. *Monsieur* has outdone himself, everyone said, and Mrs. Trevor, sighing in awe, looked longingly toward the pyramid of cream puffs obscured in powdered sugar, which were her particular favorite. To the usual plate of almond and sesame seed biscuits was added that afternoon a dish of caramel éclairs, a silver cup of cherry compote with clotted cream, and a formidable centerpiece, a whole Neapolitan cake perched atop a crystal stand. A chocolate pot of porcelain, hand painted with green vine and periwinkle, towered in the upper left corner, while to the right, a damask napkin folded in the shape of a swan embodied the most modest of the tray's offerings.

In the drawing room, where the picture by Sargent had since been restored, Mrs. Vanderbilt Belmont waited.

"What day is it?" Marjory had asked Janey that morning.

"Saturday," Janey said.

"Is it Saturday?" Her voice was hushed like a whisper. How had three whole days passed without her realizing?

"Arnault certainly knows how to please," Mrs. Belmont muttered, as Marjory poured the chocolate. A set of chubby fingers wiggled toward the cream puffs.

She was about to leave when her mistress waved a hand at her.

"Stay. I might have something for you to do. An errand to run maybe."

Marjory waited. She watched as the first bite of cake was ingested. Then a biscuit was consumed and several spoonfuls of the cherry compote topped with cream. As the compote was still being swallowed, a second cream puff disappeared into the mouth, and Marjory thought how her employer's jaws resembled a powerful machine that one might see in a factory, mashing to a fine paste whatever entered it.

She thought, as she refilled cups of chocolate, how grotesque her mistress looked. Mrs. Belmont was a woman of mature years—old with a mean face, like an embittered bulldog. You could tell, just by casting your eye over such a face, that she was a woman hard to get along with and who was used to having the rest of the world see things her way. It didn't matter that she was dressed, at the moment, in the latest creation tailored by Madame Paquin herself from Paris. Or that she wore, pinned in the center of a wide and ample bosom, a brooch of rare purple stones. There were still cake crumbs lodged in the corner of her mouth, still a dab of clotted cream stuck, like a white mole, to the front of her chin. And the lips, when they caught the light, were oily with the stickiness of the compote. The syrup from the cherries had colored her mouth a dark shade of crimson, and if one looked quickly enough, it was easy to mistake the reddish outline for fresh blood.

She had heard at breakfast that Mrs. Belmont was in a foul mood. The tray of sweets was offered as a palliative, meant to cool the breath of her fiery temper.

"Of course she's against it," Mr. Riggs had said. "You can't really see her supporting such a demonstration, can you? It's against all her sensibilities." And he enunciated the syllables of *sensibilities* as though they were separate words strung together.

"It's just a parade," Janey put in. "What's the harm in it? A lot of women marching up a few blocks?" She shrugged.

"I hear there'll be men as well," Mrs. Trevor said.

"You know she's only upset," Richard said, "because she isn't in charge of the whole damn thing."

They had laughed at this, and Richard, thinking himself extremely clever, added, "If they could only put her on top of a float with a crown on her head and a scepter in her hand, you know she would just love the idea."

"So long as it's *her* idea," Mrs. Trevor said, since the mood at the table called for a little impropriety.

"Mrs. Belmont won't be there, then?" Janey asked, cutting up the rest of the egg on her plate. "She won't walk with the other ladies today?"

"She'll be there," Mr. Riggs said. "Don't be fooled by her blowing all hot and cold now. She couldn't let something happen without her in this city. It's not her way."

"Parlor entertainments," Mrs. Trevor said.

⁂

When Mrs. Belmont rose from her chair and left the room to go out, Marjory did not take the depleted tray and its contents through the corridors and down the stairs to be washed. Instead she lingered. She looked around her, as if seeing the walls, the furniture, and the Sargent painting for the first time. She touched the Louis XVI table by Roentgen and sat, for a few minutes, in the soft velvet side chair, to rest her feet, which were sore from standing. The soles of her boots brushed against the hardwood floor, and she tapped her heels in a cheerful rhythm, listening to the music she made, of which she was the only audience.

She didn't take the tray with her, even as she traveled through the rest of the house. It was still early in the afternoon, in the lazy hours between luncheon and dinner, and she knew that everyone would be downstairs, chatting about the demonstration and Mrs. Belmont's bad mood.

The double doors of the library creaked when she opened them. The sight of books, of so much learning and accumulated knowledge contained within rows of neatly bound volumes, moved her in a way she couldn't explain, as her fingers slid over the spines, pulling out ones of interest. She caught bits of phrases she thought lovely, like a line from Catullus, and the wing span of the butterfly *Aporia crataegi*. She opened a volume of *The Mayor of Casterbridge* to a random page and lifted the book to her nose so that she could inhale the smell of leather, ink, and fine paper. With *Middlemarch* she did the same, and she walked all around the perimeter of the room, a copy of *Robinson Crusoe* tucked in the crook of her elbow, while she stroked the backs of the armchairs and touched the head of a marble bust of Horace.

In the bedroom of Mrs. Belmont, she opened bottles of fragrance from Poiret and dabbed a little of one that she liked on her wrists. Before the mirror, she straightened her cap and apron. Her hands drifted to the panels of the immense rosewood wardrobe and, flinging them open, embraced the line of furs that hung there as if they were old friends. Sleeves of mink and fox caressed her cheeks. She felt giddy, weightless. She thought if anyone, Mrs. Trevor, Janey, or Mrs. Belmont herself, stepped into the room at that very moment, they wouldn't be able to see she was there. She would be like a ghost to them, and they would feel only a slight chill in the room where she had passed over the carpet.

Her head was full of useless things. As she moved through the halls, she considered that Mrs. Belmont had had three children by her first, loveless marriage, and that the children were named, in sequence of birth, Consuelo, William, and Harold. Mr. Harold Vanderbilt sailed a yacht named the *Vagrant*, and Consuelo had cried the night before her wedding to a duke from a place called Marl-borough. When she visited, she liked a blue Ming vase of Provence roses to be placed on her dressing table. Everyone who met her said she was beautiful. Her portrait had been painted in Europe sixteen times, Helleu and Sargent among the artists.

She had learned that furniture must have names like George or Louis or Charles to be considered of value, that it didn't matter if a string of pearls Mrs. Belmont wore had been previously owned, because the owner happened to be the late empress of Russia (Cath-erine the Great). There existed a particular fork for the eating of terrapin soup, just as there existed a spoon with a serrated tip for piercing the pulp of an orange. As she wandered through another corridor, in a part of the house she didn't know, she heard again, like a whisper, the ghoulish cackling of the servants who had laughed at her in the kitchen.

In all this, there was no room for her own thoughts. For grief. No room for the recollection of how her left boot had inadvertently stepped in a palm-sized pool of blood or the bottle of dark glass, still full, because she couldn't bring herself to drink.

The irony of what had happened three days ago didn't strike her until she nearly collided with her employer in the entrance of the house.

"Here," Mrs. Belmont said, shoving into her arms a heavy coat.

"Ma'am, you're back already?" Marjory asked, taking the gar-ment from her.

"I am. Where is everyone? Where's Mr. Riggs?"

She heard herself answer and Mrs. Belmont huff away, up the main staircase to her room. If the earth swallowed her now, she wouldn't resist. She would let herself be buried and the thousands of pounds of stone and dirt crush her from above. There was no afterlife, she thought. She needed none.

I think you'll agree, Father McKinnon had written, *that some things one can't escape knowing even from foreign shores . . . Your mother and sisters say the money from you stopped a while ago, four weeks, to be precise. They don't under-stand why this is . . .*

The door to the street was still open. As she turned away, a sound came to her from outside. It was familiar—deep and reso-nant, an echoing, cyclical rumble.

The sea! she thought. *The sea!*

She was in the road, no longer a road but a grassy path scattered with wildflowers in a green land. Her mother had told her, in times of trouble, that she must listen for the sea. The sea will save you, she'd said. And it was here—finally, it was here. It had arrived when she most needed it. A cold wind touched her back, and the coolness felt pleasant to her, even as she shivered. The sound of the current, of chanting and singing and laughing just ahead, sent her heart turning with joy.

She saw waves of white, of rows and rows of angels riding the waters, arm in arm. A garlanded float, like a massive ship, followed close behind, and she saw there were more angels to come behind the ship, that banners decorated with purple and green streamers fluttered over all their heads.

In the distance, the blast of a trumpet thundered like cannon fire. The sound would signal her crossing into heaven, she thought. She shut her eyes and waited.

"Come on!" a voice shouted, and she felt a hand smooth as mar-ble grip her arm, leading her forward. "Come on now! Don't be afraid."

A sob choked her throat as she left the pavement behind. There was no going back, no time even for good-byes.

"You can open your eyes," the angel said into her ear. "You'll crash into a lamppost going this way."

The face that greeted her, wide and framed with curls, came slowly into view. A week ago, she had thought that such a face would do well behind the counter of a store. And for a moment, they blinked at each other, divinity and human, before the current of bodies forced them on ahead.

"What's your name?" the Irish shopgirl asked.

"Marjory," she answered quickly.

"Your real name, I mean."

She hesitated. "What, don't you know your own name? Forget it?" the girl teased.

All around her, as she looked, there was beauty. Those who passed her noticed her and smiled, and she did not feel that they were laughing at her or smiling because she still wore a maid's cap on her head and an apron around her waist. From behind, a woman she didn't know placed a gloved hand lightly on her shoulder.

"A wonderful turnout, isn't it?" the stranger whispered, before moving on.

When she looked back, her friend was still waiting for her reply.

"Siobhán," she said. "My name is Siobhán."

Inside, there was so much that was raw, that hurt and was painful to think about. Yet as the sound of the sea filled her ears, as waves of angels continued to stream past them and the purple flags on the top of the grand ships rippled in the wind, she felt that this, all of this, would be enough.

Yes, she thought, it was enough.

The Runaway

⚜

Christina Baker Kline

Standing on the wide front stoop of the Children's Aid Society with the others, clutching her valise, Kira gazed down the empty street.

The plan was to walk a mile uptown to Grand Central Station, where the children would board a train headed to small towns and cities in the Midwest. They were wearing their Sunday best, gray coats over white dresses for the girls and neat shirts for the boys, white socks and brown lace-up shoes. Each of them carried a change of clothes and a Bible in a small brown traveling case. But now they waited. The matron's attention had been diverted by strange sounds in the distance: a staticky noise like the roar of the ocean, the faint blaring of horns.

The matron sighed, shaking her head. "The parade. I'd forgotten it was today. They'll be upon us if we don't make haste."

"We can avoid it," her assistant said. "We'll go up Park instead of Fifth."

The matron nodded. Turning to the children, she waved a cupped hand in the air.

The kids, a dozen in all, surged forward, trailing the women from the stoop to the sidewalk like a brood of ducklings. The assistant walked at the front with the matron, conferring about directions. Kira—at age twelve, one of the oldest—hung back. When

the last of them disappeared around the corner, she hurried down
the steps and broke into a run in the opposite direction, down the
avenue toward the sound of the crowd.

⁂

Maybe she had always been running. Most days it felt that way to
her.

Her earliest memories were of foraging through rubbish bins
in Shannon for a heel of bread and scrabbling for nibs of coal at
the gates of the coal yard. Her heart beating in her ears, her breath
fogging the air. The gates were chained, but sometimes chunks slid
to the ground from the heaping piles on the trucks that left twice a
day. She fought other desperate children for them, fumbling in the
dirt with coal-black fingers, trying to avoid the kicks and shoves.
Running home with weighted pockets, one ear cocked for the bob-
by's whistle.

She would never forget the damp, burning scent of the coal yard,
the haze of yellowish smoke, sloppy rainfall splashing in puddles.

All of them were cold and hungry. Her worn-out mam and her
angry dad. Her sister and two brothers. Arguing over a scrap of
blanket in the dark, grabbing the last sliver of cheese on the plate. It
seemed to her that her parents existed in two states, sodden silence
and rage. They fought constantly, screaming and throwing things,
breaking the few odd pieces of china they possessed.

Kira was a watcher. She was the fourth child, the afterthought.
Her parents had little time for her. Her brothers ignored her. Her
sister let Kira follow her around but was indifferent. Kira had never
met her grandparents: her mother's parents were dead; her father's
family was up north—"a brutish clan," her mother said, shaking
her head in disgust, "not a decent human in the lot. Including your
da."

The glimpses Kira had of other lives—a mother's protective arm
around a daughter's shoulders at the fair, a father, pipe in his mouth,

striding down the cobbles with a laughing baby on his shoulders—
made her wonder. She knew from the Bible that she should love her
parents, but she didn't think she did. She wondered what was wrong
with her, why she couldn't love them. Maybe she was incapable of it.
Maybe she would never love anyone.

"She's your side of the family, not mine," her da said, goading
her ma. "Plain as soda bread. Serious as a sermon."

"It's an honest face, though," her ma said. "Perhaps that's a good
thing. Beauty is a curse."

When Kira scrutinized herself in the clouded glass in the out-
house, she had to agree. Skinny as an alder, ghostly pale, with brown
hair that fell in strips around her face. Brown eyes and brown freck-
les. Too serious for her own good. She tried to hide it, but how
could she? She was who she was.

One by one her siblings drifted away. Her eldest brother,
seventeen-year-old Niall, across the water to England to seek a better life, taking the family's loaf for the day, promising at the doorstep to send money back. Aileen, sixteen, her stomach blooming
under her dress, sent to a Magdalene asylum. Then Sean, caught
shoplifting at fourteen, off to a boys' home in Galway.

A few months later, Kira's mother took sick in the coldest Feb-
ruary anyone could remember, moaning in the bedroom, spitting
blood into a rag. Kira ran to get the doctor. Watched him frown,
shake his head. "Too late," he said.

Nothing to do but watch as her ma sickened and died.

After the funeral it was just her and her da. She was a nuisance
to him, he made it clear, a drain on his wallet, a stopper in his plans.
She crept around quietly, trying to be useful. Roasted potatoes in
the hearth for his dinner, stood on a stool to wash dishes, swept the
floor with a brush broom taller than she was. Pulled off his shoes
when he came home drunk and collapsed on the bed, setting them
neatly by the door.

Even so, she saw him clearly—his glassy, red-rimmed, pale-blue eyes, one front tooth chipped in half from that time he'd fallen down the stairs. The way he bit his ragged thumbnail till it bled. His Adam's apple bobbing as he drained pint after pint.

"Stop looking at me like that, high and mighty," he said.

"I don't need your judgment," he said.

She watched him count coins at the kitchen table from his job at the morgue, muttering to himself. Still youthful, he was, only thirty-four. Young enough to seek a better life. Had to get the hell out of this place before it killed him, too.

A few days later she heard him clomp out into the hallway and ring the bell of the neighbor next door. She wouldn't let him in. "What d'ye want, Mr. Kelley?" she asked, standing firm in her doorway. Kira listened as he asked in hushed tones if she'd take his little girl; he couldn't bring her where he was going, she'd be better off here in Shannon. And the neighbor's pious rebuke: "Lord have mercy, Mr. Kelley, you'd abandon your own blood."

"Not abandon, no, Mrs. Marray, not at all. I'll send money. And I'll come back for her when I have me feet on the ground."

"Will ye, now? Like that no-good son of yours did, eh?"

And then the shouting started, her da swearing up and down.

"Nothing but a gombeen, just like his father," Mrs. Marray said, to which he responded that she was a hoor and a hag and a dry shite, and she slammed the door in his face.

The next thing Kira knew, her da was prodding her in the dark to wake up and they were stealing out the door, running down the street past the gas lamps, dim in the hoary gloom, and climbing into the back of a cart with a huddle of people she didn't know, rattling and swaying all the way down to the pier.

On the ship her da disappeared with a pack of men and boys, leaving her down in steerage, bedded between two crates. Her stomach roiled with seasickness. One night she woke to find a man's knee between her legs. She shrieked so loudly, at such a pitch, that he stumbled off her, hands over his ears, and staggered away. She never learned who he was, but he didn't try again.

Cold potatoes. Stale bread. The occasional rubbery egg. Thin broth. A tumbler of lemon juice every few days from the ship's doctor. Days and days of gazing out from the railing at the dark choppy water. She witnessed more than one funeral, shrouded forms splashing into the sea.

As the ship neared land, an excited murmur ran through the crowd. The Statue of Liberty just ahead! But the day was cool and foggy; there was nothing to see. It was as if an old blanket had been thrown over everything beyond the deck rail. The crowd was quiet as they pulled up to the dock.

Kira felt a pit in her stomach. Now, once again, she'd be reliant on her da.

They stood for hours in the immigration line, unwashed and stinking in the salt-sharp humidity. She was eleven now, she realized when the official asked her age. Every year hard-earned.

That night she and her da slept in the cluttered back room of a pub owned by an Irishman, with four of his mates from the ship. Just till I get on me feet, her da told her, but the days passed and that was where they stayed. He slept until midafternoon and was seated on a barstool by four. Staggered back to the room in the wee hours of the morning, wreathed in whiskey.

The room was dark and drafty and smelled of vomit. Kira slept on a small pallet behind an overturned table, a part of her brain always alert. She only talked to the other men when she had to. Come 'ere, lass, they'd say, but she spit at them and bared her teeth. When they tried to joke with her, or flirt, she'd let loose a string of insults she'd learned from her brothers: *Hump off, ye fat-headed lobcock. Yer full of shite, ye dumb bollix. Bunch of feckers. Bleedin' eejits . . .*

She wanted them to find her hateful. They did. And eventually left her alone.

Sometimes her da brought her food, sometimes he didn't. She began helping out in the pub, washing glasses and sweeping floors before it opened in the early afternoon. The owner's wife, Mrs. Connolly, paid her in mutton stew and soda bread. The beer she gave Kira to wash it down was dark and bitter; she only gulped it to quell hunger, but she came to like how it blurred the edges.

One day Kira was stocking shelves with liquor bottles when Mrs. Connolly said, "Those don't go together. Can't ye read?"

"Course I can."

Mrs. Connolly pointed at a line of letters above the door. "Read that."

Shame burned Kira's face. She'd been faking it for a long time, relying on cues like a carnival psychic.

Mrs. Connolly tapped her lips. "Ye should be in school."

The next day she set a book on the bar. "It's a primer," she said. We'll start with the ABCs."

A few weeks after learning the alphabet, Kira was piecing together words wherever she looked: labels on boxes and bottles, storefront signs, scraps of newspaper. Within a month, the jumble of letters above the door revealed itself as an Irish proverb: *May you never forget what is worth remembering, nor ever remember what is best forgotten.*

"I need ye to keep a secret," Mrs. Connolly said. "I'm holding a meeting here tomorrow morning. A group of suffragettes. You know what that is?"

Kira shook her head.

"Women who want the right to vote. We're planning a parade. Mr. Connolly will be at the supplier's, and he doesn't need to know."

The next morning, as Kira washed the floor behind the bar, she listened to half a dozen women plot and plan as they sewed banners out of purple and white and green cloth. They were all in agreement that women bore most of the burdens and had none of the benefits of citizenship, and it was high time they were recognized and respected as full members of society.

Kira kept her mouth shut, but she couldn't see the point. The poor were poor and the rich were rich; the men made the laws and women birthed the babies, and that was how it was. A gaggle of angry ladies marching up and down the street wouldn't change anything.

Within an hour she was conscripted to cut fabric and thread needles, to iron finished banners and tuck them into boxes. As she worked, she mouthed the words on the banners:

A VOTE FOR SUFFRAGE IS A VOTE FOR JUSTICE
YOU TRUST US WITH THE CHILDREN
TRUST US WITH THE VOTE

"How many are marching?" she asked.

"Thousands," one woman said.

"Millions," said another.

"It'll be the largest gathering of women in the history of this nation," Mrs. Connolly said. "An army of women, all in white. They can't keep saying no. We'll overwhelm 'em."

That night Kira's da got it into his drunken head to swipe from the till at the pub. He was swiftly foiled, arrested, and hauled off to jail, but not before protesting loudly that it wasn't his idea; someone else in the back room planned it. He was the fall guy, the patsy. Kira was asleep when Mr. Connolly stormed in, calling her da's mates traitors and coconspirators and worse, ordering them up and out, and Kira along with them.

She never had the chance to say good-bye. Whatever else he was or wasn't, he was still her da.

"Mr. Connolly is fit to be tied," Mrs. Connolly whispered as she ushered Kira out the door. "I wish ye could stay, but there's nothing I can do. We're not a charity, he says."

"I'll be all right," Kira said.

"I know ye will." Mrs. Connolly shook her head. "I'll look for ye at the parade."

For several weeks Kira wandered the streets. Trailed chestnut carts, waiting for vendors to toss out nuts that were too charred for paying customers. Fished penny papers out of trash bins to resell. Plucked apples from the fruitmonger's display when he turned his back to make change. She offered to do errands for shopkeepers, but mostly they shooed her away. She wasn't the only stray—there were plenty. Newsies in flat caps, bootblacks carrying brushes and wax. Packs of eight-year-olds making mischief and noise to look bigger than they were. Girls no older than her simpering with painted lips, begging for change.

It was a mild autumn, at least. Kira slept on a pile of rags in Washington Square Park with the other vagrants. When it rained, they curled up under awnings or in stairwells.

Early one wet morning she woke to find two constables, one fat and one thin, bending over her.

The fat one poked her roughly with his stick. "Can't sleep here."

"I'll move."

"Where're your parents?"

"I have no parents."

He frowned. "You're on your own, then?"

She realized her mistake. "No—I live with me gram. Just thought it would be a laugh to sleep outside for a night."

"Where's your gram?"

"Asleep."

He grunted. "Don't be wise. Where's she live?"

Ahh . . .

The constables looked at each other. Then back at her. "You're coming with us."

"I'm not."

The thin one hauled her up by the arm. "You Irish are trouble."

"You're Irish yourself, ain't ye?" she asked.

"I'm one hundred percent American," he said.

They stuck her in the dark and smelly back of a paddy wagon.

"Where're ye taking me?" she shouted through the grate.

"Children's Aid Society. The only place that'll have you."

Oh, no. She'd heard the newsies talk. Rumor had it the Children's Aid nabbed children off the streets and put them on trains—orphan trains, they called them—and sent them out to work on farms in the middle of nowhere. Once you left the city on a train, you were never coming back.

The building they pulled up to was large and imposing, with a wooden front door and a broad stoop.

"Where'd you find this one?" asked the matron who came to the door.

"Washington Square," the fat constable said.

"What's your name, girl?"

"Kira."

Surname?

"Kelley."

"How old are you, Kira Kelley?"

"Nearly twelve."

The matron sighed. To the constables, she said, "Well, if she doesn't find a placement, she'll age out soon enough."

Once inside, Kira gave her a defiant look. "I heard about the trains."

The matron eyed her. "What did you hear?"

"That ye load 'em up with children and send 'em far away to work like slaves."

"You shouldn't listen to idle gossip. Hard work and fresh air are good for children."

"I'd rather be back on the streets."

"Have you started your monthlies?"

"Me . . . ?"

"Your virtue is the only thing of value you possess in the world, Miss Kelley. On the streets of New York City you'll lose it before you know it, and then you're done for." Handing her a bar of lye soap, the matron herded her toward a room with a porcelain tub. "No belongings?"

"No."

"One last thing," the matron said. "Don't talk about the trains with the others. No need to scare them."

After a cold bath, the matron handed Kira a stiff gray shift and led her to a dormitory filled with girls of all ages, where she was assigned to a metal bed with a horsehair mattress. As the matron left, she whispered: "You probably won't be chosen anyway. Females your age are hard to place. People would rather have a strong boy or a healthy baby than a querulous twelve-year-old girl."

❖

Life at the orphanage, Kira had to admit, was better than life on the streets. She wore clean, dry clothes and shoes and was given her own hairbrush. Most of the staffers, while not particularly friendly, were not unkind. Three regular meals a day, morning, noon, and six o'clock. For the first time in her life, she attended school. The girls were kept separate from the boys, which suited her fine.

One morning, a few weeks after she arrived, she was roused from bed with a tap on the leg. Come on. Time to get ready.

Standing in line for a bath, Kira tried to imagine what she was in for. She'd been born and raised in cities; everything she knew about country life she'd learned from ballads. Thyme and roses, hares and pheasants, streams and meadows; the high mountains o'er the west coast of Clare, the rocky slopes round the cliffs of Dooneen . . . Maybe the fresh air would be good for her, as the matron had said. Maybe the people who took her in would treat her kindly. Maybe she'd find a family.

But she'd experienced enough misery in her short life to doubt it.

After their baths the girls were given new white dresses and white socks, scratchy gray coats, and brown leather lace-up shoes. Ribbons for their hair. Each received a small valise with extra clothing sewn by volunteers—a dress, socks, and undergarments—and a Bible. Then they were led into a classroom to be lectured by the matron.

"You seven girls are extremely fortunate," she said. "You're about to embark on a journey to find a family who will love you and care for you as their own. But you must be on your best behavior. The more polite and presentable, the better your chances of being chosen. Put yourselves in the shoes of the people making the decision! Wouldn't you prefer a well-behaved, pious, respectful child to a whiner or a complainer?"

Nobody spoke. The question was clearly rhetorical.

The girls lined up with a group of five boys by the large wooden door.

After being ushered outside, Kira cocked her head and listened. She heard a distant shushing sound, a faint tinkle of music. Even before the matron said it, she knew it was the parade. *An army of women, all in white.* She looked down at her dress. It should be easy enough to disappear into a crowd like that, if she could only get there.

※

It was a crisp October afternoon. The trees on the avenue rustled in the wind. The side streets were quiet, drained of people. After running several blocks, Kira stepped into a vestibule to catch her breath. She'd kept expecting to hear the matron's shout, or a policeman's whistle, but no one was behind her. She knew she was conspicuous in her coarse orphanage coat, carrying the brown valise, so she tied her coat around the waist of her dress and tucked the valise in a corner of the vestibule; if she could, she'd come back for it later.

Spying an errant sash with purple and green stripes in the gutter, she put it on. *Votes for Women.* Now she looked like any parade-goer.

She hurried toward the noise, which surged to a roar as she got closer. Crowds twenty deep lined both sides of Fifth Avenue, many wearing sashes and pins. She slipped through the throng, all the way to the front, and peered down the street.

She'd never seen so many women in one place. All shapes and sizes, young and old. Row after row of them marching in formation, unsmiling, wearing floor-length white dresses, multicolored sashes, and large hats. Old women hobbled along with canes; young mothers carried children or pushed them in carriages. Some marched with American flags that flapped in the wind. Others carried placards from states all over the country: GOVERNMENT LEAGUE OF MARYLAND, WOMEN OF OHIO, NEW YORK CITY WOMEN HAVE NO VOTE AT ALL . . .

A lively brass band passed by, trumpets and trombones blaring. Then five women hoisting a large banner: NEW YORK STATE DENIES THE VOTE TO CRIMINALS, LUNATICS, IDIOTS & WOMEN. A group on horseback clip-clopped along, the horses wreathed with garlands of white flowers, the women wearing matching flowers on their hats. A group of four carried ballot boxes on a stretcher; men wearing white jackets and boater hats marched by, sporting orange-and-black buttons in solidarity.

As Kira stood on the sidewalk, taking it all in, she heard a whimper beside her. She looked down to see a young girl with ringleted auburn hair, wearing a white dress and coat and a satin sash that spelled out *Miss Suffragette City.* She carried a large brown box.

Kira stepped back a little. This girl was not her problem. But when the girl looked up, her face was streaked with tears and her bottom lip trembled.

Kira sighed. "Are you all right?"

The girl shook her head.

"Where're your parents?"

"I'm . . . I'm not allowed to talk to strangers."

"Ah."

For a moment they stood silently, watching the parade. Then the girl blurted, "I'm lost. I was with my aunt and my uncle, but I turned to take a picture of a woman on a horse, and when I turned back, they were gone."

"D'ye know your address?"

She sniffed. "I'm staying with my relatives. They have a chauffeur. I never paid attention."

"What's a chauffeur?"

The girl smiled a little. "A man who drives you around."

Kira looked at her, noticing the mother-of-pearl buttons on her creamy dress and the fine stitching on her bodice. "I see. Well, d'ye remember anything about where ye went today?"

The girl thought for a minute. "We were at my uncle's store. Called Tiffany's."

"That's a start."

"Do you know it? It's famous."

"I don't. But if it's famous, I'm sure you'll find it. Ye may need to speak to a few more strangers, though."

A woman on the other side of the girl leaned toward them. "I'm a stranger, but I promise I'm harmless." She pointed a gloved finger in the direction the parade was moving. "Tiffany's is on Fifth Avenue, at Forty-Ninth. Just follow the parade."

"Oh, thank you," the girl said. Lifting the brown box slightly with both hands, she turned to Kira. "You were so kind to me. Can I take your photograph?"

"I wasn't really, but . . . why not, I suppose."

The girl snapped a picture of Kira against the backdrop of the marchers.

Kira had seen photographs, of course, but she'd never had her picture taken. It was strange to think of her image captured inside that box.

"Good luck to ye, Miss Suffragette City," she said.

The girl raised her fingers in a wave and disappeared into the crowd.

Alone now, gazing down Fifth Avenue at the long, slow procession of women in white, Kira felt something stir within her. She thought of all the girls in Shannon who waited breathlessly for men to ask for their hands in marriage, only to end up in misery, with too little money and too many mouths to feed. She thought of her sister, Aileen, sent to the asylum for the crime of pregnancy. She thought of her mother's short and bitter life. And she thought: *Here I am, in New York City. I can read. I can work. I have two legs and two arms and a head on my shoulders. Here I am, surrounded by an army of women and some men who believe that females should have an active hand in their own fates.*

As she watched the banners waving in the wind, in the glittering sunlight of late afternoon, Kira remembered Mrs. Connolly and her hardy band of suffragettes. *They can't keep saying no. We'll overwhelm 'em.* They had to be here somewhere, marching in their purple and yellow sashes. She wondered if she would see them. Probably not. But later in the day, when the parade was over, Kira decided, she would make her way back to the pub and see if she might earn a job.

Glancing around quickly, she stepped off the curb and fell in with a cluster of marchers. A young woman holding a baby gave her a nod and moved over to make room. Looking down at her shoes, Kira matched her steps to the women's deliberate gait. Here she was, trooping up Fifth Avenue in a white dress and a suffragette's sash, chanting, *"Votes for women—Votes for women."* Maybe, for the first time in her life, she was right where she belonged.

Boundless, We Ride

✣

Jamie Ford

M ABEL LEE, BIBLE IN HAND, CLAD IN A YELLOW DRESS STILL stained with chewing tobacco from when she'd last been spat upon, led members of the Barnard Suffrage Association up the marble steps of the Low Library. The grand dome at the heart of Columbia University, with vaulted pillars and a façade of Ionic columns, was fashioned after the Pantheon in Rome, more cathedral than college, more temple than lyceum.

And like Rome, Mabel thought, *institutions of oppression will burn.*

As her cohorts unfurled a thirty-foot banner that read RESISTANCE TO TYRANNY IS OBEDIENCE TO GOD, other young women hoisted hand-painted signs emblazoned with WILSON IS AGAINST WOMEN and TODAY IS THE DAY.

Mabel blew a pitch pipe and the women began singing the hymn "Columbia's Daughters," harmonizing the lyrics:

> *Raise the flag and plant the standard.*
> *Wave the signal still.*
> *Brothers, we must share your freedom,*
> *Help us, and we will.*

Male students in matching Philo blue ties and dark wool suits laughed and jeered, shaking their heads, taunting, "Go back to the barn, you dozy cows!" and "What more do you man-haters want? You have your own school."

We do, your sister school, at a building that was once the Bloomingdale Asylum.

Mabel was more incensed by the boys' female companions who shouted, "Haven't you done enough? You've ruined college for all of us!"

Mabel had grown accustomed to the scorn and derision from the noisy, nattering minority of classmates at Barnard College, especially after she'd fought for, and won, the abolition of the Greek system on campus. After a three-year campaign, the final vote had been 244–30. Gone were the sororities that occupied so much time and attention of her peers, especially wide-eyed freshmen who saw college as a place of cotillions and ball gowns, curtsies and corsages, where their education consisted of finding a suitable husband as they auditioned for the future role of broodmare or corset wrangler.

"Now we can focus on intellectual pursuits instead of social polarization," Mabel had said in her victory speech. The first of those pursuits would be the right to vote.

As the hectoring women stepped toward them atop the library landing, pillorying them with insults, henpecking them with incivility, Mabel reached into a pocket she'd sewn into her dress and pulled out a large handful of pledge pins from Delta Delta Delta, Chi Omega, and Kappa Kappa Gamma. She cast them at the women's feet as though she were an emissary of the Persian conqueror, Xerxes, casually presenting the heads of fallen kings. Mabel kept singing and smiled as she pointed to the yellow and purple brooch on her chest emblazoned with VOTES FOR WOMEN.

"Damn, Mabel," her roommate, Sophie Gleeson, whispered as the opposing women retreated, slack-jawed, mouths agape. "You keep this up, and you're either going to get kicked out or given a scholarship."

Mabel snapped her fingers and motioned for the others to continue singing, pointing upward to indicate they should sing even louder, with more vigor.

She knew full well that the Barnard board of trustees were deeply divided, especially since its founder, Annie Nathan Meyer, and her older sister, Maud, both banking heiresses, were on opposite sides of this particular battle of the sexes. Mabel had ridden her horse, a bay courser named Quiet, in the vanguard of the city's last great suffrage parade three years ago, alongside Maud. While Annie had stayed on campus, lecturing how the moral superiority of women was enough and that voting rights were wholly unnecessary.

"Marching in a parade is a shocking and shameful thing for female students to do," Annie Nathan Meyer had argued to a half-empty hall. "It's clearly unladylike and too sordid an undertaking for a refined woman of this institution."

Since then, Dean Gildersleeve had asked Mabel to lead the student suffragettes on campus, following in the footsteps of Juliet Poyntz, who had inspired Mabel as a freshman. That odious blessing, along with a byline in *The New York Times*, had earned Mabel a place on the dean's secret honor roll of Barnard activists. As well as the school board's list of students now facing conditional probation, since for months Mabel had been organizing protests and discreetly circulating maps with directions to where students could sign up for today's march.

As more Columbia students exited the library, Mabel and her group were quickly outnumbered and the jokes and taunts turned to curses and threats.

"Are you sure you're up for this?" Sophie asked. "Things got pretty ugly last time. I can take the lead if you need to slip away and saddle up for the parade?"

Mabel looked down at the menagerie of brown stains she'd been unable to clean from her dress. She remembered the finely tailored men who spat upon her and called her a chink and a whore. The men who threw garbage at them. When the march turned into a scrum, dozens of women had been shoved, pushed, and groped, while a handful had been beaten. Meanwhile, police officers in starched blue uniforms, sporting badges of polished silver, looked the other way. They were chivalrous enough, however, to summon stretchers.

Since that day, members of the Barnard Suffrage Association had taken self-defense classes, taught by a colleague of Kitty Marshall, the British activist who believed in direct action.

"I'm fine," Mabel said, but her heart was pounding.

"You don't even have a hatpin."

"'Deliver me from my enemies, O God; be my fortress against those who would attack me.'" Mabel held up her large leather-bound Bible. "Psalm fifty-nine."

Sophie raised a worried eyebrow and continued singing.

As a group of male students in soiled rugby uniforms joined the growing crowd, Mabel chewed her lip and looked out at Columbia's great lawn. She could smell the freshly shorn grass, which had been cut in a checkerboard pattern. Her eyes were drawn to the Pompeiian grotto where an ornate fountain had been built. Adorning the fountain was an enormous sculpture of the Greek god Pan. Stretched out in lusty repose, black of beard, and uninhibited in his nudity.

Mabel thought this was as good a god as any to represent their opposition.

Then she looked up and beheld the giant, weather-worn inscription in the attic of the library. She read aloud the words of King George II: "For the Advancement of the Public Good and the Glory of Almighty God."

God is mighty. Mabel felt emboldened and popped her knuckles. As for man, well, King George was a man and he died while sitting on the privy.

The louder Mabel and her suffragettes sang, the angrier the crowd became. The more she smiled, the more the crowed turned into a well-heeled mob, a riot of hateful privilege. They encircled Mabel and her group, trapping them. The crowd inched closer as Mabel, Sophie, and the dozen students from Barnard continued singing in earnest as though the rapture might save them. They stood tall, chins out, heads held high.

Ignore the thunder, Mabel thought. But watch out for the lightning.

A barrel-chested young man emerged from the fog of noise in front of Mabel. He rolled up his sleeves. "Don't make me do this," he said as he grabbed her shoulder.

Everyone heard it well before they saw what happened—the heavy slap of old leather as Mabel, two-fisted, swung her Bible across the young man's simian jaw—so hard that pomade flew from his hair and spattered the squealing girls beside him. Followed by a pregnant silence that gave birth to the sound of a body hitting concrete. The dull thud of a one-hundred-and-eighty-pound bag of flour in a rugby jersey crashing to the ground. The assumptions of previous generations, flattened, knocked out cold.

"I will not be a midwife to violence," Mabel said in a manner so controlled, so resolute, so piercing, her words felt like lances to those on the receiving end. "But I also will not abide any man to lay hands upon my person. Ever."

In the awkward moment that followed, Mabel noticed that starlings and sparrows were singing. She heard motorcars growling in the distance. The clanging of a streetcar bell. The whispers of students as they gently revived her assailant.

"*Emgoi joi gong.*"

Mabel looked up to see who was speaking to her in Cantonese. Yet even as she searched the crowd, she realized who it was before she saw him.

"You can say that again," a handsome young Chinese man said for the benefit of his English-speaking peers as he parted the crowd. He spoke with a British accent and, like the others, wore a fine wool suit. But his blue tie had a pin in the shape of a cross with a golden sun, honoring him as a senior member of Columbia's Philolexian Society. The debating club for men had been founded by Alexander Hamilton, but the common joke was that they were only debating who would someday rule the world.

"Are you still angry with me, Ping-hua?" he said as he peered over the rims of his tortoiseshell spectacles. "Chinese only get angry about things we truly care about. I didn't know you had such feelings for me. I didn't know you were capable."

Mabel gritted her teeth. No one but her family ever called her by her real name. Not even the parishioners at her father's Chinese mission home on Pell Street. She tried to calm her emotions, but her blood was still racing. "I have more important things to do than be angry with you, Tse-ven. Like shoveling manure from my horse's stall."

He smiled as he released the button on his suitcoat and adjusted the knot of his silk tie. "How about this? I'll call you Mabel and you can call me President Soong."

Mabel hadn't seen Paul Soong in more than a year. Not since he'd defeated her in the most recent election for president of New York's Chinese Student Association. Though *defeated* was a subjective term. They both came to this country as toddlers, spoke fluent English. Both were finishing their degrees in economics with perfect marks and had been handpicked by their respective deans for leadership positions on campus. The difference was that his college admission had been bought with a sizable donation from his family, while Mabel had won a Boxer Indemnity Scholarship. She'd had twice as many supporters. Yet when the ballots had been counted behind the closed doors of the Low Library, she'd lost by a dozen votes. She was the poor daughter of a Baptist minister in Chinatown. Soong lived uptown, the princeling of one of the four wealthiest families in Shanghai. She should have known the rules would change for him. There was no way he could return to China having been defeated by a woman.

"You're speechless for once." Soong smiled, laughing. "I like that."

Before Mabel could respond, Sophie was tugging at her sleeve. She pointed at her wristwatch. "I know you want to fight every battle, but there's a war to be won today. We need to go, Mabel. It's time to get ready for the march."

"You should listen to your rabbit friend," Soong said.

Mabel tightened her jaw and closed her eyes. Then she opened them, turned, and walked back through the crowd, her face glowing red with anger. Sophie walked next to her as their group of protesters followed.

If Soong and the male student body of Columbia had more words, Mabel didn't hear them; her ears were ringing with frustration and humiliation.

"Why did he call me a rabbit?" Sophie asked. "Is that a Chinese thing?"

Mabel said nothing. She didn't want to explain the gift that had shown up on her doorstep on the eve of the student election—a copy of *What the Master Would Not Discuss*—a collection of short stories that had been banned in China. In it was the story of Hu Tianbao who, after confessing his feelings for another man, had been tortured and executed. Tianbao's spirit later returned from the underworld in the form of a rabbit.

"It's an insult, intended for me," Mabel said.

Sophie seemed to mull this over as she walked. "Well, whatever it means, I'm kind of glad he showed up. I mean, we're lucky to have gotten out of there in one piece."

Mabel stopped and held up her Bible.

"When you're down on your luck, grow a wise heart. Proverbs nineteen."

"Yeah, but . . ." Sophie said.

Mabel opened her Bible and withdrew a horseshoe that had been slipped inside the back cover. She felt its weight, then handed the rusted piece of metal to Sophie.

"I've learned to bring my own luck."

⁂

In the livery next to her family's mission, Mabel left her sidesaddle hanging on the wall and instead dusted off her father's old Western saddle. She hefted it atop her horse, Quiet. Then she adjusted the breast collar and shortened the leathers.

"It's going to be okay," she said as she scratched her horse's withers and fed Quiet a piece of ginger candy. "I know this saddle isn't what you're used to, but just like everyone else, you're going to have to get used to something new from now on."

Quiet, who never neighed and rarely even nickered, flapped her ears, bobbed her head, and flashed her tail as though in reply.

Mabel had decided she would never again ride sidesaddle. Especially after reading how Inez Milholland had ridden astride, like Joan of Arc, charging her horse through a crowd of howling drunks in last year's parade in Washington, D.C.

"If Inez had been riding like a so-called lady," Mabel told Quiet, "that mob would have pulled her down and beaten her like all those other women who were carried down Pennsylvania Avenue bleeding. Instead it was the hooligans who had to be rescued, by the U.S. Cavalry."

Lack of mobility, Mabel thought, *just another way we're kept in our place.* Lack of education. Arranged marriages. Being treated as property. A man can divorce a woman but a woman cannot divorce a man.

Mabel heard a knock on the door and was startled to look up and see Soong in the doorway. His double-breasted suit stood out against the raw timber of the stable and the horse tack hanging from the beams. She noticed him trying not to wince at the odors of hay and sweat from the horses, which to Mabel smelled better than the finest perfume.

"What are you doing here?" Mabel asked, as Quiet whinnied and twisted her head.

Soong removed his hat and then sneezed into a handkerchief, twice. He wiped his nose, then refolded the pocket square and put it away. "Would you believe me if I said I came all the way down here to make amends for that scene earlier today?"

Mabel slipped a headstall over Quiet's ears. "No. I wouldn't, actually." Soong's aspirations always came first. She'd never heard him apologize for anything, ever.

"Well, here I am nonetheless. You know me, Mabel. We used to be friends. I am many things, but I'm not one of those brutes. Though appearances must be maintained—surely you can appreciate that?" He let himself in, watching where he stepped so as not to ruin his expensive leather Oxfords. "I came down here, because on a day like today, we shouldn't be fighting. Or at least we should be fighting on the same side."

Mabel found a riding crop and flexed it. "You once told me that we're opposites. That I'm yin. You're yang. I'm dark. You're light. I'm closed. You're open."

"And I meant it. You and me—look at us—we're the epitome of dualism. I'm order, and you're . . ." He motioned to the stable of horses and bales of hay, sighing. "You're whatever this is. But we complement each other. One might even say we need each other. Together, we're stronger, more capable. I lead the Chinese students at Columbia. You lead the Chinese girls—the women—of its sister college."

"What do you want, Tse-ven?"

"I want you to give up this idea about riding in today's parade, Ping-hua. You weren't born here. Even if you win, you won't be able to vote anyway."

Mabel stared back at him, shaking her head, smiling. "That's the difference between us. I don't do things just for me."

"Then I'm sure you'll be astonished to hear that I came down here to offer you a seat next to me as my guest in the viewing stand in front of the city library. Mayor Mitchel will be there, the Board of Aldermen and their wives—"

"I have a better idea," Mabel cut him off. "Why don't you support us by marching in the men's brigade? There are thousands of men who signed up this year."

Soong smiled but Mabel could see he was trying not to laugh.

"Me, marching in a women's parade?"

Mabel hung the crop from the saddle horn.

"They won't even let you ride in this year's parade," Soong argued. "Look in the mirror. You're not Nellie Bly, or Margaret Vale, or even bloody Helen Keller. They all have something in common, in case you haven't noticed. Ever since Woodrow Wilson took office, there haven't been any colored women invited to these marches."

On campus, Mable had watched Soong win debate after debate. He could be convincing when he wanted to be, powerfully charming.

Soong cleared his throat. "Lincoln said, 'I am not, nor ever have been, in favor of bringing about in any way the social and political equality of the white and black races.' He said those words to Stephen Douglas, but those sentiments apply to us as well."

"Things are different now." Even as Mabel said those words, they felt more a wish than a statement of fact. She chewed the inside of her cheek, knowing there was an uncomfortable truth in Soong's words. She felt it strangling her, like a tight button collar, a corset, squeezing her until she felt light-headed, dizzy with discomfort. Since President Wilson had been sworn in, even maverick suffragettes like Alice Paul had been hesitant to affiliate themselves with women of color. Wilson was a southerner, after all, and to southerners, women's suffrage was a road paved to the unthinkable— black suffrage. Lincoln had been practically beatified for helping to emancipate the slaves, but he'd still been against black Americans voting, serving on juries, holding office, and intermarrying with whites. Mabel frowned as she remembered how in Washington, D.C., Ida Wells had refused to march in the back of the parade with the black delegation. Instead, she waited with spectators along the parade route and then walked into the middle of the street and took her place at the head of the Illinois group as they passed. Mabel wasn't even sure if Ida was going to bother with today's march. She couldn't blame her.

"If you sit in the viewing stand with me, the world will see you differently. I could introduce you to some very important people. We could present ourselves as a united front, representing all Chinese in the city. Not just students. All you have to do is—"

"Be your subordinate," Mabel said. "Show them all that you've tamed a suffragette. Be your pet, your pretty lap dog, but not your equal."

"Women never will be," Soong snapped, then stared at the ceiling, nostrils flaring as though he'd just revealed his cards in a poker game before the final round of betting had ended. "But . . . that doesn't mean we can't help each other. I'm trying to offer you something. But all you see is your anger. You've been bitter for as long as I've known you, Ping-hua. Even before the student election. You're a leader at school. You have Dean Gildersleeve's ear. Why are you so unhappy?"

You're Chinese. You would never understand.

"I have my reasons," Mabel said.

There was an awkward silence.

Then Quiet chuffed and stamped her hooves.

"Fine. I've wasted enough time here. If they somehow let you march, do wave when you see me. I'll be the one sitting next to Senator Wadsworth."

As he stalked out, Mabel stood wondering for a moment if she'd made the right decision. She was well regarded at Barnard. She'd planned to pursue a doctorate at Columbia, something no woman had ever achieved. But even then, she'd be seen as a mere woman. Would it be better to be seen with Soong? Visible—her photo would appear in hundreds of newspapers—instead of just another face in a crowd of thousands?

"So, that's the handsome Paul Soong I've heard so much about."

Mabel smiled when she heard her ah-ma's comforting voice. That smile vanished when her mother—still a young woman, not yet forty years old and full of joy and good humor—shuffled in with a cane in each shaking hand. Her back was stooped, curled like a question mark. She could barely walk. She could hardly leave their home to shop in the market; she could scarcely do anything outside of domestic work. Even that drudgery was a struggle since her feet had been bound as a child, soaked in herbs and animal blood to soften the tissue as her toes had been curled under, her arches folded, bandages cinched so tight that the bones in her feet had broken again and again, until they finally fit a pair of tiny four-inch lotus shoes.

All for the amusement of men.

"He gave me this as he left." Her ah-ma held up a calling card. "Everyone in the neighborhood talks about him. We should invite him back for tea sometime."

"He won't be coming back."

Not in this lifetime.

Mabel took the card. On one side was a sepia print of Soong's smiling face and his signature in English. On the back was his home address. She stuffed it in her pocket.

"That's too bad." Her ah-ma put a hand on a wooden beam to steady herself, lest she topple onto the muck-ridden floor. She rested her canes against the wall. "I brought you something."

Mabel watched as her ah-ma held up a yellow chrysanthemum in full bloom. She pinned it to Mabel's dress above her heart, hiding a dark stain.

"Good luck with that march of yours, Ping-hua. I'm so proud. And even though your father is abroad, I'm sure he'd be proud, too. I only wish I could be there to watch you. But by the grace of God, I am what I am." Her mother smiled. "First Corinthians."

※

Mabel rode through the Bowery, Quiet's hooves clip-clopping on dirty, cracked pavement until they reached Bleecker Street, where Sophie would be waiting along with dozens of members of the College Equal Suffrage League. The student suffragettes were stationed behind a gathering of letter carriers' and patrolmen's wives and in front of a brigade of caped nurses. The student group was impossible for Mabel to miss as they were all wearing caps and gowns and had their own marching band. As she listened to the brass section tuning up, Mabel noted the colors and banners, representing at least a dozen women's universities—Mount Holyoke, Vassar, Wesleyan, Bryn Mawr, Radcliffe, Wellesley, and of course, Barnard—and that everyone wore matching suffrage pins. Gathered together they looked like a roiling sea of possibility, tidal forces to be reckoned with.

The group cheered when they saw Mabel on horseback. That joyful noise exorcised the demons of doubt planted by Soong. She smiled and spun Quiet around, trotting back and forth across the street until she found her roommate.

"Hey, you forgot your Bible!" Sophie teased.

"A whip is for the horse, a bridle for the donkey, and a rod for the back of fools." Mabel held up her riding crop, smiling. "Proverbs twenty-six."

※

An hour later Mabel heard the booming of a drum corps thundering in the distance and knew the march had officially begun. A whistle blew and she and the other student suffragettes lined up, eight abreast, each row of marchers carrying hand-painted signs that delivered part of a continuous message:

WE TALK WITH YOU

WE EAT WITH YOU

WE DANCE WITH YOU

WE MARRY YOU

WHY CAN'T WE VOTE WITH YOU?

Mabel rode to the front of the student marchers, where she met four other young women on horseback, each in a yellow dress. The combined collegiate marching band assembled at the rear, their drums pounding in time with others in the parade.

The rider next to her said, "Just look at that. A three-mile-long argument for women's rights. I hear it's the largest suffrage parade ever."

Mabel nodded. Was it also large in its passivity? She couldn't help but yearn for more pointed actions, not violent like the arson and window-breaking of European suffragettes, but something akin to when British activists dropped thousands of handbills from a hot air balloon on their prime minister as he was attempting to dedicate a statue on the embankment of the Thames. Mabel smiled as she recalled how some of her classmates had stolen acid from a closet in the chemistry lab and burned SUFFRAGE NOW into the fairway grass of the Van Cortlandt golf course.

As they slowly marched past Washington Square Park, the official starting point of the parade, Mabel beheld the crowd of spectators, thousands, at least five or six deep on either side of the avenue, with hundreds more in the windows and on balconies and fire escapes. The parade watchers didn't boo or yell this time, much to Mabel's relief, but they didn't applaud either. Though she couldn't help but notice more yellow dresses in the crowd than last time, and the sparkling suffragette pins in yellow and purple, worn by quiet matrons along the way, nodding in solidarity as their husbands stood mute.

When the student band played "The New America," Mabel began to sing:

> *Our country, now from thee,*
> *Claim we our liberty,*
> *In freedom's name.*

Mabel looked back at Sophie in the front row of the marchers. She smiled as they sang back:

> *Guarding home's altar fires,*
> *Daughters of patriot sires,*
> *Their zeal our own inspires,*
> *Justice to claim!*

From horseback, Mabel could see the millenary of marchers stretching into the distance, brass bands and fleets of automobiles, traversing the ribbon of concrete known as Fifth Avenue. They looked like an army of beautiful righteousness, an armada of hope, faith, and aspiration. Mabel sat tall and proud in the saddle, confident they would be heard beyond the city, beyond New York, beyond her own expectations. But when the towering pillars of the New York Public Library came into view, she saw the enormous grandstand that had been erected atop the front steps between the great marble lions, Patience and Fortitude. Gathered in the stand were the city fathers.

Why were there never any city mothers? The joy and satisfaction Mabel had felt moments before seemed to vanish, like the fading memories of a pleasant dream. Why were there only male politicians and business magnates with their hands on the wheels of progress, steering the city and the state in the direction of their choosing at the speed they alone cared to travel? As their wives smiled in ornamental beauty?

Mabel found Soong standing atop the riser, looking down at her as she sang, "*Sons, will no longer see, mothers on bended knee . . .*"

Her voice quavered and she stopped singing.

Soong smiled.

Mabel drifted along in the current of marchers. She looked away, rocking in the saddle, staring into the distance. She felt Soong's eyes upon her, illuminating her fears and insecurities, but also her determination and convictions. Heart pounding, she pulled on the reins and turned Quiet around, veering off the parade route. She cantered down a side street as she heard Sophie calling her name.

Clear of the parade, Mabel galloped down vacant streets. Quiet's hooves echoed through the canyons of brick and mortar, leaving marchers and spectators and music in the distance. She rode hard, back to Chinatown, until Quiet's neck was wet with perspiration. She was comforted by the sights and sounds of home, the smells of freshly caught fish and sesame oil. But home was not enough. She dismounted in front of her family's mission, bursting through the front door, shouting until she found her mother.

Thirty minutes later, Mabel returned, nearly out of breath as she caught up to the parade, which was far from over. She slipped through an opening in a crowd of spectators who had gathered at the crossing of Forty-Second Street. There she found a space just ahead of a group, two- or three-thousand strong, carrying banners representing Empire State Teachers. That group was marching behind the delegation from New Jersey. Mabel knew that the New Jersey suffragettes had just lost their referendum by fifty thousand votes, though if they had been discouraged by their setback, they didn't wear their defeat. Instead they wore smiles, proudly marching in purple and yellow gowns, and had a horse-drawn victory float adorned with a Junoesque woman dressed as the Scales of Justice.

Mabel was happy to be back, walking beside Quiet, lead rope in hand.

In the saddle sat her ah-ma, beaming.

"Are you certain we're allowed to do this?" her mother asked.

Mabel had to adjust the leathers on the saddle since her mother's bound feet were so tiny and narrow they wouldn't rest in the stirrups. Her feet risked slipping through entirely, so Mabel kept her eye on them as her mother held on to the saddle horn with one hand and waved to the crowd, who seemed amused and delighted by her presence.

"What do you think, Ah-ma?"

Mabel looked up as her mother sighed happily. She hadn't been uptown in nearly a year. She didn't like to travel, even on streetcars, and had never taken the subway, which began service ten years ago. Boarding on and off was simply too hard.

"I think I am blessed to have you as my daughter."

Mabel looked up as the sun began shining through the pale October sky.

They followed the New Jersey delegation, which began singing as they passed the grandstand. Mabel's eyes once again met Soong's. She smiled, knowing she was right where she was supposed to be, no matter what, and that she wouldn't trade this moment for all the vainglorious pretensions in the world.

Soong simply nodded, tipping his hat.

Then she heard a soft *click* and looked down.

In front of the crowd of onlookers, halfway into the street, stood a little girl, no more than seven or eight, in a white dress and coat fringed with lace. She was magnificent in a sash of purple, green, and white that read *Miss Suffragette City*. The girl was peering down into the viewfinder of a small handheld camera.

She looked up, delighted. "That's going to be a good one. Would you like me to send you the photograph when my auntie gets the pictures finished for me?"

Mabel stopped her horse. She glanced at her ah-ma, who was still in awe of the parade and being part of such a grand occasion. Then Mabel knelt down, held the little suffragette's hand, and said, "Thank you. I'd like that very much."

She reached into her pocket and found Soong's calling card. Then she handed it to the little girl. "Please be so kind as to send it to this address, at your convenience."

Mabel stood and led Quiet back into the parade, waving good-bye, searching for an appropriate scripture. Something about a little child, leading the way. Mabel forgot the verse and for once it didn't matter.

American Womanhood

༜

Dolen Perkins-Valdez

O N THE MORNING OF THE NEW YORK CITY PARADE, I WAKE up early and open the dining room windows. The breeze billows the sheers. I did not sleep well, but the cool air refreshes me. I have been following the planning of the parade closely in the Chicago papers, and I know they are expecting a crowd. Not being in New York feels like adding insult to injury, but I refuse to let it get the better of me.

On Saturdays, my family typically enjoys a late breakfast, and the whole house smells of bacon. I hope the scent will awaken my daughters and remind them of their morning duties. We take all our meals in this dining room, and though our sons are older now, with their own schedules, I still manage to gather the family for weekly Sunday dinners. Our table is set with a lace tablecloth every day of the week. On the wall above the sideboard hang portraits of me and my husband in oval wooden frames.

"If you do not eat much, you will not have the strength to work today," I tell Ferdinand as he takes his seat at the table. He has been working late all week, and exhaustion sits beneath his eyes in dark rings. His new case involves a Negro man who was fired from his job after white union workers claimed the position. Last night, Ferdinand admitted he may not be able to win against the powerful union.

I am worried about my husband. His hair and mustache have turned entirely gray in just the past two years. He has spent the better part of the year working on behalf of colored laborers while I worked on city council and mayoral races. Both of us are tired, but there is no time to rest. After the elections, the racist film *Birth of a Nation* was released in Chicago theaters. Then I became involved in defending a prisoner, Joe Campbell, who had been accused of murdering the prison warden's wife and, in late August, I learned of the lynching of a Jewish factory superintendent, Leo Frank, in Marietta, Georgia. No, there was no time to rest at all for either of us.

"I see the way you look at me," he says suddenly, jarring me out of my thoughts.

"You do?"

"I will get through this. But what about you, Ida? Have you come up with a plan to keep the Negro Fellowship League afloat?"

"Not yet," I say. I have been out of work for months, and our funds are running low. My decision to fund the league out of my salary as a probation officer was supposed to be a temporary solution, but I had been too busy working to find an alternate source. First, men needed housing and jobs. Then there were political meetings to be held. Voters to organize. A women's suffrage club to run.

Ferdinand and I are a comfort to each other when the sun goes down, but each of us must march out alone in the morning. The newly elected alderman, Oscar De Priest, promised me a judgeship for Ferdinand if he were elected. I worked day and night to canvass black voters and get De Priest elected as Chicago's first black city councilman. In the end, black women in the city cast over twenty-five hundred votes for De Priest. My Alpha Suffrage Club played a significant role in his election, and everyone knows it. Becoming a judge is Ferdinand's dream, so I merely tried to accomplish two things at once by offering my candidate support while also enabling another worthy colored man to rise in the ranks. Wasn't that the purpose of enfranchisement for women? To open the doors of powerful political opportunities for colored people in the city? I am still hoping the alderman will deliver on his promise, but there have been troubling signs. I have not mentioned them to Ferdinand.

I am disappointed by the way colored women are being treated by the politicians we helped elect. After the debacle at the Washington march two years ago, I decided to focus on local politics, help the women in my own city. Now even that city has forsaken us. At our meeting today, I must help lift the morale among the clubwomen.

I kiss Ferdinand on the forehead. His hand shakes and he spills a little coffee on the table. The brown liquid spreads on the lace, to the vinyl beneath.

"I'm sorry, darling."

"It's fine," I say, though I waste no time blotting the stain with a napkin. My husband has been married to me long enough to know that my household has to maintain a certain rhythm of efficiency. I just wish my entire life were as simple as running a household. I kiss him on top of his thinning hair before I leave, glancing at the clock as I put on my wrap. The women at the parade in New York are probably preparing to walk to their meeting points. They are having the last of their breakfast, chatting excitedly among themselves. They are hopeful, optimistic, newly recharged with their mission. Parade or no parade, I need to do the same for myself.

※

When I arrive at the State Street building where the Alpha Suffrage Club holds our weekly meeting, I am early, but there are at least a dozen women milling about. The meeting is held in the reading room of our Negro Fellowship League building. It is a long, rectangular room with a line of bookshelves along one wall. Typically, the tables are surrounded by chairs, but now the tables are adjacent to one another and covered in a long white tablecloth. Two women arrange plates of food. At the end of the row, a third club member sets up a beverage station. As the president of the Alpha Suffrage Club, I am not expected to help with the refreshments. I go to the lectern and consult the program for the meeting.

My assistant, Bettiola, has written everything out. The young woman is a poet and journalist, and at twenty-four years old—twenty-nine years my junior—she reminds me of myself when I was her age: opinionated and fiercely committed to the cause. She has no interest in marriage, though her beauty is well known. She carries herself with a steady sense of purpose. What I also like about her is that she is one of those rare young people who listens.

"How are you feeling today?" she asks me.

"I am feeling much better," I say. I had been a little sick with a cold, but thankfully, the weakness has passed. I am too busy to tolerate illness.

"Why are there only three people speaking tonight?" I ask. "That will hardly fill the entire first hour."

"Mary will perform a recitation that is quite long. Each of the other two women will speak for twenty minutes. I have left time for discussion."

More women enter the room. They remove their stoles and hang them on a rack. The din of conversation grows.

"You penmanship is difficult to read. Did you hear back from Mr. De Priest?" I ask her.

"I did not. I have sent him three letters now requesting a meeting."

"Maybe you should appear at his office in person."

"Yes, Mrs. Barnett. I will do that."

I know I am difficult. My daughters say this about me. Yet this world countenances very little patience for inept colored women. We must be excellent in all areas, or we shall be trampled. This is especially true when we are trying to be taken seriously by men. Even so, I must be honest. I am especially churlish today because I am not in New York marching with the other women. The current financial affairs of the Negro Fellowship League also weigh on me. I am unsure how to take a step forward when the walls are closing in on all sides.

Bettiola glances down at the paper, as if she wants to take it and correct her errors. I soften. She only wants to please me, and I appreciate all that she has been doing to help with the club. The young lady has proven herself indispensable.

"Thank you, Bettiola."

"You're welcome." She looks at me for a moment.

"Is there something else?" I ask.

The women begin to take their seats. The chairs are lined up in rows, and they scratch against the wood floors as everyone settles. Most weeks, we welcome over a hundred women to our meetings. We use the first hour for club business and the second hour for socializing and eating.

"There is a march planned in New York City today. Did you hear?" she asks.

I have not spoken to Bettiola about it because I did not want to alarm her. But of course she knows. She reads the papers as regularly as I do. I have planned to mention it in my speech today, but I had hoped to keep our business limited to Chicago's own woes. I want to convince the women that this parade is too distant to be related to our troubles. Folly, I know.

"There are always parades of one kind or another," I say.

"This one is big. They are expecting thousands of people. Perhaps it will even be larger than the one in Washington—" She stops.

I purse my lips. Even now, two years later, the pain of that humiliation lives with me. Bettiola knows this. Yet she also understands that if I am to lead this meeting, I need to be aware that the topic of this New York parade might arise. And she does not want me to be embarrassed or caught unawares. I am grateful for the warning, though it is not something I don't already know.

I look out over the women who are chatting among themselves as they await the appointed meeting hour. I observe Mary, who must have knocked on over one hundred doors on behalf of Oscar De Priest's campaign to be the first black city alderman. I see Vera, who led a band of twenty women into churches all over the city to ask for votes in the mayoral election. Now those elected politicians have barely offered us a crumb of the spoils. It is outrageous.

I have been so busy with my efforts to make the best use of our limited enfranchisement in Chicago that I have put aside the efforts of national white women's organizations such as the National American Woman Suffrage Association. We still must attain a constitutional amendment so that women in every state will have the vote. I understand the urgency. Yet I still remember how our white suffragist sisters barred us from attending their conventions in 1901 and 1903. I remember how they refused to condemn racism while simultaneously expecting us to put gender before race when, in fact, both are hurdles for us. How can we work together in such circumstances?

The clubwomen quiet and look up at me. Bettiola takes a seat in the front row next to an empty chair where I will sit once the speakers are introduced.

Shall I talk to them about what happened in 1913? Shall I mention this New York City parade? Or shall I ignore those efforts the same way they tried to ignore us in Washington, D.C.?

"Ladies. Welcome to the Alpha Suffrage Club meeting. Today is October twenty-third, nineteen fifteen, and I am Ida Wells-Barnett."

⁂

Two years earlier, on March 2, 1913, I arrived in Washington a day before the parade. The March wind cast a chill in the air, and the sky was overcast with the threat of rain. I had arranged to stay at the home of my friend Mary Church Terrell, while the rest of the Illinois delegation stayed in a hotel. Two months prior to the trip, I had founded the Alpha Suffrage Club, whose mission was to educate colored women in Chicago on their civic responsibility and help elect public officials who would advance our cause. But I was the only colored woman traveling with the Illinois delegation. My suffrage club was still recruiting members, and I could not convince any of my colored friends to make the journey with me. I did travel with two friends, however. Among the Illinois delegates were two white women who helped cofound my club: Belle Squire and Virginia Brooks.

The city was filled with people. The march organizer, a young Quaker woman by the name of Alice Paul, had shrewdly planned the march for the day before Woodrow Wilson's inauguration. In addition to the suffragists, thousands of men had arrived for the inauguration. The swell of visitors to the city was impressive; it was a relief to get out of the crowds and make my way to my friend Mary's house.

When she opened the door, she swiftly took my bag out of my hand.

"Ida Bell, if you don't get in here so I can hug you!"

Mary was from Memphis, not far from my hometown of Holly Springs, Mississippi. In fact, her father, the late Robert Church, was born in Holly Springs. We were nearly the same age. I had always felt a sisterly affection for her, and as soon as I walked into her house and saw the logs burning in the fireplace, I was glad not to be allowed to stay in the same hotel as the white delegates. Mary was stunning in looks and intellect. We had worked together on numerous occasions, and though we did not agree on everything I knew she felt as strongly as I did about race work. I looked forward to an evening of lively discussion with her, and I said as much.

"Oh, it won't be just the two of us tonight. I have invited some very special guests," she said.

"Who?"

"You shall see."

Later that evening, a group of students from Howard University arrived, and Mary served them several different kinds of cake. The women were members of a newly founded sorority that called itself Delta Sigma Theta. The twenty-two young women were planning to use the march as their first service event, and they were abuzz with excitement. As the senior women there—both Mary and I were in our fifties—we looked upon them as daughters. They were so well dressed and respectful that I was proud to think they would represent our cause in the parade the next day. Their talk was filled with ambition, how they planned to use the platform of their sorority to work within the suffrage cause. Their enthusiasm energized me.

After they left, Mary showed me that she had obtained a copy of the march's official program. I carefully read through the twenty pages, looking at the pictures and examining the biographies of the women. Then I turned to her. We were both sitting next to the fireplace in her parlor. The embers were waning, and the window shutters were drawn. The house was eerily quiet after having been filled with the chatter of young women all evening. Though I had enjoyed the activity, I relished being alone with my friend, finally.

"They say the theme of the march is the 'Ideals and Virtues of American Womanhood,'" she whispered.

"American womanhood? And yet they do not include a single reference to or picture of a colored woman in the entire program," I replied.

"And they use the word *ideals*."

"As if we are not the ideal."

"As if we are not women."

We expressed our anger to each other, but our emotions did not prevent us from retiring to rest up for the next day. Mary and I were used to channeling our frustrations. There was work to be done, and we had to rise early. She was planning to accompany the sorority, and I had to meet the Illinois delegates for a drill practice.

On the morning of the parade, we dressed in the early light. I donned a long black dress and draped a white silk Illinois banner around my neck. On my head I placed a hat trimmed in stars that peaked into a point at the top like a crown. When she saw me, Mary smiled and said, "If only our parents were here to see us." At the corner of Rhode Island Avenue and Seventh Street we parted ways with a kiss on the cheek. The streets were too crowded for us to take a carriage.

I was surprised to see that the streets were already filled with people at this early hour. Groups of men carried large floats. Street vendors hawked hats. Policemen barked at gatherings blocking the walk paths. The sharp scent of roasted nuts wafted in the air. Marchers wrapped their shoulders in American flags. A mounted brigade trotted by.

Our delegation had been given a time in the morning when we could use the second-floor drill hall in the suffrage parade headquarters. We all arrived fully attired in our dresses and hats. There were sixty-two of us, so it was quite a large group. Two would march at the head—Laura Welles and Grace Wilbur Trout, the president of the Illinois Equal Suffrage Association. The rest of us lined up in neat rows of four.

Laura shouted orders: "Attention! Forward march!" And we matched step. When she shouted, "Turn!" we practiced an orderly turn. We could hardly contain our excitement, but she hushed us when our chatter drowned out her voice, because we did not have long in the hall. We were to report to our assigned location by two that afternoon, and another state delegation was scheduled to use the hall right after us.

The parade would begin at the Peace Monument. We would march to the Treasury Building, then on to the White House before ending at Continental Hall. Our delegation was large enough to house different contingents—from the Chicago Political Equality League to the Cook County Suffrage Alliance. Virginia, Belle, and I would carry the Alpha Suffrage Club banner.

Just as Laura began to shout another order, Grace rushed in.

She had been missing for some time, and the look on her face was panicked. She asked Laura if she could have a private word with her. The rest of us grew silent, waiting to hear what had caused such consternation. Finally, Grace turned to us, and the words she spoke struck dread in my heart.

"We have an issue that has arisen regarding Mrs. Barnett's participation in the parade."

A murmur arose among the women. I did not look right or left. I just looked straight at Grace. I had a feeling I knew what was coming.

"Many of the eastern and southern women here greatly resent the fact that there are to be colored women in the delegations."

My eyes burned. *Do not cry, Ida*, I told myself. *You are more dignified than this.*

"Some have even gone so far as to say they will not march if Negro women are allowed to take part."

It was as if every eye was on me. This was what it felt like to be the only Negro woman in the room. I did not understand why she was talking about Negro women as a group, as if the attention was not entirely focused on me at that moment. I tilted my hat down over my eyes so that they could not see my face. I had preached to my daughters so often to stay strong in these situations. I was a leader in my community. A journalist and teacher. Yet here I was about to lose my composure in front of a room filled with women. I wished for my friend Mary and wondered if she and the sorority were also being banned from the parade.

"Who has said this?" someone demanded. I did not recognize the voice. My ears felt as if they had been stuffed with cotton. I could hear people speaking, but I could not make out the words. Finally, I heard Grace speak up again.

"Mrs. Stone of the National American Woman Suffrage Association and the woman in charge of the entire parade have advised us to keep our delegation entirely white. So far as Illinois is concerned, we should like to have Mrs. Barnett march in the delegation, but if the national association has decided it is unwise to include the colored women, I think we should abide by its decision."

They were still doing it, talking about me as if I were not standing right there. Grace looked around at the women, as if to solicit their opinions. I watched her from beneath my hat. She would not look in my direction.

"You are right. It will prejudice southern people against suffrage if we take the colored women into our ranks. We must not allow it," said one of the women.

My friend Virginia, who helped cofound the Alpha Suffrage Club, came to my side and took my arm. "But it is entirely undemocratic," she said. "We have come all the way here to march for equal rights. It would be autocratic to exclude her. I think that we should allow Mrs. Barnett to walk in our delegation. If the women of other states lack moral courage, we should show them that we are not afraid of public opinion. We should stand by our principles. If we do not, the parade will be a farce."

I could not hold back the tear that escaped my lash. I quickly wiped it away and pushed my hat up as I turned to look at them. Virginia's words had strengthened me. I had something to say. I straightened the banner around my neck. My throat hurt with the shame of it, though I knew I had nothing to be ashamed about. I had not done anything wrong. Still, it was hard to get the words out. Finally, my voice came to me.

"The southern women are always trying to evade the question by giving some excuse or other every time it is brought up. If you, women of Illinois, do not take a stand now in this great democratic parade, then colored women are lost. Do not do this. I urge you," I said.

Grace spoke slowly. "Mrs. Barnett is right, ladies. It is time for Illinois to recognize the colored woman as a political equal. You shall march with the delegation, Mrs. Barnett."

The women began to whisper. I did not know what to do. There were no chairs in the room, but I really needed to sit down. I tried to breathe. Virginia put an arm around my shoulder. "Do not worry," she whispered to me.

Grace and Laura huddled with a group of women. I watched and waited. When Grace turned around to speak, she sounded embarrassed as she conveyed the will of the group's leaders. "It will be undemocratic if we do not let Mrs. Barnett march with us. On the other hand, it is imprudent to go against the law of the national association. We are only a small part in the great line of marchers, and we must not cause any confusion by disobeying orders. But Mrs. Trout and I will go to the march leaders and make the case once more. They are just downstairs. Give us a few moments, please."

The two women exited. Belle and Virginia led me to a window that was open just enough to let in a slice of cold air. I leaned my face down toward the windowsill. Someone brought me a glass of water, and it cooled my throat.

Grace reappeared, and this time she addressed me directly. "I am afraid that we shall not be able to have you march with us, Mrs. Barnett. Personally, I should like nothing more than to have you represent Illinois. But I feel that we are responsible to the national association and cannot do as we choose."

"It is outrageous," exclaimed Virginia. The women began to whisper.

"Quiet, please." Grace looked at me. "The march leaders have offered an alternative. They have suggested that you march with the colored delegation. At least you will be able to participate, Mrs. Barnett. You can still carry your banner at the back of the parade."

"At the back of the parade?" The water and air had returned me to my former self. I straightened my back and faced her. Grace was a fair woman, and it seemed cruel of me to oppose her in front of the group. Yet I was long past the point of sparing white women's feelings when it came to my oppression, no matter how good-hearted they were. "I shall not march at all unless I can march under the Illinois banner. When I was asked to come here, I was invited to march with the other women of our state and I intend to do so or not take part in the parade at all."

"Oh, come now, Mrs. Barnett," said Laura. "If I were a colored woman, I should be willing to march with the other women of my race."

"There is a difference, Mrs. Welles, which you probably do not see. Either I go with you or not at all. I am not taking this stand because I personally wish for recognition. I am doing it for the future benefit of my whole race."

My entire body trembled. I tucked my hands into the folds of my dress so no one would see them shaking.

"If you walk in the colored delegation, I will walk with you," declared Virginia.

"I shall join Mrs. Barnett and Mrs. Brooks," said Belle. "I think it would be a disgrace for Illinois women to let Mrs. Barnett march alone when the parade is intended to show women's demand for the great principles of democracy."

I looked over at my friends gratefully. None of the other women in the room offered to join us, and that made Belle and Virginia's actions even more touching. If these two women marched with me at the back of the parade, I would accept this defeat. I would manage it. I just worried about those young sorority sisters from Howard University who would show up at the parade today and discover that gender equality did not apply to women of a darker hue.

After we left the drill hall, I wandered around the city attempting to calm myself. A line of trumpets backed by two drummers played "America the Beautiful." A part of me wanted to go back to Mary's house and sit quietly in front of the fireplace with a book for the rest of the afternoon, but I had not traveled all the way to Washington, D.C., to run away and hide.

It slowly dawned on me that despite my promise to the women, I could not march in the back of the parade. I just could not. There was something in my soul that rejected this proposition. It defeated the purpose of attending the march. If colored women did not stand up to this outrage, we would not be granted the right to vote if a constitutional amendment were ratified. Then everyone would have the vote but us.

As I thought over my decision, I tried to make my way to New Jersey Avenue, where the Illinois delegation had been instructed to wait. All the delegations had been given an appointed meeting location at which to line up an hour before the parade was set to begin. I tried to find Virginia and Belle, but the crowds were so thick I could barely make my way. Hundreds of men walked toward Pennsylvania Avenue. There may have been thousands, but I could not tell. Alice Paul was getting her wish. The parade would be a spectacle. But I wondered if she had underestimated the number of spectators.

Finally, I spied the delegation making their way down Pennsylvania Avenue. The march had begun. I saw Virginia and Belle walking slowly, holding a single banner between them. The crowds surged from all sides. Some of the men even spilled over into the parade's route. The police did nothing to hold them back. At times the women stood at a complete standstill because the route was so blocked. I was only able to reach the delegation because no one was moving.

I slipped in beside Belle and Virginia, and they both turned to me in surprise. "We could not find you," Virginia shouted. Some of the other delegation members frowned, but I did not care. We started to move again and I could see a float in the shape of Lady Liberty ahead. Yes, indeed. Our own liberty would come, that of white and colored women. There was nothing anyone could do to stop this momentum. And just as the nation would be forced to sit up and take notice of this great movement, the Illinois delegation would march with a colored woman in its ranks despite the misgivings of some. And that was that.

I had defied the parade organizers by marching with the Illinois delegation that day, but I never forgot the humiliation. Even if they picked me up on a magic carpet, I would not go to the New York City parade. I understand the purpose of the event, but black women suffragists have learned the hard way that we have to chart another course.

As thousands of white women line up to demand the right to vote in New York, I stand at a lectern in Chicago and look out upon nearly a hundred colored women. Their bright faces gaze up at me expectantly, and I realize I have been quiet too long, too lost in my memories.

"Thank you to Mrs. Fortson," I say, and nod at Bettiola, "for putting together such a lovely program. I will not speak long because we have invited guests today. My dear friends. You may have read about the women's suffrage march happening in New York City today. Once again, colored women have not been included in this important work. Our voices are excluded, pushed to the margins. Two years ago, we experienced this rejection firsthand during the march in our nation's capital. Despite these wrongs, I ask you to maintain your faith in your civic responsibility. Work remains to be done. We must be a united sisterhood that works together in all ways possible to uplift the race. Your labor, your commitment, your intellect are sorely needed. The conscience of this country needs your voice. Do not give up, my dear sisters. We must fight on. Thank you."

I leave the lectern and sit beside Bettiola as the women clap. I am angry that we were not included in the New York march, but my anger is tempered by envy. If only colored women could have those kinds of numbers and create such a spectacle. If only we could organize ourselves in such a way to demand our rights. But our resources are constrained by broader racial fights. And when we do succeed in those fights, we often do not share in the victories. I suppose I am just admitting to myself that I get tired sometimes. My constant reach for acknowledgment and recognition makes me weary. And today is one of those weary days.

On the other hand, I am unable to deny my pride. I remember the soaring feeling on that day in 1913 when I marched alongside thousands of women. Despite the outrage, I was inspired to see so many women march together in their beautiful dresses, carrying their banners. I wonder if the women in New York are accompanied by marching bands. I wonder if there are brigades. I wonder if they have a grand marshal in the front riding a white horse and wearing a white suit, blue robe, and gold tiara.

We Shall Take Our Lives into Our Own Keeping

Ֆ

MEGAN CHANCE

EILEEN WAS GLAD TO BE OUT OF THE COLD YET STIFLING FLAT, away from the stink of Da's sweat and the pungent glue Ma used to make her artificial flowers, but mostly away from her parents' questions about why she was home on a Saturday and how she'd managed to win the day off. Still so much suspicion, even after all this time.

She swallowed her resentment, grateful for the excuse of Troop as she took the dog into the hall and down the narrow stairs, which stank worse than the flat. The front door wouldn't close properly, no matter how many times they'd complained to the janitor, and the cool October air whisked in the noisomeness from the cesspool. A tangle of sounds—a dozen languages, shouts, and babies' cries, that old German man and his wife fighting down the hall—assailed her ears, but she was used to this, and she followed Troop as he bounded out the back, where the floor had sunk and the rains had created a mini lake that the homeless or those too drunk to make it up the stairs or dogs like Troop used as a latrine.

Eileen waited for the dog to finish and then do his usual sniffing and prowling about. The day was sunny but cold; she hugged herself against the breeze that blew trash and bits of straw and filth into growing piles against the walls and into corners. Troop growled at someone out of sight. Eileen stomped her foot. "Come on, boyo. It's cold."

The dog ignored her.

"Troop! Troop, come on!"

The dog stiffened, his short tail stilled, and Eileen was swept with the strangest feeling. Not a premonition, and not quite dread or apprehension. It was more . . . something about the way the air felt, the way the breeze pressed her skirt into her stockinged legs, or perhaps it was the sudden shade of a cloud moving over the sun and then the light again shifting through the laundry strung overhead. Familiar, like a moment she'd lived before, or a nostalgia that was not welcome, but cruel and bittersweet, and then she caught the scent above that of the cesspools and the mud and the harsh soap of drying laundry.

Lavender. And she knew.

Or thought she did. Eileen whistled sharply for the dog and dodged back into the building. When he didn't come, she left him there, desperate to disappear, panicked now, walking quickly for the stairs but not wanting to run, not wanting to appear afraid. Unconcern, that was what she wanted. Seeming obliviousness. The stairs were just ahead, and she had the ridiculous thought that if she made it to the second floor, to the landing, it would be far enough for escape.

It was not.

"There you are, Eileen," came the voice she had thought never to hear again. "Rory told me you were still here. I didn't believe it."

Eileen stopped and turned slowly. "He didn't tell you. He wouldn't have told you anything."

Maeve. Maeve of the curling hair, dark fire to Eileen's straight, fine strawberry blond, Maeve Murphy, Maeve the One Who Dared, Maeve who had squirreled under Eileen's skin and stayed and who she never expected to see again, never wanted to see again. The scars on her palms itched. The past was gone. Let it stay the past.

Maeve considered Eileen, then said, "Tom, then. Tom said you were here."

"None of them would have told you."

"You won't let me have my safe little lie?" Maeve's smile was wistful. "You've grown so cold."

"No one wants you here."

"No," Maeve disagreed. "No one wants me around you. It's a different thing, you know."

Troop came shuffling over, whining, always whining, like some damnable skipping record. He made a wide circle around Maeve, sniffed at Eileen's boots as if to be certain she was still she, and then trotted up the stairs toward the flat, ignoring them both.

Eileen turned to follow him. "Good-bye." She could not say the name. Her tongue would not physically form the word.

Maeve touched her hand. Static shocked them both. Maeve leaped back; Eileen snatched her hand away, startled. Maeve laughed, and the whole thing was so absurd that Eileen could not keep her mouth from quirking.

"You see? We're still setting fires together," Maeve said—the wrong thing; it sobered Eileen immediately—and then Maeve reached out. "No, I'm sorry. I'm sorry. Please, Eileen. I've come here all this way to see you. I had to see you. Please. Just . . . will you walk with me a small ways?"

It seemed such a nothing thing to ask, but it was not a nothing thing. The whole neighborhood would talk to see them together again. Even if she told Da and Ma a lie, they would know the truth by the end of the afternoon. Her brother, Scully, would hear of it, and his Go-to-It Boys' Club. Rory would know. She'd promised to keep her distance from Maeve Murphy. There had been a time when it was what she herself wanted most of all.

But then . . . there was that plea in Maeve's dark eyes and that wistfulness that had always been Eileen's undoing before. Maeve had always pretended to be so vulnerable. "*I can't do it without you, Eileen.*

We have to be together always." But now Eileen knew better. Maeve was indomitable. When the world was burning, Maeve would be the one standing in the ruins. It wasn't her vulnerability that had called to Eileen's yearning for things she could never have, for an impossible life. It was Maeve's strength. The excitement of her.

Eileen had weaned herself off that addiction with care. She did not want to lose herself again. But this was only a walk, and the whole neighborhood would know, and in the end, that was her guarantee that nothing would come of it.

"A quarter hour," she said.

Maeve broke into a smile—ah, that smile! Like the smell of lavender, it said *Maeve.* It was part of the addiction. That smile that said, *You are the best thing I know.* "Of course! Yes. Thank you!"

Eileen turned away. "Let me tell my folks."

"Must you? They'll just say no."

Eileen didn't bother to disagree. "Wait for me here."

She went up the stairs to the flat. Her parents were exactly as she expected to find them—they never moved, morning to night, as if they were fastened in place by the glue from the artificial flowers they made by the dozen. Ma at the table, deftly turning bits of fabric into roses, her fingers stained a muddied purple from the cheap dyes. Da half snoring on the broken-down sofa near the window, the curtains drawn to protect his damaged eyes from whatever sun managed to eke its way into the swampy inner courtyard of the tenement, the pile of wires he'd been twisting for Ma's flower stems tangled on the floor beside him. Troop was nestled again at her mother's feet.

"Ma," Eileen said quietly, "Maeve is downstairs."

Was she imagining the color draining from her mother's face? "Eileen—"

"I won't be long. A quarter hour, that's all."

"A quarter hour?" Ma glanced at Da, and Eileen saw her mother's anxious desire to wake him, for Da to put his foot down, to say no, because she herself could not do it, and she wanted to.

"I promise," Eileen said.

"Eileen—"

"It's been five years," Eileen reminded her softly. "Everything's different now."

"Is it?" Ma asked.

But she said nothing to keep Eileen, and she didn't wake Da. Eileen felt her mother's worry trailing after her as she went back down the stairs, and she felt guilty for it, because she wished she had the strength or the will or the faith to convince her mother there was no reason for concern, but if she truly believed that, then why now was she half wishing that there was no Maeve waiting at the bottom, that Maeve's appearance had been an illusion bred of a waft of lavender and a strange and bitter nostalgia caused by a play of light? If she was truly to believe that, why then that mix of joy and fear when she caught sight of the deep blue of Maeve's skirt, the gray jacket, the relief and dread when it was no stranger who greeted her but the old friend she knew better than to see? Why then, after so long, did it trouble her that the connection between them was still strong enough to spark?

Maeve asked, "Did they tell you not to come?"

She had to know already the answer to that, and so Eileen did not bother to enlighten her. Instead, because she did not really want to meet Maeve's gaze, nor to see what it held, Eileen led the way out onto the broken stones of the street, turning to go toward the river.

Maeve said, "Not that way."

So then it was Maeve leading, and though Eileen thought it was best not—wasn't Maeve's leading always the problem?—she followed.

It was just like any other Saturday, the warrenlike streets with the peddlers and the women gossiping on the stoops and the children racing about like small demons while dogs chased them, barking excitedly. But the farther they got from home, the more women swept onto the sidewalks, many all in white with sashes of green and white and purple worn across their chests or tricolor ribbons fluttering from brooches or armbands. They flocked, chirping animatedly, heads bobbing, movements quick and breathless. The parade marchers. The suffragettes. The *harridans*, Da called them, as did the boys at the Go-to-It Boys' Club, *"Like biddy hens, picking and pecking. 'We want the vote bwwaaawwwkkk! Give us the vote bwwaawwkkk bwwaawwwkk!'"* How Rory had laughed at Scully's tease. How they'd all laughed. Tom Boyle had grabbed up his cornet and said he was joining the anti-suffragists, who planned to shout and play loudly enough to drown out the parade protests. *"They'll have to make a lot of noise to be heard over us."*

Da saying, *"The polls are no place for women. It's too rough. If a woman tried to cast a ballot, someone would try to stop her, and someone else would try to protect her, and God save us all, there'd be wars all over the city."*

Ma had said, *"Alice told me that the suffragists are threatening that if they don't get the vote, many of them will be told to commit suicide every year until men agree."*

"You see? They should be in a madhouse. Aye, a bunch of nonsense is what it is. Women don't know enough about the world to know what it needs."

Eileen had looked at her father, half-blind and ensconced on that sofa as if he'd grown into it. He'd once dreamed of owning a saloon and going into politics, which was the same dream of every Irishman in New York City, but she'd believed in him. When she was a small girl, he'd talked of it all the time. She could not remember the last time he'd stepped into the world beyond this room. What could he possibly know of it now?

Today the protesters were everywhere, rounding every corner, laughing as they grabbed their narrow-brimmed hats against a sudden gust—white, too, and straw, bought at Macy's for forty-eight cents; Eileen had seen them in the window display. They waited with dancing feet to buy the shiny brown pretzels stacked on Mr. Meyer's wooden dowels. They oohed over bags of roasted peanuts from the man who sang out *"Votes for women!"* though Eileen suspected he was doing so just to sell peanuts, and not because he actually cared for woman suffrage. The smell of those nuts took the edge off the chill and set the taste of salt on Eileen's tongue.

"How happy they look, don't you think?" Maeve asked, and again Eileen heard that pensiveness in her old friend's voice, that yearning. "Like they're embarking on an adventure. Like we used to be. Do you remember, Eileen?"

Did she remember? When did she not? "Of course I remember."

"I wasn't sure," Maeve said.

"Yes, you are," Eileen protested, not bothering to hide her irritation. "You know very well I haven't forgotten. Why did you come, Maeve? What do you want?"

The tenements of Hell's Kitchen turned to shops and houses, and the rush of men and women hurrying to the parade grew heavier. How fresh and blooming they were against rusty brown leaves and tattered broadsides, feathers and rags and dust spinning and rustling down the filthy streets. Some bore signs, others struggled with yellow banners. One sign saying WE TRUST OUR WOMEN, DO YOU? twisted in the breeze, becoming a sail that pulled the young woman holding it into a trash-filled gutter. Her friends pulled her out again, all of them laughing.

"I wanted to show you something," Maeve said. "Something to change your life."

"I've had enough of such promises. I don't want to change my life."

Maeve went quiet. She stopped to adjust her skirt. The gesture sparked a memory, Maeve's little restlessnesses, her pauses for thought, always accompanied by some small fix—her hair, a boot, a collar. Maeve sitting on the step of the old passenger car, laughing, unfastening her boot to cast out a stone, wiggling her white toes through the holes in her black stockings. "*That was a close one!*" and her voice echoing in the swollen, subterranean darkness lit only by the weak spitting of the fire Eileen had cobbled together from bits of rag and paper to light the oil lamp they kept in the cavernous ruin.

Then the rasp of the grating cutting through Maeve's laughter.

Eileen could almost feel the hard edges of the long-ago necklace in her hand, the stones pressing into her fingers, the clasp biting against her thumb.

"No, I don't guess you do," Maeve said, straightening. "I guess you've everything you want now with your factory job."

"Yes." Eileen pretended she didn't hear the contempt in Maeve's voice.

"Why, I guess it's every girl's dream, working in a candy factory."

Eileen said nothing, waiting for Maeve to make her point.

"He must be a decent boss, to give you a day off on a Saturday. Did so out of the goodness of his heart, did he?"

Eileen gave Maeve a sideways glance—how did she know? But then, for a long time, that had been the best thing between them. That knowing without speaking. That understanding. Eileen did not like it now, the way it made her feel small and compromised. She did not like the echo of Da's question that she heard in it. *What did you do to get it?*

What did she do? It was more what she hadn't done. What she hadn't done was respond to Mr. Martin's brushing against her as she stood on the line, placing cherry-filled chocolates and caramels and nut-studded divinity into frilly white paper wrappers. What she hadn't done was smile big enough when he leaned over her shoulder to show her precisely how he wanted things, though she'd been working there for two months and there was no need to show her anything. What she hadn't done was let him corner her on her way back from the toilet. Instead, she'd crossed her arms over her breasts and told him that she had a beau when he'd asked her to go dancing. He'd only said, *"Why, I don't think he'd mind if you went with me to opening night of the Empire next week, lass, now, would he? He wouldn't begrudge you a dance with your boss. Just to show your appreciation for your job, you know."*

"Take tomorrow off, Eileen," he'd told her last night as she'd pulled on her coat. *"And maybe Monday, too, unless you think maybe you want to go with me to the dancehall."*

The thought of it filled Eileen with such dread that she'd actually gone happily to Scully's club in the basement of Randall's Hardware last night, where she'd sat next to Rory on the beat-up old sofa and contemplated the lights flickering on the fake fireplace they'd made of balsa wood. When Rory had put a record on the Victrola and drawn her close and murmured in her ear about how things would be when they were married, she thought of Mr. Martin and his threats and the world seemed to narrow and choke until she couldn't breathe, but when she'd said she needed a breath of air, Scully had said, *"You aren't going out there alone, Eileen,"* and so she'd sat there scrunched between Rory and Gemma Boyle, who was thirteen if she was a day, but who sneaked out of her parents' flat and put up her hair and let down her folded skirts in the stairwell—the way Eileen had once done—and pretended to be a grown woman, and Scully pretended she was, too, even though he knew better, because Gemma let him kiss her, and perhaps other things, and that was how Scully was going to end up with a family before he knew it.

Maeve went on, "And your Rory. Still such a good boy?"

Oh, that mockery. Eileen's marriage to Rory had been talked of nearly since she had been born. He was revered by both her parents. *"He's such a good boy!"* And such a handsome one, too, with his black Irish looks. Ma sometimes wondered aloud what their children would look like, given how pale Eileen was. *"Bairns with some color to them! Can you imagine!"*

Again Eileen felt that crush in her chest, that strangled breath. "He's just what I want."

"You used to want so much more."

"I was thirteen. I didn't know what I wanted."

"Yes, you did," Maeve told her, starting to walk again. "We had such plans."

Eileen fell in beside her. "They were never going to come true, were they? We were just stupid girls. Better to just accept that."

"They're not accepting it." Maeve pointed to another gaggle of suffragists emerging from a crossing street. "You didn't even try."

But Maeve didn't know, did she? She couldn't know. She hadn't seen Ma's worry, or Da's anger. She hadn't understood Eileen's shame, or her guilt that she had let her parents down, that everything they'd given her she was throwing away, and what for? What she'd wanted was impossible. What had she thought, that one day the world would simply open up for her? That she was special? That there was something she was meant to be or do, or some fantastic fate that the world had waiting for a child of Irish immigrants whose father had been struck nearly blind from flying sparks, for a girl who'd followed the wrong person down a rabbit hole and almost lost herself?

Thank God she'd realized it in time.

But still . . . so many things she could not forget. The two of them huddled around that little fire, blowing on it to make it bigger. The damp cold of the old Beach Pneumatic subway tunnel. Maeve had said they were explorers, the first to discover it, though of course they hadn't been. There had been trash there from others before them. An empty package of Camel cigarettes, a tossed Sunshine cookies wrapper, a broken smoking pipe, and a pair of drawers that had been mostly destroyed by rats that Maeve had kicked aside with an "Eeww!"

But those days, it had been their own place. Their hideout. Maeve had heard about it from some other street Arab, a rumor of the old tunnel that had served as an experimental subway for nearly three years, with a car that went one block. It had been closed down for lack of money, bricked up. The legend was that a boy had gone down there and been eaten by rats, and once Eileen and Maeve heard that, there was nothing for them to do but find it. It had taken weeks of sneaking out, exploring every alley and rusted grating, and then—oh, then! The joy of discovery and the thrill of fear and surprise as they'd ventured down the short tunnel lined with brick, the musty, underground smell, that frightening abandonment, the certainty that around any corner they might find that boy's skeleton (*"Except I heard rats'll eat everything, even the bones!"*), or even worse, an army of rats waiting to devour them, for which Maeve had brought a big stick, and Eileen "borrowed" Scully's pocketknife, expecting any moment to see a crowd of yellow rat eyes staring at them from the darkness...

None of those things had materialized, but instead something more magical. Desolation. Silence and solitude. A sense of having been forgotten that surpassed any notion of time or place. That it had once been elegant was obvious. The brickwork had been laid with care, though it was crumbling now. They could not get to the main station; the building above had caught fire years ago and collapsed upon it, but still there remained a bit of platform here and there, as well as the old passenger car, its upholstered seats rat-bitten, with springs that creaked and squeaked. That was where they made their hideout, where they kept a small oil lamp and things to make a fire in the old rail track.

They explored every inch. There, they brought the treasures they'd found. Nothing very valuable, cheap rings that turned their skin green or watches that broke within days or hair ribbons or, more usual, pretty stones. Whatever it was, it went into a small bag that they kept tucked into a hole in the passenger seat, and each time they came, they laid the things out in a line on the platform and told their future by them.

"We'll take a ship to Paris," Maeve would say.

"We'll explore the seven seas." Eileen's addition.

"I'll never do piecework!"

"I'll never make an artificial flower as long as I live!"

"We won't be like everyone else."

"No, we'll never be like anyone else."

Dreams and dreams and dreams. They'd counted their treasures greedily. Never enough. Never close to enough, but the more they spoke of such things, the more they consumed Eileen's hours. Grubbing in that short tunnel beneath the ground, following rail tracks that went nowhere, the world became so very big that she could not hold everything she felt about it inside. Her longing threatened to explode, and only Maeve could contain it. Only Maeve knew how.

"We can't just wait for things to happen, Eileen, we have to make them."

Eileen had never stolen anything in her life. She'd never thought to do so. When Maeve first suggested it, Eileen had been horrified, and Maeve had scorned her horror so thoroughly that the only thing Eileen could do was prove herself, and so she had. She'd been good at it, too, better than Maeve. *"You're braver than I am,"* Maeve said to her once, as they hovered around their little fire, faces lit in the dusky darkness. She'd leaned close, her lips grazing Eileen's cheek in a way that even in memory made her shiver. *"You'll do things I wouldn't dare."*

It wasn't true, but Eileen had felt warm and brave and special.

Which was perhaps why, when they'd seen the coat laid so haphazardly on the bench in the square, and the man to whom it belonged talking to someone in a carriage at the edge of the park and paying no attention, she had dared what even Maeve would not have dared.

It was cold, that was what she told herself, but the truth was that the stealing had become an addiction, too. She had begun to crave the excitement. She wanted the rush of fear and the cold sweat that came after, that giggly *I can't believe it; let's do it again,* and Maeve beside her, pulling her through the grate to their subterranean hideout, falling into each other's arms giddy with success. And that afternoon, in broad daylight, no less, oh, how heady it had been! To take that coat, to run off with it, to hear the man shouting after them as they dodged through the streets and alleys, Eileen's footsteps pounding into her skull along with her heart, and that man not stopping, not giving up as they expected, calling for the police as he chased, and suddenly that daring had turned to fear, and Maeve had ordered, *"Leave the coat!"*

Eileen had thrown it aside, and the necklace had spilled out, and yes, she should have ignored it. It was obvious that was why the man was chasing so hard, and now there were policemen, too. But the blue stones glittered, and Maeve's eyes glittered, too, and though Eileen heard *"leave it,"* she saw that desire in her friend's eyes, and she heard their dreams in her head, and so she grabbed it and shoved it in her pocket.

Instead of the start of their dreams, that moment had been the end of all of them. It was only that Eileen hadn't known it. She hadn't known it until they were in the tunnel, safe and victorious, laughing with relief and delight as she built the fire and lit the lamp, the necklace slinking between their fingers, the answer to everything at last. *"You see what I mean? We make our own dreams . . ."*

Then the terrible sound, the rasping of the grate echoing in the tunnel, and the man calling out, and a police officer shouting, and after that . . . well, it was all a nightmare after that. There was no other way out but that grating, but she and Maeve knew the tunnel so much better than anyone else. Every nook and cranny. They hid in the abandoned passenger car, and while the men tried to find their way in the dark, she and Maeve dashed past. Which one of them kicked over the lamp, Eileen never knew. The two of them slithered out; Eileen stamped the grate hard into place to slow the men down, and they ran. Two blocks, and then she remembered the necklace.

"I left it there!"

The horror on Maeve's face made Eileen sick to her stomach. In a panic, she raced back. She thought only of the necklace, of their dreams disappearing. She barely heard Maeve's *"No! Eileen!"* She heard nothing but the rush of her own breath.

The smoke coming from the grate alarmed her, but she hurried to it; it wasn't until she was right there that she heard the men shouting. She grabbed the grate—it was so hot it seared her hands. She dropped it in confusion—how had it gotten so hot? It rattled back into place. The necklace. The necklace. She had to save it. She reached again for the grate, but now someone was grabbing her, pulling her back, Maeve.

"Eileen, no, you can't go in there. Look!"

Eileen looked wildly about, uncomprehending. Maeve wrapped her arms around her, holding her tight, falling with her into the street. Eileen's hands burned, the grate had imprinted itself on her palms in blisters, her skin a weird white and red. She stared at them in dumb surprise, and it was only then that she realized others were running to the opening, calling to each other, gathering for rescue. It was only then that she saw the flames and realized the men were still down there.

Maeve pulled her away; they'd melted into the gathering crowd. For days, with bandaged hands and under Ma's watchful, worried gaze, Eileen waited for a knock on the door, for a police visit that never came. She listened to Da saying again and again, *"What have you done, lass? You were with her, weren't you? I've told you not to get mixed up with that one. Running around the city like a hooligan. I tell you, she's not right,"* when what he really meant to say was *"Something's not right with you when you're with her."*

And Ma saying nothing, but looking at Eileen as if something rotten had burst in the flat, or worse, with this great sadness that gripped Eileen from the inside out.

"I'm sure they got out," Maeve had reassured her. *"But even if they didn't, Eileen, you couldn't have saved them yourself."*

Eileen had stared at her, disbelieving, and then felt sick all over again with mortification and fear when she realized that, for once, Maeve did not understand.

She did not understand that Eileen cared only about the necklace.

She had not seen that Eileen hadn't considered the men at all.

It was the first time since they'd met that Eileen felt them as separate beings, and nothing would put that right.

"Don't you ever think about it?" Eileen asked Maeve softly now.

Her old friend said, "You've got to put it behind you, Eileen."

"That's what I've done."

Maeve shook her head. "You've never let it go. You're punishing yourself."

"You don't understand."

"Sure I do. It was the necklace. It was always the necklace. You've never let it go. It's like you said, we were just thirteen and stupid. Don't make it worse by living your whole life stupid."

The words were a little shock. A spark through years of confusion.

They had reached Washington Square, the start of the suffrage parade. The grounds were full of white. Floats parked along the streets. Bands tuned their instruments. One played a rousing song while nearby marchers practiced their one-step. People cheered and talked. Banners luffed in the breeze and women fussed with their tangled and blowing skirts. Everywhere were white hats, yellow banners, city flags of blue and white and orange, and signs reading DENVER VOTES, WHY NOT NEW YORK? and VOTES FOR WOMEN! and people looking for their standard bearers, winding through the streets to take their places, to wait their turn to march. Whistles and the blaring horns of automobiles made a festive noise. Eileen had lived in Hell's Kitchen all her life and she could not remember when she'd seen so many people. So many women. Had she been asked, she would have said there were not this many women in the world.

Maeve touched her hand. Again, that electricity, and Eileen was transported back to their fervent whispers, their dreams that took form in the ashy darkness of the old subway as they bounced on the old seats, the scurrying of rats and cockroaches providing background music. Such things they'd hoped for. No tenement flats with boarders sharing rooms and chipped dishes or going to the tavern in the afternoon to fill the growler with beer for a man too beaten down or injured to stir himself from a chair. No gossiping with other women on the stoop while the men gathered in the saloon and the children played in septic puddles and chased dogs and feral cats in the streets. No worry about money. No being told what to do day in and day out. No being cornered by lascivious bosses or being cajoled into dances one didn't want to dance or marrying a man because your parents wanted it just so you could live their same life again.

Eileen took in the protesters gathered before her, the signs for the actresses, the singers, the women's trade unionists, the clerks and the lawyers and the writers. Peddlers sold yellow paper chrysanthemums and balloons. Babies raised their little fists either in solidarity or excitement or temper tantrums.

"Look!" Maeve whispered, close now, and Eileen did not move away from the familiar warmth of Maeve's breath against her ear, fluttering the loose wisps of her hair so they tickled, not realizing until that moment how much she had missed that feel, that voice, that lavender scent—or perhaps it was not those things, but simply Maeve's presence, the tingle she kindled in Eileen's blood and her fingers, the excitement and the wanting that had disappeared from her life the moment Maeve had dragged her from that burning grate. "This is what I wanted you to see. This is how we make the world, Eileen. We won't be like anyone else. Remember?"

How often Maeve had said those words. How often Eileen had said them back. Their charm, their spell against complacence, against a world that conspired against them, that kept girls in their place.

"We did it the wrong way last time," Maeve told her. "Now we have the chance to do it right."

Someone in the crowd began to sing. Eileen thought of Mr. Martin. Other girls in the candy factory had wanted the day off to march. He had refused them all. *"If you want to march, go ahead. But don't expect to have a job when you come back."*

What if she marched? What if she didn't come back on Monday? Why did she keep that stupid job; why did she bear him? There were so many jobs. Jobs that didn't need a heavy, sticky apron, or mean that she had to breathe sugar all day until she was sick with it, or fight off a boss who wouldn't take no for an answer. Maeve was right. She was afraid. Afraid of how much she *wanted*. Afraid of what she'd been willing to do to have it. Afraid that no one could understand, not even Maeve.

But Eileen had been wrong about that, hadn't she? Maeve had understood. She had understood.

Eileen stared at the crowd and felt the excitement in the air, the palpable sense of doing something, of achievement, of knowing that whatever the outcome, they had tried. They had not simply accepted the world as it was.

Yet there were consequences for that. Eileen knew it better than most, and the reminder never faded. She looked down at her hands, at the too-white scars against her already pale skin, the outline of the grate evidenced in the blisters that had healed yet never left her. But . . .

They'd nearly disappeared, she realized. Why, in the cold sunlight, she could hardly see them. When had that happened? Why had she failed to notice?

"Over there," Maeve said, taking Eileen by the hand, curling her fingers around tightly, as if she couldn't feel the scars at all, just as she had that day the two of them lay in the street, watching the rescuers work to save the men in the tunnel.

Maeve took them through the crowd, past a group of women trying to maneuver a banner proclaiming A VOTE FOR WOMEN IS A VOTE FOR JUSTICE. She stopped at a tall woman in a black coat standing near the sign announcing the Women's Trade Union League. The woman wore the green-white-and-purple-striped sash of suffrage and carried dozens of them looped over her arm, and when she saw Maeve, she smiled. "There you are, Miss Murphy! Is this your friend you've spoken so much about?"

"Eileen Quinn," said Maeve, pulling Eileen forward.

"We're so pleased to have you join us," said the woman, putting a sash over Eileen's head without asking permission, and then reaching behind her for a sign. She held it out to Eileen. "This one's for you to carry."

Eileen looked up. The sign was yellow. In big black letters, it said: STANDING TOGETHER, WE SHALL TAKE OUR LIVES INTO OUR OWN KEEPING.

"Well?" Maeve asked. "What do you think, Eileen? Shall we?"

Maeve's expression shone with hope. The scent of lavender was everywhere.

Shall we?

Eileen pulled her hand gently away. The hope in Maeve's face fell into disappointment. How silly, that she did not understand now, when she had understood that long-ago day, enough to return now, to show Eileen there was another way, a way she hadn't seen at thirteen, and not until this moment. A way to change her life, to save herself. A way like *this*.

Eileen touched Maeve's arm, just a slight touch, and then opened her palm, holding it out for her old friend to see. "Look," she said wonderingly. "The scars are gone."

Maeve's smile returned, brighter than the blinding-white dresses reflecting the sun. "Then it will be easy to carry a sign."

A Woman in Movement

☙

ALYSON RICHMAN

THE BLUE INK FROM THE PRINTMAKING PRESS WAS STILL visible on Emma's fingers when she ran down the steps of the Art Students League. Only after she emerged into the blazing sunlight of Fifty-Seventh Street did she stop and tuck the stack of flyers underneath her arm and pull on her gloves.

A surge of adrenaline rushed through her. No longer in her artist smock, Emma felt transformed, wearing a long sage-green skirt and the white cotton blouse that she had dyed lavender the week before in the bathtub of her boardinghouse. Emma aspired to embody the suffragette movement as much as possible, and while some chose to wear white in its honor for that afternoon's parade, Emma chose the more vibrant colors of its political party because they made her feel confident and bold.

She believed color and images were another form of language, just like poetry or music. For months she had juggled her classes at the league with her part-time job at the ad agency, hoping to find a way to put her artistic skills to good use. It had not been as easy as she thought it would be when she first left the safety and security of living with her parents. New York City was a far cry from the bucolic setting of her Connecticut childhood. The bustling streets, the expense of living and studying in the metropolis, and the need for her to gain street smarts were all things she had been forced to navigate on her own. Under Ida Sedgwick Proper's mentoring, she had learned so much, and now she realized all the hours she had spent in the printmaking room, perfecting the illustration that would not only be printed on the flyers, but also on the cover page of *The Woman Voter* journal, had not been in vain. She felt quietly victorious, not just because Ida had ultimately chosen her image, but because she knew she was now stronger and more confident after having created it.

For months, Emma had worked on her print for the contest. After several misguided attempts, she arrived at her final version, one of three female figures: a little girl in a pinafore, a young woman close to Emma's age, and an older woman, with a carefully detailed face, whose lines were meant to represent wisdom. All three had their hands interlocked and were facing an enlarged wooden ballot. "Fight not just for one generation," it announced in bold black letters. "But for all!"

As Emma started walking down Fifth Avenue, she pulled out flyers from beneath her arm, offering them to men, women, and children alike; she believed she was channeling a little bit of Ida's spirit with each hand that reached out for one of the sheets of paper. "Come to today's parade!" Emma added with boundless enthusiasm. She wanted everyone to feel the sense of purpose that she now felt. Ida's energy and determination had been infectious, affecting nearly everyone who came into contact with her. It was hard for Emma to believe it had been only four months since she'd first walked through the office doors of *The Woman Voter* to find out more about them before crafting her submission for their contest. The journal was seeking an original image to be printed on all the promotional flyers for the suffragists' October twenty-third parade in Manhattan. It was the lure of the fifty-dollar prize that first caught Emma's attention when she saw a notice about the contest, as that amount of money would be more than three months' salary at the

Speyer Creative Agency, where she had been working part-time to pay for her studies.

Emma had been desperate to find an extra source of income to support herself and prove her father, who had remained skeptical of her artistic pursuits, wrong. When she first arrived in New York at the start of the school year, she combed the classifieds looking for work. How many times had she arrived at the reception of a particular creative agency, only to be turned away when they saw she was a woman? Emma didn't have enough fingers to count the rejections. It was only after she had nearly given up hope that she found herself in the office of Lewis Speyer's ad agency.

Speyer had greeted her himself, claiming his receptionist had already left for the day. A large man wearing a wool sack suit that was far too small for him, the buttons of his jacket strained to keep his voluminous belly locked beneath the chalk-striped fabric.

"You must be Miss Kling." He appeared to appraise her before his eyes settled on her face. Then with an exaggerated flourish of his hand, Speyer motioned her to follow him to his office.

※

"So . . . you're the artist applying for the job?" he asked her briskly, and told her to sit down. "Studying at the Art Students League? Is that right?"

"Yes, sir," she answered. Emma was proud to respond affirmatively. She would have struggled to have the confidence to call herself an artist when she lived at home. But now that she was officially a full-fledged student at the league, she felt she could legitimately claim the title.

"I've been sketching ever since I could hold a pencil in my hand."

Her eyes scanned the framed newspaper ads from New York's leading department stores that Speyer displayed on the office's buttermilk-colored walls. These ads featured hand-drawn illustrations of women wearing beautiful dresses and hats, their hourglass bodies exaggerated for effect.

Emma knew she was capable of creating similar sketches; she just needed Mr. Speyer to give her a chance. As she looked at him perched like an overstuffed owl at his desk, forehead glistening with perspiration, she forced herself to remain focused. She would see past his rapaciousness if he'd just see past her gender and give her the job. She loved drawing fashion sketches. Her mother had always sewn her own clothes, and Emma knew how to re-create the drape of fabric and the movement of a skirt on paper. She was confident she could make those fashions come alive; her imagination began to spin with the excitement of the unfurling possibility of being employed there.

"I brought my portfolio." She handed him the leather case with her drawings and watercolors. She had also brought along her sketches of models that resembled the ones framed in Speyer's office. "As you can see, I love capturing a woman in motion."

Speyer unlaced the leather folder and glanced at her drawings. He did not study them carefully like her professors who assessed her work, but rather looked quickly, shuffling through the pages like they were a card deck. He then folded his pink, pulpy hands in front of him.

"This is the deal, Miss Kling," Speyer explained matter-of-factly. "You do the drawings for our clients . . . bold drawings of the models wearing the latest fashions for our large clients—B. Altman, Lord and Taylor, all the big names who advertise in all the major papers—and it's great work." He paused. "But, there's just one other detail you should be aware of . . ."

He leaned back in his dark black chair, unbuttoned the two jacket buttons of his wool sack suit, and lit a cigar. "I sign my name to the drawings. You get paid, of course. But the client won't know you did the work. Does that sound amenable to you, Miss Kling?"

Emma's face reddened with indignation. Had she even heard Mr. Speyer's words correctly?

"My clients wouldn't feel comfortable knowing a woman was sketching the illustration . . . so I consider my offer a generous one, don't you think, Miss Kling?"

She looked at Speyer's face, which had now become engulfed in shadow as the afternoon sun descended in the window behind him. Had she a piece of charcoal in her hand, she would have sketched his face in dark, smoky smudges.

"What do you think?" he asked her again, fixing his gaze hard upon her. Little red embers burned at the end of his cigar as he rotated it between his two fingers.

Emma fell mute for a moment. She was still trying to silence the voice inside her head, which was raging: *Wouldn't being paid for your work and getting credit for it be a better deal?* But she held her tongue. This was the first interview she had gotten in weeks. She needed the job.

"I just want to make sure I understand you correctly, sir." Emma formed her words slowly. "Your clients believe they are hiring you to do their drawings for their advertisements?"

"Yes."

She swallowed hard. "But, in fact, you employ others like myself to do them under your name?"

"Correct." He sucked at the cigar and blew circles of smoke in her direction. "A lot of ambitious, artistic women have been delighted to have the opportunity, Miss Kling." He smiled again, his tobacco-stained teeth reminding her of a soiled paint rag. "It's what I'd call a mutually beneficial arrangement, one that I'm happily extending to women exclusively."

Emma knitted her hands together. A visceral repulsion swept over her. She was nauseated by his unctuous gaze and unfair work proposition. But she had been looking for a job like this ever since she arrived in New York, and had not found a single person willing to employ her at all. She needed the money, and Emma realized that if she was left with just this one option, at least it was a chance to do something she loved.

No matter what, she refused to entertain the thought that she would be forced to return home and admit to her father that she couldn't support herself. That would mean the end of her dream of ever becoming an artist.

She thought of her parents back in Connecticut and how she had struggled to convince them to allow her to go to Manhattan for art school. Her father had been particularly resistant. Emma would do anything now to prove to him that she could manage on her own; she'd make nearly any sacrifice to achieve her goal of becoming a working artist. How many afternoons had she not eaten lunch because she wanted to save the money to instead purchase one of the more expensive tubes of pigment for her oil class, like cobalt blue or cadmium red? She knew her parents had made certain sacrifices when they decided to leave their home country and start anew in America.

Her parents, Elsa and Milos, Hungarian immigrants, had come to America before Emma was born, frustrated by the failure of reform and lack of safety in their home country. The deprivation they had experienced in their childhoods was hardly ever mentioned, as they forged ahead in a new country that inspired them with its sense of possibility, tolerance, and hope. Now they owned a small hotel in Stamford, where they channeled their European background into creating an ambiance of old-world elegance and hospitality.

Yet, even as they put the past behind them, they still experienced difficulties as they tried to adapt to their new surroundings. The English language proved difficult for them to master, and guests often struggled with their accents or sometimes seemed put off by the foreign-sounding dinner options of beef goulash and kohlrabi soup that Elsa prepared. But Elsa was determined that their guests see beyond their broken English and their foreign traditions. She had a natural sense of style and a talent for sewing, a gift she used to transform everything from her own wardrobe to the rooms in the inn, which she described as "nests of beauty." Each guest room had its own palette. She pulled colors from nature for her inspiration, telling Emma that the blue in one room was meant to evoke the same shade as a robin's egg. Another room was painted bright yellow to resemble marigolds in bloom. Emma learned to see the world through her mother's naturally artistic eye. And although she did not inherit her mother's talent with a needle and thread, ever since Emma was a child her hands were always grasping for a piece of chalk to draw on any surface she could find.

As she grew older, Emma yearned to draw from real life. She painted still lifes of the delicate Herend pitcher in the kitchen and the vase of seasonal flowers in the living room. Other times, she would sit in the kitchen with her sketch pad and draw the faces of those who came in to help her mother prepare the food and clear the dishes.

Soon she began to experiment with pastels and watercolors, and by the time she was eighteen, she had started to work in oils, learning to blend the pigments to re-create what she saw in her mother's garden. It was a hotel guest who first took notice of one of Emma's small landscape paintings framed and on display near reception, and told her parents she should consider enrolling in classes at the Art Students League in Manhattan.

The gentleman wrote down the name and address of the school, telling them that his own son had attended classes at the league and was now a successful portrait artist in Boston. The following morning, when he was having breakfast in the dining room, he pulled Emma aside and told her what he had shared with her mother and father.

"You have a gift, young lady," he reminded her. "Don't squander it. I see something in your paintings that I saw in my son's work. I would hate to see your talent used only to decorate the walls of your parents' hotel. That would be a real shame."

His words affected her. For the past few years, her life had seemed particularly shuttered. Ever since Emma had graduated from high school, she had ceased to interact with many of the girls she had known since childhood.

Her mind had swirled with the prospect of traveling to New York to study art more deeply.

But the following evening, when she broached the subject with her father, he could not muster a single ounce of enthusiasm for the idea.

"Absolutely not," he told her. "It is out of the question."

Milos had a whole litany of reasons why he would not even consider Emma's wishes. "It's not a stable life for a woman to be an artist," he retorted quickly. He imagined Emma following in her mother's footsteps, using her gifts to make their surroundings at the inn more beautiful. He wanted her to marry, have children, and eventually take over running the hotel with her future husband, whoever he may be.

Emma had heard her father mention how friends and family members back in Hungary had cautioned her parents about leaving for a country they knew so little about. But Milos had not been swayed from what he believed to be the right course of action. He had been brave—some might even say adventurous. Now he was telling his daughter to be the complete opposite of what he himself embodied.

"Papa, I can't improve as a painter unless I learn from others who know more than I."

The possibility of a whole new world beckoned, and to Emma it was almost within reach. She had tried since she was a teenager to expand her horizons, finding enormous pleasure in the books she had taken out from her local library. It was in those pages she had first learned about artists like Mary Cassatt and Berthe Morisot, who were Impressionist painters just like the more well-known

Monet and Renoir. Emma longed to travel to Paris. She imagined the energy of the big city. Her spirit yearned to be unbridled.

But Milos sought to diffuse the high emotions of his only daughter.

"It's too dangerous," he insisted. "You'd be living unchaperoned. Impossible."

Emma's mother stared at her hands, looking at them as though she had just let something slip through her fingers.

While her father's words infuriated Emma, her mother's silence pained her even more deeply. She had stormed off and retreated to her room after her standoff with her parents. The apricot-colored walls that her mother had painted years ago and then matched with sage-green drapes now seemed to trap her.

"Emma?" Her mother gently rapped at the door. "May I come in?"

Emma ignored the request, but Elsa turned the doorknob and entered cautiously anyway.

"Don't be angry at him, darling." She sat down on Emma's bed and placed her hand on her daughter's back. Emma pulled away from her mother and lifted her hand to wipe her tears.

"A stranger told me I had talent. He instructed me not to squander my gift!"

"I know. He told your father and me the same thing."

"New York is only a few hours away. I am not asking to return to Budapest."

Her mother squeezed her hand. "Your spirit reminds me of myself when I was your age."

Emma could hardly imagine her mother acting in any way but that of the graceful woman with the high lace collar and sweeping skirt sitting behind her Singer sewing machine or arranging flowers.

"I will talk to him, I promise. Just let me figure out the best way to make him understand." She threaded her fingers through Emma's hand. "It's not easy to be a woman with a dream that stretches beyond the living room or nursery." Her gaze fell away. "I understand that more than you probably realize."

Later that evening, Emma overheard her parents having a heated argument in their bedroom. "We came to America to have greater opportunity, Milos," her mother pushed in her native tongue.

"You and I are supposed to be united on how we raise our daughter, Elsa. I want you to talk to her and stop this nonsense! I'm not telling her she has to stop her watercolors or sketches. She can do that right here in Connecticut."

Elsa continued to try to convince him. "Just sleep on it, Milos. Please."

Minutes later, her mother returned to Emma's room.

"I've tried my best to get him to at least consider the possibility," she lamented. "But your father can be so stubborn, you know that ..."

Emma pulled herself up from under her covers. She was exhausted from all the fighting. "Yes ... I do know that. But is it so wrong of me that I dream of another type of life than yours?" She did not say what she really thought, which was that she never imagined a life of domesticity like her parents'. She instead yearned for a life of infinite possibility, where every day presented itself like a blank page thirsty for new strokes of color.

Elsa fell silent. There was much she had never shared with Emma. Like the fact that as a girl back in Budapest, she had dreamed of studying costume design. She imagined herself creating the sumptuous costumes for the Royal Opera House or the National Ballet. Her imagination always flickered with her own interpretations on how she would dress Brünnhilde in Wagner's *Ring*, or Papageno in Mozart's *Magic Flute*. Elsa had even been granted a rare invitation to apprentice under the opera's wardrobe mistress, an opportunity that still pained her because of her own parents' refusal to permit it.

Her mother and father had spoken nearly the same words then as her husband did now. Elsa could easily recall that terrible memory of having her dreams cut down by the very people she loved the most. That feeling of despair, from over twenty-five years before, still felt like a fresh wound when she thought back to that time in her youth. And while she ultimately channeled her artistic spirit into making curtains and coverlets to evoke beauty and elegance at the inn, she knew it could never compete with the joy of fitting a live model or creating a gown that would come alive onstage.

Over the course of several days, Elsa struggled to convince her husband to let Emma at least attend class for one semester. At night, after the last hotel guest had retired for the evening, she'd find her husband at the foot of the bed, massaging his tired feet, and she would gently advocate for her daughter's studies.

"We must let her try, Milos. If she doesn't succeed, she will always have the hotel to return to," her mother reasoned.

At first, her father still refused. But when yet another customer commented on his daughter's talent, and then another, Milos started to feel that perhaps he needed to listen to his wife and give Emma a chance to further her studies.

"If things don't work out the first semester, then promise you'll return home." Her father believed this to be a fair compromise.

But Emma would do anything to make sure that would never happen, even if it meant working for men like Lewis Speyer.

The months she spent at Speyer's ad agency had been a challenging ordeal. At his insistence, she had to do all her drawings in the office, often during the nighttime after she had finished her classes. He would hover over her as she worked on her sketches, sometimes placing his hand over hers as she put pencil to paper.

Emma hated the sensation of his cigar breath on her neck. His swagger and his brash way of speaking similarly annoyed her. But by far the worst part of her employment was when she handed over her sketches to him to deliver to the client.

He would take the heavy stock paper and lift it to the light, examining her careful and deliberate strokes. She tried to make the drawings look effortless and carefree, but they each had taken several hours, to make sure the artwork embodied the elegance of the particular dress or conveyed a sense of motion and vitality to the image. The goal was to entice women to visit the store for that particular piece of clothing. Emma strove to capture that desire in ink on paper, and it often took many revisions before she got it just right.

And then—after all that hard work, all those endless drafts that ended up in the wastepaper bin—she was forced to endure watching a smile appear on Speyer's lips as he took out a fountain pen from his breast pocket and signed his name with great satisfaction. In those few quick strokes, he rendered her invisible. No one would know it was her hand that had created those images, and she despised him for the deception.

So it was a mixture of curiosity and self-preservation that made her take pause when she noticed the ad tacked to the bulletin board at the Art Students League.

> Contest! Suffragette newspaper looking for original artwork
> to promote October 23rd New York City parade. Image must
> embody spirit for the passing of the 19th amendment. $50
> prize money. Submissions must be delivered in person to *The*
> *Woman Voter* by May 30th, 1915.

Emma wrote down the address in her notebook. She had leafed through copies of *The Woman Voter* on occasion when one of her classmates, Mildred Stein, handed them out after class periodically. Milly, as her friends called her, was in Emma's printmaking class, and was an outspoken suffragist. On more than one instance, she had tried to corral Emma and another female classmate of theirs to attend a meeting downtown.

She spoke on a first-name basis about women whom Emma knew very little about. The names Florence Guy Woolston and Vida Goldstein often rolled off her tongue. As well as the names Ida Sedgwick Proper and Gertrude Vanderbilt Whitney, who were artists themselves. Emma had been impressed by Milly's zeal for women's rights and the need to have their voices recognized by the government, but she never made time to attend one of the meetings that Milly spoke so passionately about.

Emma had been so preoccupied during her first semester with finding a job, and then later started working for Lewis Speyer, that the thought of making time to attend a suffragist meeting seemed untenable. But now the fifty-dollar prize money made her infinitely more curious about them.

She pulled Milly aside after one of their classes together.

"I'm thinking about your invitation to go to one of the suffragist meetings . . . I'd be honored to go to one with you if you're still open to taking me . . ."

Milly, never one to mince words, smiled and said, "Ah, I see you noticed the announcement I posted on the bulletin board for the image contest."

Emma blushed. "Well, yes, I did actually see that."

"Ida Sedgwick Proper, the art editor of *The Woman Voter*, asked me to put that up. She was a student here herself before traveling to Paris to study further."

Emma's heart quickened. Just hearing about a woman who had pursued her artistic training in France gave her an enormous sense of hope.

"Paris?"

Milly laughed. "Yes, Paris!"

Emma shook her head. "I've so dreamt of going there myself, but just getting my parents to let me come to New York City was difficult enough."

"Ida has had her own trials—her father was a Lutheran minister who thought there was no reason for her to go to college, but she persevered and put herself through school. She's always reminding us to stay the course for what we believe in." Milly's voice was imbued with a mixture of respect and awe for the journal's art editor. "It was her idea to create the contest to bring a little more attention to trying to pass the Nineteenth Amendment, but also to make sure that a woman's hard work would be rewarded by the prize money."

"I assume you're entering the contest, too?" Emma queried.

"Are you kidding? I started working on my image even before I tacked up the announcement on the bulletin board." Milly patted the front of her canvas satchel. "But it's not just the competition; it's the comradery." She gave a little pump with her fist. "There's a meeting at *The Woman Voter* next Tuesday. I'll meet you after class and we can go together."

⌘

Tuesday arrived and Emma found herself taking the subway downtown with Milly. They walked through Washington Square Park as mothers strolled in pairs with their enormous prams and men in their black suits and hats smoked pipes as they conversed on park benches. Milly talked excitedly about all the artistic and political activity being done by women in Greenwich Village. "Gertrude Vanderbilt Whitney has a sculpture studio on MacDougal Alley!" Milly chirped ebulliently. "Can you imagine that? An heiress creating her own artwork on a street where, only a few years ago, horses were eating hay!" Milly laughed.

Emma couldn't imagine it. Her experiences in Manhattan had

been limited to the exuberance of attending classes at the league and the wretchedness of working for Speyer. She had spent a few exhilarating hours wandering the halls of the Metropolitan Museum, where she found inspiration in the paintings of the Dutch Masters and the ink scrolls from the Orient. But she rarely had the time or money to imagine all the possibilities the city had to offer or the people who were as wealthy and as trailblazing as Gertrude Vanderbilt Whitney.

"It's like what Professor Clark said to us yesterday: the most important quality for an artist to have is the curiosity to see. You're helping me open my eyes, Milly."

Milly beamed. "It makes me happy to do it!" She squeezed Emma's hand and gently tugged her in the direction of the meeting.

When they arrived at *The Woman Voter*, the smell of fresh newspaper ink greeted them, and the room buzzed with activity. Women in long, dark skirts and lacy white blouses were working at wooden desks, scrutinizing page proofs and conferring with one another with great intensity. An immediate spark ignited inside Emma as she felt the energy and sense of purpose in the room.

Women immediately approached to greet Milly. One girl with fiery red hair came over and embraced her. "We've been working all night on the journal. Come here and see."

"Let me first introduce my friend Emma."

Milly began making informal introductions and took great pleasure telling the other women that Emma was also an artist at the Art Students League, just like her. "It took Ida's image contest and the fifty-dollar prize money to whet her interest, though," Milly said, and laughed.

"You brought another artist?" A strong, confident voice suddenly emerged from behind the circle of women. Ida stepped forward and looked to Emma. "I'm sorry, I didn't catch your name."

"Emma . . . Emma Kling, ma'am."

Ida extended her hand. "A pleasure to meet you, Emma. I'm so glad Milly brought you to see what we're doing here at *The Woman Voter*. Did I hear Milly correctly that you're a student at the Art Students League?" Ida's eyebrow lifted with curiosity.

"Yes, ma'am. Milly and I are in the same landscape and print-making classes."

Ida smiled. "How wonderful! I'm so happy the contest enticed you to come down and see some of our work." She gestured toward the printing press in the far corner of the room.

"I'm very fond of the league. I took classes there myself, as did our fellow suffragette Gertrude Whitney. That's why I told Milly to put up a notice about the contest." She folded her hands in front of her. "I'm indebted to many of the teachers I had there. Professor Merritt Chase is the one who encouraged me to continue my studies in Paris."

"Milly told me you were in France. It's always been my dream."

"Paris truly is an extraordinary place." Ida's face softened as the memories returned to her. "I hope to go back one day. But in the meantime, I have my work set out for me here with the vote." She motioned to the posters set against the brick walls and the copies of journals stacked on the front table. "I'm looking forward to seeing your contest submission, Miss Kling. Often an image has more power than words."

"That's what I think, too!" Emma blurted out. She found herself blushing at her inability to contain her enthusiasm.

"Good! That's what I like to hear from my girls. Come spend some time with us," Ida offered. "Look around at what we do, read the paper, speak with some of the other suffragists, and learn what we're doing to get us the vote. You're a woman. You're an artist. I'm sure you know how hard you have to fight to be heard."

Emma did, in fact, know that, and for several hours after she had left *The Woman Voter* office, she still heard Ida's words ringing in her ears.

※

That evening when Emma entered Speyer's office, her sketches from last week were on the reception desk with a note saying they were to be delivered to the executives at Bonwit Teller. Lewis's prominent signature appeared on the corner of each and every one of them.

As she sat herself down at her drawing board, she thought about the suffrage movement. It had seemed so abstract to her in the past, but now she realized its objectives mirrored her own desires. Wasn't fighting for the right to vote part of a desire to be heard? To be justly represented? In her employment with Speyer, Emma struggled with this every day.

Her drawings were bringing him not only praise and income, but also a sense of accomplishment and recognition, despite his never having touched the paper with a single stroke of his pen. She hated how he took such delight in signing her sketches and taking full credit for her work. She had been denied recognition for her own drawings because of this dreadful man. He had rendered her voiceless by signing his name where hers should have been.

Now with the office to herself, Emma took out her pencil and began to sketch. And this time it wasn't for Speyer's client—it was for the contest. Her desire to create something that embodied the spirit of all the women she had just met took over. She wanted to have her voice heard just as much as they did.

※

As the deadline for the contest approached, Emma began attending weekly meetings downtown with Milly, finding herself drawn to the courage and independence of the other women there. She didn't share with them the details of the horrendous deal she had made with Speyer in order to pay her bills, but every time she went to a meeting, she felt herself growing stronger as she threw herself more into her sketches for the contest, hoping that she might win.

Many of her first sketches, however, found their way into the waste bin. She drew a woman standing next to the Statue of Liberty with her hand similarly raised in the air. She depicted a woman dressed in an American flag, and another one waiting in line with men to cast a ballot. But none of the images appeared powerful enough to Emma. She knew that the graphic had to embody more than just a woman's right to vote, but also the entire spirit and vision of the suffragist movement.

It was, oddly, during a visit home to her parents, a place that felt so far removed from the women's movement, that she finally found her seeds of inspiration.

She had just shared a cup of tea with her mother in the kitchen, and Emma was struck by how her mother's face looked more lined than the last time she had visited and her expression appeared more reflective.

Elsa spoke softly. "I know you have often felt frustrated by your father and me. But I want you to know that when you speak of trying to get women the right to vote, it inspires me. When I was your age, back in Budapest, I think I had already given up dreaming of so many things."

"You've done so much to inspire me, Mama. You create beauty with everything you touch."

Her mother lifted her hand and touched Emma's cheek. "In the case of you, that is true."

"Mama . . ."

"Listen, Emma. What you're doing with Ms. Sedgwick Proper is wonderful. I assumed when you went off to study art, you would learn more technique, and strengthen your own artistic style, but I never dreamt you would also find another voice inside yourself."

Elsa paused for a moment.

"You're not yet a wife or mother, but your work is not just for the young women of today. It is for every woman. Young and old."

Emma absorbed her mother's words. They were simple, but there was so much truth in them.

Instantly, Emma could envision an illustration to accompany them. Three generations of women. Their hands threaded together and their message floating in unison above.

She leaped up to retrieve her sketchbook from her satchel.

"Mama, that's just it. I think the image I needed just came to me!" Her excitement was bubbling forth. "Would you mind letting me sketch you for part of it?"

Her mother's expression changed. "Of course not. But, really, me?"

"Yes, you'll see. Just wait."

No longer did Emma see the thin feathering of lines on her mother's face. Instead, Elsa's face beamed. Transformed like a beacon of creative light.

Emma took out her pencil and began to draw.

※

Emma worked the whole weekend on perfecting her sketch. She used her mother as the model for the older woman, and sketched herself for the middle female. But for the child who represented the youngest generation, for whose future they were all now fighting, she found herself struggling to get the girl's face just right.

Elsa walked into the kitchen where Emma was working, her robe tied tightly around her waist, her hair protected by her nightcap. "I was searching for this photograph upstairs while you've been drawing. I have been thinking about it all evening." Elsa handed her a small sepia photograph of two girls nearly the same age, wearing dark wool dresses and with their hair in braids. The photograph was creased, but Emma was sure the face of the older girl was her mother's. She put down her pencil.

"Mama, is that you?" Her finger hovered over the person in the left corner. She had the same eyes as her mother, and her expression was eerily familiar.

"Yes, it's me."

Emma squinted at the other girl, who had to be around three or four years old in the picture. "But who is this other person?"

"It's my sister, Fanny," she uttered so softly that Emma at first thought she had misunderstood her. "Fanny died two months after that photograph was taken. She was always so full of life, running all over the place. She had the most infectious laugh . . ."

"But . . . but you've never mentioned her before."

"I know, Emma. There is so much of my life in Hungary that I haven't shared with you, like Fanny's death. We both took sick with the measles. I survived. But she didn't."

Elsa's voice broke midsentence.

"My parents forbade me from doing so many things afterward. They worried about losing their only remaining child. They wanted me to have a family. Many of the same things your father and I worried about when you went to study in the city were the same fears as my own parents'. But now I look at you and you make me so proud. Maybe you'd want to draw Fanny into your sketch for Ms. Sedgwick Proper's contest?" Elsa dabbed her eyes with a handkerchief. "I would love to think that Fanny is contributing somehow for a woman's voice to be heard, since hers was silenced so young."

Emma took the photograph from her mother. She looked at the two girls sitting side by side, their neat braids framing their faces, their collars trimmed in white lace. Their expressions were somber. But beneath their formal reserve, Emma began to imagine their distinct personalities and hidden layers. As an artist, she yearned to bring those qualities to life.

She tore off another sheet of paper and began sketching the three female figures with a renewed vitality. When she finally finished, the women were arranged in descending age, their hands were threaded together, and their expressions were united in conviction. Yet the figure inspired by Fanny would prove to be her favorite, for she would symbolize not just the face of the young, but also of the women in Emma's family who came before her. Her spirit permeated each stroke that Emma put down on the paper.

When Emma submitted it for the contest, she was no longer fixated on the prize money. She felt she had given a voice to her mother and to Fanny. That was the wonderful thing about art; it had the capacity to transcend time and even defy death. Looking at her drawing, she felt she had not only resurrected a part of Fanny, but had given three distinct faces for the cause. That was what drew Emma to a creative life, the ability to believe that anything was possible.

Weeks later, Milly and Emma took the subway down to the journal's office for the grand unveiling of the winning submission. Emma had invited both her parents to attend, but she discouraged them from undertaking the special journey.

Don't make the trip or special arrangements for coverage at the inn, she had written her mother. *There are so many talented artists submitting entries. It's doubtful I will win.*

Her mother had written that she would try to figure out a way to come. *Your Papa has his hands full with the guests, as you might imagine, but how I would like to come and support you, my darling,* her careful writing scrolled on the page. But the following day another letter arrived saying they wouldn't be able to make it. *How I wish I could be with you when the winner is announced,* her mother lamented, *but you know how he doesn't like me to travel without him. In his mind, Manhattan is teeming with pickpockets and other menaces . . .* Emma had read the last letter quickly and then placed it in the back of her desk drawer.

On the day of the awards ceremony, Emma and Milly entered the office and discovered nearly a hundred people standing in the

long, narrow room. Many of them were familiar faces, fellow suffragists who came in frequently to assist with the journal, but there
appeared to be family members of some of the artists she recognized
from the league. She told herself that her parents would have been
far too uncomfortable in such a crowded space, but when Milly's
parents surprised her by attending the ceremony, she felt her heart
sink. Even though she'd told her mother she didn't need to come,
she now wished she had.

"Attention, everyone!" Ida stepped to the podium. "I am so
thrilled to be here this afternoon to announce the winning submission." She pointed to an easel draped in a heavy dark cloth.
"Beneath that veil is our winning image!"

The crowd rustled with anticipation.

"This has been such an honor to have so many artists enter our
contest. We at *The Woman Voter* wanted an image that would unite
the generations fighting for the vote, and I believe we found just the
right one." She took a deep breath and smiled. "Thank you, Miss
Emma Kling!"

Ida pulled away the cloth and revealed Emma's detailed drawing.
As the sound of clapping permeated the room, Emma's head spun.
She was incredulous Ida had announced her name. Milly threw her
arms around her. "You won! You won!"

Emma walked to the stage, her heart beating loudly within her
chest.

Ida handed her the prize money and whispered in her ear, "Aside
from the prize money, know there is a part-time job as a junior
artist on staff at the journal open to you, too."

That night, as she came home to her boardinghouse, she was
able to use the public telephone to call home and tell her parents
the news. She could hear the disappointment in her mother's voice
that she had not been there to witness her daughter winning the
prize.

"I'm so proud of you," her mother said, her voice breaking with emotion. "And knowing Fanny is part of your image makes me think you've given new life to her."

"Thank you, Mama," Emma answered. She still felt dizzy from the news.

"Before I put your father on, please tell me where I can send a note to Ms. Proper and tell her how grateful I am for recognizing the talent I've always known was inside you."

Emma gave her mother the address of *The Woman Voter*, then straightened her back in anticipation of speaking with her father. When he finally got on the phone, Emma made sure she not only mentioned the fifty-dollar prize money she had been awarded, but the new part-time job as well. Sharing with him the news of her new-found employment, something that was a direct result of her artistic skill, made her latest victory that much sweeter.

❈

Emma's real triumph, however, was witnessed by no one besides herself. With her new job at the journal, Emma could now do what she had been dreaming about doing for months. She walked into Speyer's office the next morning and told him that she was quitting.

"I wanted to give you notice," she explained with a confidence that caught him off guard. "I will no longer be working here as of today."

His face fell into a scowl. "You can't just leave. We have three drawings due tomorrow! You promised them to me last week!"

Emma folded her hands in front of her. "I don't owe the client anything, sir. You do." Her face lit up in a smile. "It's your name on the drawings, Mr. Speyer, not mine."

His face matched the flame of his cigar. "Get out!"

❈

"Out!" he had cried at her, and the sense of liberation she had when she left Speyer's office for the last time was now extended into the exhilaration she felt as she walked toward lower Fifth Avenue to meet Milly and her other friends who were marching in the afternoon suffragist parade. The crowd had begun to fill the streets, and the music of marching bands filled the air. One could sense the excitement lifting off the skin of everyone who had come out to show their support.

Hundreds of people were lined up already for the parade, and thousands were expected to witness as spectators. Emma saw groups dressed like Grecian goddesses with gold leaves woven into their hair and sandals on their feet. Others from the Women's Trade Union League wore washboards across their chests emblazoned with the call for the vote. Women who looked to be around Emma's mother's age wore suffrage slogans printed on their aprons, and younger ones pushed baby strollers with their infants tucked inside draped in the suffrage movement's banners. Flags were hoisted into the sky, and row after row of handheld banners called for women's suffrage. Emma was surprised by all the men who had also begun to fill the streets in anticipation of the march. She passed one with his daughter on his shoulders waving a sparkler.

Emma felt that the joy on the little girl's face was contagious. She eyed her watch, as it was already nearly two and she knew she was supposed to meet some of the other women from *The Woman Voter* near Washington Square Park.

She had one last flyer left. "Can I have one, miss?" one of the men on the sidewalk hollered out to her.

Emma went over to him, happy to give one out to another man who wanted to give his support. As she approached she could smell alcohol on his breath. His face was yellow as a wax bean.

"Aw, girly, thanks ever so much," he said, and winked at her. She went to walk away, but he interrupted her movements. "Wait! Hold on a second!" His voice was slick and oily. "Watch this!" he announced loudly.

With a great, exaggerated flourish, he raised the flyer in the air and tore it straight down the middle.

"Good luck today!" he muttered. A gap-toothed grin spread across his face. Before Emma had a chance to walk away, another one of his friends stepped forward and added: "Stupid women should keep their mouths shut and their hands off the ballot!"

"Tear it all you want! We're still going to get the vote!" Her anger flared. She went down to pick up the torn pieces of paper before they tumbled ahead.

A teenage girl knelt down to help her. "Don't get too upset. We're the majority here. Not them!"

A group of teachers with sandwich boards that read *Women teach little boys to read. Grown men owe us the right to vote!* were walking in front of her. With each passing minute, the streets were growing more crowded and harder to navigate.

Emma glanced at the large clock above a bank entrance. It was nearly two p.m., and she still had fifteen more blocks to walk until she got to Washington Square Park to meet the others before they officially began marching.

Emma looked enviously at the women who were sitting on large floats and the rare group on horseback. Her feet ached. Her outfit that she had been so proud of when she set out that morning was now soaked with perspiration. She had been walking for what seemed like hours, and she wished she could have taken the subway, but the lines were so long, it would take hours to even enter the station. Why hadn't she left for the parade earlier that morning? She was irritated at herself, but she could have never imagined so many people outside at one time.

Finally, when she approached the meeting place for all the women from *The Woman Voter* marching together, she thought she was witnessing a mirage.

She saw Milly and some other women holding posters with her

image printed on it. But what truly amazed her was the beauty of their costumes. The twenty women were wearing sumptuous silk capes in the most radiant jeweled colors. Deep violet. Forest green. Blue and gold.

As they congregated near the park's fountain, the hems of their cloaks lifted off the ground and fluttered like the wings of exotic birds. They looked majestic. And Ida looked like a queen in the center as she held aloft a gold banner of the American Woman Suffrage Association.

But it wasn't just the banner that took her breath away. Nor was it the sight of a woman marcher raising a poster with her winning illustration. It was the sight of someone Emma never expected to see there, marching arm in arm with Ida.

Beneath a garland of green leaves in her hair was the shining face of her mother, who was resplendent in a purple dress.

Elsa left the others and raced over to greet her beaming daughter. She took the crown of verdant ivy off her hair and placed it atop Emma's head. "I made this one just for you."

Just Politics

☙

Chris Bohjalian

She no longer dreamt in Armenian. She dreamt now in English.

And so, as a language teacher, she knew there was a difference between a scream and a shout, just as there was between a groan and a purr. But a moan? In this tongue, once her fourth but now her first, it could be an exhalation of ecstasy or despair. Of pleasure or pain, of longing or lust.

The transformation had taken barely half a decade.

Initially, she interpreted the sound as screams, not shouts, and her head had whipped around reflexively, her mouth open, her eyes wide. It was Adana again, six years earlier, the neighborhood two blocks distant from the mosque and the staging area for the Otto-man soldiers, and the screams had preceded the gunshots by sec-onds. Seconds. But then the screams had continued—as had the shots.

But these were shouts (and mere shouts, she thought, only shouts) and she brought her fingers to her mouth to warm them, and closed her eyes for a moment in relief. She wished that she had remem-bered her gloves, threadbare as they were, and her breath felt good on the skin by her nails. When she opened her eyes, she studied the women who'd shouted: there were easily a dozen of them, and they were shouting in glee because they had found one another near the arch. She guessed they were her age, late twenties, and she could see by their shoes and their furs—yes, three of them were wearing fur shawls—that they all came from privilege and wealth. Some had sashes across their chests that boasted they were from New Jersey, and at least one of the sashes was hanging awkwardly beside the face of a dead fox against the woman's rib cage. Others were from Connecticut. She wondered how they all knew each other, and imagined a ball. A cotillion. Had these women once upon a time been . . . debutantes?

They were wearing white dresses now—she was, too—but these were not gowns. For a moment, in her mind, she saw them in gowns. Elbow-length gloves of the sort she'd studied in the magazine drawings. The advertisements. They were being presented to their suitors, the appropriate and eligible bachelors in their tuxedoes.

Mostly, she was happy for them: they were so delighted to discover one another that they had literally shrieked when their paths had crossed in this crowd. But a small part of her pondered how much of this was but a parade for them. A social gathering as meaningful as a picnic or, yes, one of their galas. No, that was unfair. This was a parade, yes, but no woman (or man, because there were men here, too) had ventured to this arch and this park just for fun.

"Ani?"

She smiled at her friend.

"You looked like you'd seen a ghost," Catherine was saying.

She nodded in the direction of the women whose shrieks had caused her to turn. "It was them. They surprised me, that's all."

Catherine raised an eyebrow, and in the shadow cast by the bill of her straw hat, Ani could see the worry in her friend's gaze.

"Don't fret," she added, and she rested a hand and her chilled fingers on Catherine's forearm. "I'm fine."

She looked beyond the women to the arch. Someone had told her that the monument had been built in 1892. That meant that it was six years younger than she was. The marble on the south side reminded her of the marble wall of the mosque in Adana, and that instantly conjured an image of the reeking dead in the pile down that block. But this city was nothing like Adana, nothing at all. The buildings spread in all directions, and a mere twenty or so blocks from where they had gathered was that magnificent Metropolitan Life Tower, an edifice an astonishing seven hundred feet tall with a gold beacon at the pinnacle. There were elevated trains and some that ran in tunnels under the ground. There was also water: the city (at least the part where she lived and worked) was a slender island surrounded by rivers and then that harbor with its great statue of the woman with her torch. Yes, Adana had the Seyhan River, and it was beautiful, but mostly Adana had dust: it was a city built at the edge of a desert.

And, of course, the differences between then and now, between here and there, were built as well on what was nowhere to be found in New York City. There were steeples here, plenty of steeples. And there were plenty of statues, including the one of George Washington on the north side of this very arch. But there were no Armenian domes, because there were no Armenian churches. Not a single one.

"There won't be any violence," Catherine was reassuring her now, and Ani tried to focus on what her friend was saying.

"Tell me something," she said.

"Why certainly!" Catherine agreed cheerfully.

"What did William decide?" she asked. William and Catherine were going to be married in a month. He disapproved of this march, Catherine said yesterday at the school, and thought the idea of women voting was ridiculous and would lead only to greater absurdities: women wanting to be soldiers or firemen or (a particular peeve of his, apparently) baseball players. She had met William; Catherine had introduced the two of them. He was a foreman at a bakery that turned out thousands of loaves of bread each and every day. His hair was just starting to thin, and he was wide-necked and broad-shouldered: he stretched the fabric of his coats. She could see in those magnificent blue eyes of his just how dismissive he was of this whole idea. He had a big laugh, but still he frightened her a little bit. He took none of this seriously: it was all an absolute waste of everyone's time, in his opinion, and perhaps even unseemly.

"He decided the world didn't need him standing around on a street corner gawking at a bunch of women asking for things they don't need," she replied. "Which is fine. The world doesn't need him here if he isn't interested."

"Are you disappointed?"

She chuckled. "No. I think I'm relieved," she said. Then she leaned in to her and continued. "No one's going to hurt you, Ani. No one's going to hurt any of us. This is just politics. I promise. That's all. We're just marching for something we deserve."

"No. I know that," Ani agreed, and she smiled ever so slightly, though she could hear her heart thrumming in her head and wouldn't have been surprised if she'd glanced down at her hands and seen they were trembling. Because she didn't know that no one would hurt her, she didn't know that there wouldn't be violence. She didn't know that at all. Her brothers, both of them, and her father were killed because of politics. Just because of politics. She saw one of her brothers in that great, awful mound—decomposing carrion for the birds—and she saw her father's corpse as it dangled by a noose with four other men's bodies like the strands of a beaded curtain. Just politics. There had been a new government in Constantinople, and her father and her brothers believed that the new regime was going to change the laws that relegated the Armenians to second-class citizens. There was even talk that Adana's corner of the empire on the Mediterranean Sea might once again become an independent Armenian nation. She would never know precisely what triggered the massacres that nightmarish April, but by the end of the month, thirty thousand Armenians were dead and the Armenian quarter had been reduced to rubble or burned to ashes that looked, when it was over, like firepits the size of whole blocks. The

Ottoman authorities would call it an insurrection, but she knew that most of the Armenians had been unarmed. Everyone did. No one was rebelling. No one was doing more than . . .

This. Gathering.

In fact, it was dramatically less than this.

No one in Adana was asking that women be allowed to vote. No one.

In the Armenian school where she taught, the most subversive gathering they'd held was the April seventh production of *Hamlet*. The students knew Shakespeare, but the conservative Turkish officials who came to the production did not. It was clear they regarded Hamlet's uncle as some sort of stand-in for Sultan Abdul Hamid II. When the king's throat was cut onstage—the cast had used a gleaming letter opener—they actually viewed it as a political threat. A warning.

Catherine had insisted all week when they discussed it that nothing like the Adana massacre would happen here, because this was America. But Ani had done her homework; she always did her homework. Two years ago, at a march just like this in Washington, men had stormed the women to block their way, and at least a hundred of the protesters had been hospitalized. Just last year, nineteen coal miners had been killed in Colorado when they went on strike to protest their working conditions. It was but a quarter century ago that somewhere between one hundred and three hundred Sioux— perhaps half of them women and children—had been slaughtered by American soldiers at Wounded Knee.

Since the end of April this year, she had read almost daily yet another story in *The New York Times* about the butchery—race killing, some reporters were calling it, an attempt to exterminate the Armenian race—that was occurring in places in her homeland most Americans had never heard of and needed the maps the newspaper provided to pinpoint on the globe. Places like Bitlis. Erzurum. Kharpert.

Her beloved Adana.

Someone banged a pair of cymbals together and a small band—all men, in this case—began to gather. A French horn and a tuba glistened in the early afternoon sun. The men wore red-and-blue uniforms and stood out like flowers against the sea of women in white.

"This will be fun," Catherine was saying. "Besides, you should have the same rights as those men. *We* should have the same rights. We're smarter—at least you are." She was giggling when she finished.

"I understand," Ani murmured. "I do."

"Come on, then, let's find the others. They're about to start."

Two policemen on horseback were watching them. Watching all of them. Ani couldn't meet their gaze, and so she looked down at her boots. Pigeons were clamoring about her feet. Then she looked Catherine in the eye, wondering how in the name of God her friend wasn't terrified.

✺

Ani hadn't planned on marching. She had thought she might attend as a spectator: she imagined herself standing on the sidewalk somewhere on Fifth Avenue and watching the women in white and the floats and the bands as they marched north. But she would be sure to be near a corner with a cross street, so she could run if it ever became necessary. So she could flee if they started shooting.

But Catherine had talked her into it. Catherine taught history at the girls' school on Forty-Eighth Street, while Ani taught French. Without exception, the students in their classes came from the city's most prestigious families, and at least six of their mothers were going to march in the parade that coming Saturday, as well as three of the teachers—including Catherine. The mothers and the teachers would not be marching together: the mothers represented one class of society and the teachers another, and they all understood this unspoken distinction. But if Catherine was going to do this and wanted Ani to join her, then, in the end, she would. Catherine had taken Ani under her wing when they'd met at a speech in Boston soon after Ani had arrived in America in 1909.

She was also inspired by these suffragettes, because she would always associate them with the women and men in this country who cared about her people back home. Ani had cousins in Boston who had immigrated to Massachusetts soon after the Hamidian Massacres began in 1894, and they were her sponsors and took her in when she arrived. A woman named Julia Ward Howe was at the speech in Boston that night, though she was ninety years old, as was Clara Barton, who was about to turn eighty-eight. Barton had traveled to Constantinople after the Hamidian Massacres, helped to found the Friends of Armenia, and—along with Ani and her cousins—was one of the only people in the hall who'd ever set foot in the Ottoman Empire. The two old women didn't speak at the event, but their presence had inspired the other Americans who were there.

When Catherine learned that Ani spoke French as well as English, needed work, and had survived the savagery in Adana, she brought her to Manhattan and lobbied for months to get her a job at the school. Ani understood that the woman who had opened the school and her board viewed her as an exotic curiosity, but the founder also saw that she was well-mannered and pretty—if a bit darker-skinned than the headmistress might have preferred, her eyes shaped too much like almonds. And she was (in the founder's words) "a clever girl." No one was going to need her to speak Armenian or Turkish at the school, but the fact that Ani could had impressed the founder, and so she'd been given a chance and now, five years later, was still there. Her timidity, born after a massacre had sent her as a refugee into a new country on the other side of the globe, was deemed an asset by the school's board. She was well behaved and demure. Unlike some of those other young teachers—or, dear

Lord, unlike some of the students' mothers—she wasn't ever going to cause any trouble.

※

It was striking how most of the women and men and children lining the streets seemed to be dressed in dark clothing; it was such a stark contrast to the suffragettes in white. There were women who were very old walking with canes—in some cases, still moving at a pace that was brisk—and babies in prams and, walking beside their mothers, some of their own school's girls. There were women who had their dogs beside them on leashes, including a massive Great Dane with a sash that read *Leading My Lady to Vote.*

She had been marching fifteen minutes, and Catherine and the teacher who taught domestic science, a woman named Rose, nearing fifty, who was much harder on the girls than the younger faculty, were pointing at two little boys atop their fathers' shoulders who were clapping. The other women speculated that their mothers must be somewhere in the throng that stretched on forever: the group from the school was somewhere in the first quarter of the march, Ani guessed, and she presumed that there were still marchers assembling back at the park by the arch, even now. The crowds along the sidewalks were extraordinary: mostly they were cheering or smiling, rather like those two boys and their fathers. There were people watching from the windows and balconies. This was a parade. Yes, it was a parade with a purpose. But it was still just a parade. Ani was beginning to think this would all be fine. The sun was high, and the biggest problem (and it was a small one, it really was) was the havoc that the wind was causing: it swelled their skirts, it pulled at their hats, and it caused the banners to billow like sails.

It was then, however, that she heard the thud, followed by the—and here was that word—scream. A scream. She turned and saw Catherine falling to her knees and bringing her hand to her cheek. But it wasn't Catherine who had screamed: it was a woman behind them. Had there been a gunshot and she hadn't heard it over the sound of the bands and the cheering and the applause from the spectators along the sidewalk? That was her first thought. A gunshot. It was all about to begin, the violence, the slaughter.

And yet when she turned to aid Catherine, the woman was pulling her fingers from her cheek and Rose was lifting a piece of fruit off the street.

"One of those rascals threw an apple at me," Catherine was saying to Rose. She sounded more surprised than alarmed.

"I should paddle him," Rose said, and she pointed at a pair of teenage boys trying to work their way through the crowd to the escape of a side street. "You're going to have a bruise, my dear."

Ani could feel the women marching ahead, streaming beyond her and her friends as if the three of them were but rocks in a river, when she realized that Catherine was fine. It was just a scallywag, someone was saying. Just a scamp.

"Why, Ani, you're shaking," Rose said. "What's the matter?"

"Nothing," she replied. "I should have worn gloves."

"Yes, you really should have."

Catherine stopped rubbing her cheek and took the apple from Rose. A side of the apple had caved in, either from Catherine's cheekbone or from where it had bounced on the ground. She showed it to Ani and said, "It's nothing, Ani. It's silly. A couple of—"

"Rotten apples," Rose said, finishing the sentence for her. "Just a couple of rotten apples."

Catherine laughed and locked her arm through Ani's, their elbows linked *V*s. "Come," she said. "It's a parade, which means we march!"

※

Ani might have stayed in Adana after the slaughter if her mother hadn't died four weeks later. Typhus. Ani had nursed her in the ruins of their home—a mob of Turks and Kurds had set all the houses in that part of the Armenian Quarter on fire, using the kerosene the military had given them—but only half of their home had burned. The second story had collapsed, but a part of the living room remained livable, if you could endure the stink of the accelerant and the smell of the ash. Ani used the divan as her mother's bed. She took the latticework from the upstairs windows that had fallen into the rubble but hadn't been part of the conflagration, and burned it in a pit she dug in the small courtyard in the back so she could boil water for tea, but soon there was neither wood nor tea. She honestly couldn't recall anymore which had run out first. Then she had scrounged among the wreckage of her neighbors' abandoned homes, burning the legs of tables and whatever brush she could find so she could have hot water for the sponge baths she gave her mother and so they would both have clean water to drink, but soon the quarter was nothing but the sooty rubble of timbers and crumbling white brick and stone, and there was nothing left to feed the small fire.

By then the children were gone. Long gone. Her students. They were in the orphanage with the missionaries or wandering aimlessly like packs of wolves in the night, invisible during the day. They, too, were going to starve.

Her mother did die, and so Ani emerged from the house and might have walked into the desert to die, too. Didn't other animals do that? But instead, as she wandered aimlessly amid the ruins, looking for a familiar face among the living who hadn't fled, she was spotted by a small group of well-dressed women and men from Constantinople, Armenians who had journeyed to Adana specifically to assess the carnage and see how they could help—what could be done. One of them was a writer, and when the woman learned that the only family Ani had left lived in America, she paid for her passage there. The writer's parting words to Ani before she left Constantinople for Boston and the writer left for Paris? "Our people have no future here, none at all, so don't look back. It's only going to get worse." Then she embraced Ani and sent her up the sloping gangway of the ship.

※

It was when she was a block west of that magnificent Metropolitan Life Insurance Company building with its numinous tower, at Twenty-Fourth Street, that the three men barged into the parade from the park on the east side of Fifth Avenue and grabbed Catherine. It happened with such speed that the violence was almost secondary. One second, Catherine was on her right, Rose on her left, and then the men were whisking Catherine from the parade and toward the trees, and she was yelling at them to stop, to let her go. She was not wailing; Ani had heard wails. She could parse the fine distinctions between the wails of the terrified and the wails of the grieving, and this was neither. Catherine was furious, not fearful. She was indignant. And it was then that Ani realized that one of the men was William. The woman's fiancé, the bakery foreman. He and another fellow had each taken one of Catherine's arms and hoisted her off the ground as they pulled her from the parade, her feet bicycling above the earth like a toddler's, the third man walking behind them and scowling, daring any woman to follow. But William was laughing. He had been almost howling, he thought this was so funny.

"Let me go, William! Have you lost your mind?" her friend was saying, and it was the last thing Ani heard before Catherine was gone, separated from her by the marchers and the crowds. And all the while the bands played on, a horse whinnied, and the crowd continued to cheer. The spectators on the east side of the street parted for the men with their prey, some of them laughing, too, and William and his two accomplices pushed through them with his struggling fiancée. It was, to them, comical. Utterly comical. The woman's outrage was a source of merriment, the most uproarious thing they had seen today. Ani turned toward Rose, but it had happened so quickly that the older teacher hadn't even noticed: she was chatting with the woman to her left and waving to the people on the west side of the broad avenue.

"They've taken Catherine," Ani told her. "William—her fiancé."

"I know who William is," Rose chastised her, as if that were the element of her news that mattered.

"She's gone!"

"She's not gone if she's with William," the older teacher said, and now they were nearing Twenty-Fifth Street. The parade was proceeding, and it was moving on without Catherine, and no one seemed to have noticed other than Ani. No one seemed to care.

"She didn't want to go," Ani continued. "They just took her away!"

Rose thought about this a moment, and then shook her head. "That's disappointing and I expected better of him. But Catherine knew the risks. Some men are more enlightened than others."

"He's not her husband. He's only her—"

"He's going to be her husband," Rose said, cutting her off.

"But she wants to be here."

The woman beside Rose leaned over. She was tall, an English teacher at another elite girls' school, who, Ani had learned as they started to march, only graduated from college last May. "Then go get her," she said, her eyes playful and wide. "Retrieve her!"

Rose scowled at the younger woman and then at Ani, but Ani saw the logic in what this English teacher a good seven or eight years her junior had proposed. But she knew also there was a soundness to Rose's reasoning: William was going to marry Catherine. Would she herself have disobeyed her husband, had she lived in Adana long enough to marry there? Of course not. It would have been unthinkable. And even here in America, Catherine was unlikely to teach once this school year was finished, especially if she were with child.

More important, Ani knew better than most of these women around them—maybe all of them—how quickly violence could escalate. A few minutes ago, Catherine was hit with an apple; now three men had forcibly taken her from the parade. What was next? The gendarmes, the army, the guns?

As they reached the corner of Twenty-Fifth Street, in a reflex born of protectiveness—an impulse that trumped her natural inclination to lower her eyes and listen to Rose—she turned from the parade and ran southeast into Madison Square Park. Catherine had always looked out for her; now it was her turn to look out for her friend.

※

The past week, there had been another story in *The New York Times*. The headline, all capital letters, had taken Ani's breath away for a moment when she first read it on the way to the school:

MASSACRES RENEWED, MORGENTHAU REPORTS

The very last sentence of the article was even worse: "The writer says that the American Consul was told that the Turkish Government intended to exterminate the Armenians." And in between that headline and that sentence? The stories of, among others, the thirty thousand Armenian exiles dying or already dead by the train station at Merkedjle.

Thirty thousand. That was roughly how many people were supposed to be marching right now on this very avenue. A number so vast it stretched for miles. It was also the same number of Armenians massacred six years ago in the city where she grew up and expected as a child to live her whole life. (She recalled how so much of the Turkish and Kurdish mob, when they had joined the military to murder the Armenians back in Adana, had been dressed in white, too. They appeared wielding hatchets and axes and swords, with white scarves around their heads or wrapped like swaddling around their fezzes.)

Just politics? This is where "just politics" led. To the destruction of Adana, to the dead beside the railroad at Merkedjle. This was what men did. Not women—men.

She would never know whether the extermination of her people back home—the murder of her father and her brothers, the death of her mother as the city's Armenian survivors one by one succumbed to disease within the rubble that had once been their houses—was in fact born of just politics or a deeper loathing. Religion was obviously a factor, but so long as the Armenians—as well as the Assyrians and the Greeks—had stayed in their place, mostly no one cared all that much. The Armenian school where she'd been teaching almost a year when the slaughter began was at the edge of the quarter, close enough to the mosque that she'd hear the beautiful call of the muezzin during classes, and some months she would stare up at the building's magnificent minaret as she was walking home and the sun was setting.

The week before last, there had been an article in *The New York Times* that was even worse than this one. That headline?

800,000 ARMENIANS COUNTED DESTROYED

Lord Viscount Bryce, the former British ambassador to the United States, told the House of Lords that "virtually the whole nation had been wiped out," and that it had been "the deliberate and premeditated policy" of the Turkish government.

She had nearly fainted when she had read that story. She'd heard the reports. Everyone had. But a crime this hideous—a crime of this magnitude? How did one even begin to conjure the death of a nation?

She sighed. The idea of voting was an act that seemed at once so vast and so small. All the men she had met since landing in Boston could do it. If they wanted. Fifteen million men had voted in the country's presidential election three years earlier. Did any one of those votes on its own matter? It honestly wouldn't have occurred to Ani to vote if she were still living in Adana. But here? It seemed absurd to her that she couldn't. (Perhaps it would have seemed absurd to her back home, as well, since only men could vote there, too. But how could one worry about suffrage when it was proving hard enough as an Armenian woman simply to survive in 1915, as the slaughter spread like plague across an empire, as their men were shot and their children starved?)

If William could vote, shouldn't Catherine? Although their school taught only girls, the city was filled with schools in which women just like her taught boys, or girls and boys together. If she were smart enough to teach, didn't that, by logic, make her smart enough to vote?

When she had been deciding that week whether to march or to watch, as she was reading the arguments in the newspaper both for and against the idea of women voting, she'd come across one essay that suggested women should vote because they would civilize the voting process: because they were the "fairer sex," their votes might lead to the election of more civilized officials.

The writer didn't say whether he thought that America had a long history of electing uncivilized officials. And Catherine and Rose had both been annoyed by the argument that women should vote because they were gentler or kinder than men. "We should vote because we're grown-ups, pure and simple," Catherine had told Ani.

But a thought lingered in Ani's mind, like a dark plume rising up from the smoldering ruins of Adana: Men did that. Men. Not women. The endless sea of cadavers beside the railroad at Merkedjle? Men did that, too. Not women.

No, at this moment, Ani could be neither gentle nor timid. She could not be the sex that was fragile and delicate. *Fairer* was one thing; *fair* was another. Words and their nuanced distinctions were everything; they were all that she had.

If she wanted to transcend fairer and reach fair, one small step was retrieving Catherine. Telling William that what he and his friends had done was no laughing matter. It was unacceptable. If Catherine wanted to march for the vote, she should.

❖

The side of the park adjacent to Fifth Avenue was packed with spectators standing five and six and seven deep but was less congested once Ani was behind those who were there to cheer or, in some cases, to gape. Or throw apples. Nevertheless, she had to press between people milling about on the concrete walkways and the grass, already an autumnal brown, her eyes scanning the direction in which the men had been moving when they had taken her friend. She called out Catherine's name once, twice, but her voice was lost in the cacophony from the crowds and the parade—someone was tooting the horn on his automobile, someone else was banging cymbals together—and so she simply pressed forward, her neck craning as she stretched as tall as she could.

And there they were. The three men had Catherine surrounded, but they were no longer clutching her arms and carrying her as if she were a recalcitrant child. The small group was leaving the southern corner of the park, crossing the avenue there and continuing east. And so Ani hitched up her skirt and ran, pounding across the grass and then the street, catching them as they reached the far side of the avenue.

"Catherine, wait," she heard herself pleading, and the four of them stopped and turned.

"Ani," Catherine said. "It's fine." But she had been crying. Her eyes were red and her voice quavered when she said Ani's name, and with the back of her gloved hand she wiped at her nose like a child. Like one of their youngest students.

"This isn't your concern," William told Ani. His glee at what he had done had apparently been soured by Catherine's tears. "Go on now."

"Maybe it isn't my concern," she replied. "But neither is it yours."

William's friends, both stocky, probably worked with him at the bakery. Perhaps they worked for him. They looked back and forth between Ani and William, and Ani had the sense that one of them wanted to strike her, to lash out, and she recalled what it had been like to watch the gendarmes beating a pair of young mothers six years ago, and how reflexively she had tried to shield them from the rifle stocks. Her shoulder and back would be sore for weeks as she scrounged for wood and watched her mother die, because then they had beaten her, too. She had tried to use her back as a buffer as she curled into a ball, her hands a hood upon her skull, but still one of her eyes was blackened and swollen shut, and one of her fingers was broken.

"Not my concern?" William asked rhetorically. "This girl will be my wife in a month. *My* wife."

"That doesn't mean you can stop her from marching in a—"

"Who is this, Bill?" one of his friends asked, cutting her off.

"Some darkie from the Middle East who works at Catherine's school," he told him.

"Washerwoman?"

He scoffed. "If the school had any sense, yeah. But, no, she's a teacher."

"No shame in washing clothes," she told them both. This she knew for a fact. "Nor is there in baking bread."

"Ani, stop," Catherine begged. "Really, I just want William to walk me home now. That's all I want. I don't even want to go back now. Really, I don't."

"There you go," her fiancé said. "Now, be gone. Shoo. Skedaddle."

"No."

"No?" he asked. "Do you really think you can bully me into—"

"I've lost more than you'll ever have," she said, this time interrupting him. "Catherine, if you can look me in the eye and tell me that you honestly don't want to come back and rejoin the march, I'll leave. But if you want to return, speak now and we will."

The question hung there, floating milkweed, and for a moment the other schoolteacher glanced back and forth between her fiancé and her friend.

* * *

The Irish thought she was Italian and the Italians thought she was Polish and the Polish thought she was Persian. Some of her neighbors on the Lower East Side saw her on the street and wondered if her parents might have been slaves. No one, when they met her, could pronounce or spell her last name, though a few had at least heard something (though they could never recall what, precisely) about Armenians being massacred. Hadn't that nurse, that saint, Clara Barton, worried about them fifteen or twenty years ago?

Ani actually had been a washerwoman when Catherine first brought her to New York City. She'd worked in a plant that cleaned the bedding and the towels and the table linens of Manhattan's upscale hotels until Catherine had been able to convince the school's founder that Ani could replace the married French teacher when she left because she was going to have a baby.

Had her world in Adana not unraveled—no, it hadn't unraveled, it had been burned to the ground—she most likely would be married now, too. She would no longer be teaching, because she'd have a husband and children. There were men who were interested in her and whom she, in turn, fancied. There were matches that her family and theirs would have encouraged. Facilitated, in fact. She would be managing a house, and it would be a house with a servant to assist her. Would her husband have been Armen or Antranig? Both men intrigued Ani. Both died in the first hours of the rampage.

Of the two, Armen would have been more comfortable with the notion of her voting. He might even have seen the logic and reasonableness of the idea. But not Antranig. He would have thought it totally unnecessary, since women were married to men and men could vote. But he also wouldn't have stopped her if the law had changed. He wouldn't have physically prevented her from marching in a parade like this, the way William had kidnapped Catherine.

But there would never have been a parade like this in Adana. Not in Adana or Dikranagerd or Constantinople. She could count on one hand the nations today that permitted women to vote, and there was certainly no reason to believe that the Young Turks would ever allow such a thing. They had shown their true colors that spring and summer when they initiated the massacres that already dwarfed even the firestorm of Adana.

And her mother, what would she have said about a march such as this?

She would have been perplexed. But, in the end, she would have wanted her only daughter to vote. She might even have voted herself.

※

And just as her voting would not have compromised her marriage to a man such as Armen or Antranig, she liked to believe that if she ever found a man in America, he would not be the sort who would oppose her voting here. But as her eyes took in Catherine and William and the man's two coworkers or friends, the radical subversiveness of what she was doing on this corner grew painfully real. Not the marching: retrieving Catherine. It was, arguably, too subversive. Too radical. She had gone too far and may have risked digging a chasm between these two people who were betrothed. What right had she to force her friend to make this decision?

None. She had no right at all.

The fact was, whenever she had attempted to transcend her natural timidity and what may (or may not) have been the natural order of things, it hadn't ended well. She would carry inside her forever the scars from Adana: her heart was racing now. A part of her wanted to say her friend's name, this time apologizing—to her and to William—because she had overstepped her place and her right. But she couldn't. She wouldn't. She had come too far. They all had.

And in the vacuum, Catherine spoke.

"William," she said, her voice huskier than usual, a little hoarse from crying. "I know you think this is funny. I also know you don't want me here. But, please, let me do this. Let me do this anyway."

"Catherine, why?" he asked. "Why?"

"Because you love her," Ani answered quickly, speaking for her friend, hoping this was true. "And because she wants to."

"Well, there are many things I want—"

"And because you're a man, you've a better chance of grasping them," she told him.

The baker's two friends looked at her. She was responsible for this confrontation, even if now a part of her feared her presumption was going to have ramifications. Then they looked at William. He was wearing a tweed cap and he removed it and held it in his hands, staring inside it as if the solution to his soon-to-be wife's rebelliousness was right there in the lining.

"She takes such good care of me here," Ani told him. "Since I came to America. And, every day it seems, at the school. If you're worried about her safety, William, I'll be beside her." Her voice was as soft as she could make it, as she fabricated for him a reason for his behavior that he could look back on and justify. *I was worried you might get hurt, Catherine, that's all. I was worried.*

"You," he said, looking up. He smiled ever so slightly, but it was not a withering, angry smile. It was bemusement. "You'll protect her."

"Me," she said simply.

One of his accomplices glanced at him, realized that William was softening, and wanting to be on the right side of the man's opinion, said, "It's just politics, Bill. Right?"

"Politics is no place for a lady," he muttered, but it was wholly without conviction.

"Then view it as a parade," Ani offered. "Just a parade."

"You want this that badly, Catherine?" he asked her.

"I do," she said, and nodded. "Very much."

"Girls won't ever vote, Bill," his other friend reassured him. "It really is just a parade."

William returned his cap to his head. He sighed epically. "Then fine. Do what you want."

"You mean that?"

He nodded. "Where does this thing end? Remind me."

"The library. Forty-Second Street. The mayor himself—"

"I know. The mayor himself will be there. You told me. Fine. I'll be there, too. East side of the avenue so we can get out of this madness right quick."

For a moment, none of them moved. Then Catherine stood on her toes and kissed her fiancé on the cheek, before taking Ani's hand and pulling her back across the street and toward the parade.

"I almost asked him to go to the arch or the back of the line, wherever it is now, and join the men there—the men who are going to march and bring up the rear," Catherine was saying, as together they scurried west through the park.

"I think it was wise that you didn't."

"Probably, yes. Thank you, Ani."

"You're welcome."

"He is a good man, you know."

Ani did not know that, but she remained silent. She said nothing about the way he had plucked Catherine from the line and carted her off. That was mob behavior—mob mentality—and she knew where mob mentality led.

"And this is just a parade," Catherine went on.

"And this is just politics," Ani murmured, a hint of sarcasm in her voice, the intimation so slight that Ani doubted her friend caught it. But in the same way that she knew the difference between a scream and a shout, the way that words had particulars and distinctions, she paused on the word *just*.

Yes. This was indeed *just* politics. This was *righteous* politics. That was precisely why they marched.

The Last Mile

꩜

FIONA DAVIS

"WHAT A HIDEOUS HAT."

Mrs. Alva Erskine Smith Vanderbilt Belmont had been about to step off the curb and join the swarms of women in white marching along Fifth Avenue, when the man's words stopped her cold. She turned to look at him, but now he was murmuring something to his friend—she couldn't quite hear it—before they both burst into laughter.

Was he talking about *her* hat? She lightly fingered the brim. She'd bought it earlier this week, admiring the two long feathers that curved out from either side, after the mealy shopgirl told her it "framed her face." It'd been seven years since dear Oliver had passed away, and Alva hadn't been complimented, even once, since then. Something warm and small inside her had given way and she'd purchased it on the spot.

She really should have known better. Over the years, Alva had been compared to a bulldog and a frog, animals she respected for the way they stayed low to the ground, unyielding. Now, at sixty-two, Alva's nose and mouth, too small to begin with, were slowly fading into the folds of her thickening jowls. Not that it mattered anymore. She'd never been one of those pretty girls, not like her daughter, who'd been painted for posterity wearing a vapid, ethereal expression that drove Alva mad. Consuelo was like a delicate vase you wouldn't dream of putting flowers in, lest you ruin the finish, serving no useful purpose whatsoever. Alva still found it odd that such a gorgeous creature had sprung from her loins.

The cheering, the noise from the parade, the man's nasty comment—it was all too much, and a tightness gripped her chest that had nothing to do with her corset. One could never tell when a terrible illness might strike, as with Oliver, dying six days after an operation for appendicitis, his body septic and ravaged. She shouldn't proceed, not if she were about to fall dead. No, it was better to return home at once.

Alva stomped up the limestone steps to her Madison Avenue mansion, stopping midway to note that one was chipped. Was nothing done correctly anymore? They'd all be quite sorry when she died of a heart attack right here and now because she'd had to stop and examine the tread for cracks, instead of going right in and calling for the doctor.

On top of all that, the front door was ajar. She stepped inside and unpinned her hat, leaving it on the Calacatta marble side table. The feathers drooped like two broken wings. It was hideous; the shopgirl had known it and tried to trick her.

"Ma'am, you're back already?"

Marjory, one of her maids, held out her arms to take Alva's coat.

"I am. Where is everyone? Where's Mr. Riggs?" Her butler was usually stationed at the front door.

"Sorry, ma'am, but he went off to watch the parade."

"Did he, then? Taking advantage of my absence. I'll dock his pay. The front door was left open; anyone could've come in."

"I'm sorry, ma'am, I'll watch it until they return. Are you not marching, then?"

"No, I'm not marching. They look like ladies of ill repute, out there gallivanting, letting men gape and gawk, just as I'd warned. I refuse to be part of the spectacle. Besides, I'm unwell."

Marjory slid a sympathetic look onto her face, although Alva could tell it was devoid of true empathy. "Let me get you settled upstairs."

"I will settle myself. The front door needs to be watched—have I not made that clear?"

"Of course, ma'am."

It didn't matter that Alva had promised to march, that she'd assured the committee members that she would lead a group of shopgirls who didn't get off work until later in the afternoon. It was simply not feasible, not at her age. All these women, acting as if tromping up Fifth Avenue in their pretty white day dresses would make a difference. No, if you wanted to change the world, you had to do it like a man. Pay off the politicians, get militant like the English, push and not be pushed. Had all her work since joining the women's suffrage movement the year after Oliver's death been for naught? So supposedly decent ladies could display their wares like common streetwalkers while men laughed and mocked?

This was not the way to get the vote.

"And have James look at the front steps. There's a chip that must be fixed."

"Yes, ma'am."

Up on the second floor, Alva paused to catch her breath. Yes, it was certainly angina. No doubt in her mind. She hoped she could ring for the doctor before it got worse.

She was turning in to her sitting room when strange clanking noises came from down the hall, the sound of heavy metal on stone. Someone was messing about in the armory.

She considered calling for Marjory but dismissed the thought. Probably one of the maids was dusting a suit of armor too roughly. Alva imagined one of the steel arms yanked off, clattering to the marble floor, and her indignation spiked. Oliver had carefully curated the pieces over the years, and she'd created the room to honor his memory.

Opening the door, she stepped inside, and already her pulse settled. The diffuse gloom from the stained glass windows was offset by the soaring ceiling. At the far end, two coats of armor had been mounted on taxidermized horses, looking just as they had in medieval times, ready to storm a castle at her slightest command. The chain-mail suits embossed with gold work were her talismans, pieces of Oliver that remained behind after he died to protect her. As he had in life.

As rows of chairs remained in place from the Congressional Union for Woman Suffrage meeting earlier in the week, when she'd tried to convince them that they must ride into battle like Joan of Arc, heckle and mock the politicians, prove to men that the world will no longer be arranged around their comfort and ease. Put a stop to the predation. The women had murmured uneasily among themselves. Not the response she'd hoped to elicit. In the end, they'd voted to march like ninnies up Fifth Avenue, and there was nothing Alva could do to convince them otherwise.

A sniffle, like a mouse with a cold, drew her attention to the near corner. A figure huddled underneath a table displaying an array of weaponry and other artifacts.

Alva bent over, hands on her achy knees, and stared into the darkness. If this was a thief, it was a small one, probably a street urchin who wandered in during the riot of noise and nonsense from the parade.

"Step out from there at once," she said.

The mouse sniffled again.

"I said, out."

The creature, a girl, looked up at her with big eyes, but most of her body was hidden in the shadows. She blinked but didn't move. A glint of light caught Alva's eye. The child had taken hold of one of the weapons—a sword, by the looks of it.

"You're going to cut off your own finger with that. Is that what you want, blood spurting all over, ruining my floors and tapestries?

I'll make you clean it up yourself, don't think I won't. Now hand it over."

The girl still refused to move. Alva reached down and got a good grip on her arm and dragged her out. She squealed but otherwise stayed mute, slowly rising to her feet.

This was no street urchin. No more than four feet tall, the child wore a white coat trimmed with lace. In the dim light, Alva recognized the familiar purple and green sash of the suffrage movement. Her hair was the same color that her daughter, Consuelo, had had at that age, a rich chestnut that turned auburn in the sun, and she wore something clunky around her neck, some kind of box. One of those Brownie cameras that were all the rage. She didn't let go of the sword, even raised it slightly, so the tip pointed at Alva's knees. The girl had gumption.

"What are you doing in my armory, child?"

When she finally spoke, her voice was deeper than Alva had expected, not the high-pitched singsong typical of her age. "I saw the knights from the street and wanted to see what they were. I thought it was a museum."

"Did you see a sign on the front door that said *museum* anywhere? Did you?"

"No, ma'am."

"That's right, because this is my house."

The girl offered up a shrug. Her lack of amazement bothered Alva to no end. She'd chosen every finish, every piece of furniture, all the art other than Oliver's collection, and the very least this puny trespasser could do was act impressed, like the committee ladies had. Upon closer examination, Alva could see that the white lace trim of her coat was delicate, expensive. She came from a good family.

"I take it from that hue that you were part of the spectacle outside."

The girl nodded.

The thought of young children being paraded in the streets, against anyone's good sense, set Alva off once again. "I can't tell you how angry this makes me, young lady. This is simply not right." She grabbed the sword out of the girl's hand and placed it back on the display table. "Now, let's go. We'll take you home. I'm sure your parents are terribly worried. As they should be."

The girl shook her head.

"What? You don't want to go home?"

She shook her head again, her mouth in a stubborn pout.

Enough with this nonsense.

Alva indicated that the girl should follow her and led her back into the foyer. Alva's coat lay on a nearby chair, no sign of Marjory anywhere. She put it on and buttoned it up. The hat would have to do as well. Really, this day had everyone topsy-turvy, not a soul willing to attend to her. Thank goodness her driver, Richmond, was waiting outside in the Pierce-Arrow, one of the favorite automobiles of her fleet. He dashed out as soon as he saw them descending the steps and opened the door. Perhaps all was not lost.

"Take us to the police station, Richmond. We appear to have a trespasser in our midst."

She hoped the threat of the police would get the child to reveal where she lived, or at least whom she belonged to. But no luck. Once inside the car, the girl stared out the window at the sidewalks pressed with people.

"We'll have to cross the parade route to reach the police station, ma'am," Richmond answered. "Unless you want me to head north and then loop back."

She checked her timepiece. Half past six. "The parade should be over by now. Take the direct route, please."

The automobile crawled along, stymied by the volume of people in its way. The girl straightened out her sash and placed her hands on her lap, completely at home, as unmoved by the automobile's luxurious interior as she'd been in the Madison Avenue mansion. Exactly what the world needed, another child of wealth and unctuousness, although Alva had to admit she'd brought three such children into the world, with varying degrees of success.

"Do you know the meaning of the colors of your sash? Or are you as ill-informed as the rest of them?"

The girl lightly traced the colors on the fabric with her finger. "Purple is for royalty, which is in every woman's veins, no matter what her station. White is for purity of heart and purpose. Green is for hope, renewal."

"Well, you're right." Alva sniffed. "But that makes it all sound so pretty, like a garden party. I've said it before and I'll say it again: the only way to achieve suffrage is to get the votes from the politicians, by whatever means necessary. Grandstanding, bribes, shaming, blackmailing, I know every trick in the book. I'll tell you what won't work: making young girls who don't know any better walk up Fifth Avenue on a bitterly cold day."

The more she stewed over it, the more heated Alva became. Children these days were oblivious to what had come before them. This one, for example, would have a decent life handed to her on a silver platter, all because Alva's exertion on behalf of women's rights had eventually paid off. The girl would prance through the world, unaffected by isolation and cruelty.

Luckily, as long as they were stuck in this car together, Alva could take full advantage of the opportunity to straighten her out. "You appear to come from a family of means, so you probably have no idea what it's like to fight for something truly important." She waited until the girl stared up at her to continue, hoping to shock her. "I married first for money—after my father lost his fortune and my family was left practically penniless—then later, for love. Husband number one was a philanderer, and when I insisted on getting a divorce, I had to convince even my own lawyer I was serious. My settlement rocked the establishment—full custody of the children, a generous financial settlement, the house in Newport—such terms

were unheard of in those days. I showed all these ladies what it's like
to demand respect, to get their own way, just as I'm doing now—"

The girl cut her off. "You're sitting in an automobile." She
pointed outside, to where figures in white still teemed along Fifth
Avenue under the shimmering streetlamps. "When you ought to be
out there marching with them."

How dare she? The gall of this child.

The gall of this child. Exactly the phrase Alva's father had said many
times about Alva, who'd rejected the tedious life of restriction most
girls her age led, and misbehaved dreadfully, committing acts that
she would never have tolerated from her own children. Like the
time a boy pelted her with apples in a Newport orchard one summer, angry that she'd been accepted into the gang of miscreants
who liked to climb trees and spread mayhem. Alva had thrown her
attacker to the ground, choked him, and then stomped on him,
hard, until she had to be pulled off by the others. The fire that
poured through her body as she pounded on him had exhilarated
her. She'd wanted nothing more than to keep punching and kicking.
That would show them all.

That would show her father, who'd been bereft when her brother
died at thirteen. Alva had tried to comfort him, but apparently a
daughter was not worth the same as a boy. The loss of a son super-
seded the presence of a daughter, even one standing right there in
front of him, hoping to provide what solace she could. She knew
instinctively that his grief would not have been as vast if it had been
she who died.

Ever since, she'd forced people to pay attention to her, whether
in Newport or Europe or New York, which made it even sillier that,
as the girl had pointed out, Alva hadn't had the courage to set foot
in the parade.

At that moment, when Alva had reached the curb, it had been as
if an invisible blockade had prevented her from moving forward. A
visceral foreboding had enveloped her, that if she joined the parade,

she would be swallowed up by it, lost forever. All these years she'd fought so hard against being invisible, first because of her looks, now because of her advancing years, and as she'd stood frozen in place, her heart had begun to thump and she'd had to go home.

Because of a health condition, that's all it was. Not a lack of nerve. Angina ran in her family, she reminded herself. And now to be questioned by a child for her commitment to the cause?

"Let me tell you something, dearie. I get the job done, and I get it done better than anyone else. Where other women are content to decorate their fancy houses, I build them. My vision is paramount, even to the architect's, and when I'm finished, my buildings inspire awe. The highest ceilings, the largest ballrooms." The girl nodded gamely. She was a tough nut, this one. As Consuelo had been. Alva found herself desperate to impress her. "And that's not all. Where some mothers marry their daughters off to respectable but dull businessmen, I infiltrated English royalty. My daughter is now the Duchess of Marlborough, presiding over a palace in England with one hundred and eighty-seven rooms."

"I would get lost in a home so large." The girl turned away again, pressing her forehead to the window.

There was no end to the insults. Alva was about to lash into her again when the girl let out a small sigh, enough to fog up the window ever so slightly. Then a single tear worked its way down her pale cheek.

Alva sat back into the leather seat, defeated and spent. Her bitterness came from missing Oliver. That's what Consuelo had said in a fit of frustration the last time they'd seen each other, when Alva had harangued her for some trivial matter. And she'd been exactly right. No cause, no fight, could replace the kind man who'd loved Alva like none other, the only person who'd been undaunted by her rough edges. She was filled with a desperate desire not to let him down. "Tell me your name, child."

The girl wiped away the tear with her sash. "Grace."

"I'm sure your family is very worried, Grace."

"My uncle will be very angry with me."

"Why will he be angry?"

The girl took a moment to respond. "I ran into the parade, when he told my aunt I wasn't allowed to march."

At least the girl's guardian had some sense. Still, it was a bold move, to run off like that. She had reckless courage, something Alva knew something about.

Alva raised her eyebrows. "You have a mind of your own, it appears. Do you often get yourself into trouble?"

Grace broke into a mischievous grin. "Last summer, when my governess told me I wasn't allowed to swim, my friends distracted her while I thumbtacked her dress to the bench where she sat. Then we ran into the water. You should have heard her squawking when she realized she couldn't come after us."

It was the most she'd spoken all day, on a subject of which Alva wholeheartedly approved. Perhaps there was hope for future generations. "Well, that's one way to accomplish one's goals."

Grace pointed to Alva's chest. "Your pin is beautiful. It's just like my aunt's."

Alva traced the jewels of the suffrage pin with her fingertip. She'd bought the bauble from the man who made jewelry for Tiffany's, and wore it every day. "Tell me, what is the name of your uncle and aunt, and we'll take you home directly."

"There he is!"

In a flash, the girl was out the door, the rush of cold air stinging Alva's cheeks. She tried to reach out and grasp her, stop her from running into the mob, but she was too fast.

"Richmond, drive after her," she ordered.

He gestured to the crush of bodies that now surrounded the car. "There's nowhere to go."

"Oh, for goodness' sake." Alva yanked open the door and heaved herself out. Grace was nowhere to be seen, lost in a sea of white, even this late, when it should all have been over and everyone back home preparing for that evening's entertainment, whether a trip to the opera or an intimate dinner party for twenty.

Alva pushed her way through, hoping to get a better view. The sidewalks on both sides of the street were impossibly crowded with dark-clad spectators, rooted in place. The parade's participants glided between them like a river of white.

Without thinking, she stepped off the curb and was swallowed up by the marchers.

She was marching.

Her heart pounded and her breathing grew short, as if she were dying. As Oliver had.

She screamed the girl's name, but a band playing behind her drowned out her cries. The women around her were staring, concerned, as if she were a madwoman. Alva stopped yelling and glared back. How dare they? These ridiculous ladies, showing off their tiny figures in silk and chiffon, attracting all sorts of insults and derision. Alva straightened up and kept moving forward, not that she had much choice in the matter; it was like being enveloped in a stream of molasses.

They'd all be mocked in the newspapers tomorrow, Alva was certain. If they wanted to win the vote, they had to act like men, not Gibson girls.

Just as she'd done with husband number one, the Vanderbilt heir who'd had affairs right under her nose and done whatever he wished, after she'd spent years single-handedly lifting the family name up to the top of the social register, holding extravagant balls and planting fawning stories in the press, doing whatever it took to succeed.

The first Sunday after the divorce had been granted, Alva had walked into church expecting to be heralded by her peers for leading the way toward women's independence. No longer would wives have to suffer silently while their husbands' philandering ruined their good name. With her settlement, Alva would live life as she chose. Wasn't this cause to celebrate?

Apparently not. They'd literally turned their backs on her, left her seething in her pew. Then, at parties, women whom she'd once considered her friends openly snubbed her. Even now, Alva's cheeks turned red with rage at the memory. The desolation of their rejection still stung, twenty years later. Right when she'd most needed support and a kind word, she'd been ostracized, made fun of, and belittled for having threatened the social mores of the upper crust.

Ahead, a flash of auburn hair under lamplight caught Alva's eye. The girl wasn't far, only ten or fifteen feet away at best. Alva pushed through the crowd and took hold of the girl's shoulder, so bony and fragile even under her coat.

"Unhand my niece at once."

Alva looked up to see Mr. Charles Tiffany on the other side of Grace, holding her hand tightly in his. She'd met him several years ago and had ordered countless pieces of jewelry from his family's store. She'd been especially pleased to see his wife at several women's suffrage meetings, looking serious and attentive, able to hold her own during their lively discussions.

A wave of recognition passed over his face. "I'm so sorry, Mrs. Belmont, I didn't mean to be rude."

"Mr. Tiffany." She nodded at him. They were pressed closely together, the three of them, surrounded on all sides by marchers as the parade funneled to its end point at the southeast corner of Central Park. The proximity was ridiculous and embarrassing, as this entire day had been.

"Grace, where on earth have you been?" he asked of the girl. "I've been sick with worry."

"I was with her." She looked over at Alva.

Alva pursed her lips. "That is correct. Your niece was found on the premises of my home, hiding under a table."

"What?"

"I saw the knights and thought they could save me," Grace said. Mr. Tiffany screwed up his face, confused.

"I have an armory," Alva explained. "She must've seen it from the street and crept in."

"Right, my wife told me of your exhibits." The condescension in his voice was unmistakable. "Grace, you should have never run away. We must find Mrs. Tiffany and get out of here at once. My God, if the papers see me . . ."

His discomfort pleased Alva greatly, and distracted her from her own. "You're not going anywhere, Mr. Tiffany. We're trapped until we get to Fifty-Ninth Street."

He looked around wildly. "The men at my club will ridicule me—this is untenable. I do not support women's right to vote, under any circumstances. Period. Now, if we can only move over to the right, it looks clear over there."

"No, Uncle, I want to march to the very end." Grace looked up at him, frowning.

Alva blocked him with her shoulder. She didn't want him to have the last word, for the girl to think a man could bulldoze his way through a crowd or out of an argument.

"If the papers see you, Mr. Tiffany, you'll have more women buying jewels in your store in the next week than you ever imagined. We support our supporters."

He tried again, but she blocked him with her entire body this time. He wasn't going anywhere but forward.

"Please, I must get by."

"Mr. Tiffany, I'm surprised your wife hasn't schooled you properly on the basics of our cause."

"How dare you?"

"When a man brings home disease or muddies a woman's good name by his immoral actions, we must be able to support ourselves, free and clear. At the moment, we're at the mercy of mercurial politicians whose interests don't align with ours. This nonsense has been going on far too long. We must have the right to vote."

"What do you mean, 'brings home disease'?" asked Grace.

"Do not listen to this, Grace." Mr. Tiffany looked as though he were about to levitate into the air, fueled by indignation and bile. "Mrs. Belmont, you are corrupting young ears with your talk. We men are here to protect you from your own worst interests, including your outrageous statements. What if you were on the *Titanic* as it sank into the icy sea? Would you prefer that the men leap ahead of you into the lifeboats, leave you and your children to die?"

Alva answered without pause. "If a woman had designed the ship in the first place, there would have been enough lifeboats for everyone."

Mr. Tiffany sputtered and gasped, and for a moment Alva thought he might be having an attack of angina himself. Then he shook his head, a reluctant smile on his lips, conceding ground. "You have a point, Mrs. Belmont. You have a very good point."

"A woman and a man are equal." Alva spoke with candor, affected by the forced intimacy and the waves of progressive energy flowing off the women around her. "When my older brother died, I knew my father secretly wished it had been me instead, the daughter, not the son. I found that unjust, and still do."

The parade had ground to a halt, and Mr. Tiffany turned to face Alva. "My older brother also died, but as a baby. I was given his name at my birth. Perhaps we both understand what it's like to never have measured up."

Such intimacies would normally never be exchanged in the confines of polite society. Not in the parlors nor dining rooms, not over steaks at Delmonico's, nor during a carriage ride in Central Park. But today's riot of free expression had cracked the façade of that rigid world.

The parade shifted forward once again and the moment was broken.

Grace placed herself in between them, taking hold of each of their hands and humming to herself as they trod slowly forward. Alva spotted the signpost for Fifty-Eighth Street—one more block to go.

She put her free hand to her chest, feeling for a flutter, then let it fall to her side. Her heart was strong; no doubt she'd live to see another decade or two. Her fear earlier that day had arisen not from a physical ailment, but something else entirely. She feared another rejection by the women around her, that they once again wouldn't allow her in, or were only humoring her because of her vast wealth. For decades, she'd resented having to plow the way forward time and time again, and not get an ounce of gratitude for her bravery in return.

However, if she really examined it, taking the lead had been her way of keeping control of her life, ever since she was young.

If she built her own mansion, then it wouldn't crumble to the ground.

If she secured her own fortune, she'd never be beholden to another soul.

But nothing was ever certain. Oliver's sudden death had shown her that. Even within the suffrage movement, factions had broken away, as women with separate agendas formed their own committees and organizations, diffusing what little power and sway they held and infuriating Alva in the process.

Maybe she'd been wrong. Perhaps all these women, no matter which branch of the organization they supported, were part of a giant wave, one set to topple the status quo.

And maybe that was fine.

Well, as long as Alva could be the foam cresting at the very top. After all, someone had to be in charge. Still, these women weren't turning their backs on her. They were offering up smiles and encouragement, and even after having walked three miles in the cold, they locked arms, uncomplaining.

Alva wasn't invisible. She was an integral part of this moment in time, as were all the hopeful faces around her. Each woman had to find her own destiny, her own voice, her own cause. And then kick and scream until she was heard.

Ahead of them, a woman threw back her head and howled. A terrible, unseemly noise. But the sheer freedom of the gesture rippled around them, and as the sound echoed up the canyon of Fifth Avenue, other marchers joined in. Grace gave out a surprisingly loud howl, and then Alva did as well, the sound emerging from deep within her, out her throat, and up to the sky, like a banshee soaring to heaven.

They exchanged smiles. Alva unpinned the jewel from her shirtwaist, leaned down, and pinned it on Grace's sash. Grace looked up at her, her mouth in an *O*.

"Is this for me?"

"When you're old, like me, tell your granddaughter that you marched in the streets for her right to vote. Promise?"

"I promise."

"Grace!"

Mr. Tiffany, Grace, and Alva looked up to see Mrs. Katrina Tiffany waving madly from the sidewalk that bordered Central Park. Mr. Tiffany, holding tightly to Grace's hand, charged over, leaving Alva behind. Halfway across, Grace stopped and turned. She lifted her camera to her face. Alva stood perfectly still as the girl took her photograph. Then the crowds shifted between them, and the girl, her uncle, and her aunt were lost from view.

❈

A month after the great parade, Alva was settled in her parlor sifting through the numerous invitations for the holiday season when a thin package caught her eye. She sliced it open. Inside was a carefully written note from Grace thanking her for taking care of her the day of the march, along with a photograph.

It was of Alva, standing like a sentry in the middle of Fifth Avenue, her ridiculous hat looking as if it were about to take flight. The women in motion around her in the photo appeared like blurry angels, a stark contrast to Alva's defined silhouette. Alva's expression was not one of pique or displeasure—her usual mien—but that of someone she barely knew.

That of a young girl, pleased with herself for standing up for herself.

And of an old woman imagining the troubled but triumphant future ahead.

A Note from the Authors

Time to separate fact from fiction. While all the authors wrote stories true to the time and place, some used actual people and locations.

Lisa Wingate's characters are fictional, though the Reverend Octavia Rose was loosely inspired by a study of the real-life Reverend Olympia Brown, who was the first woman ordained as a minister with the official approval of a national denomination. Born in 1835, she was one of the few early-day suffragists to witness the culmination of a long-held dream. She was able to cast her vote after the Nineteenth Amendment became law.

In Steve Berry's "Deeds Not Words," the Dictograph machine did, in fact, revolutionize how conversations could be recorded. The incident on the bus with Margaret is taken from an actual court case that was reported in the newspapers of the time. The Flatiron Building exists and continues, to this day, to be an architectural marvel. The Men's League of Women's Suffrage existed and worked hard to convince other men that women deserved the right to vote. The National Association Opposed to Woman Suffrage was headquartered in New York, just not on East Thirty-Fourth Street.

In Katherine J. Chen's story, the character of Siobhán is fictional, along with the other members of Alva Vanderbilt Belmont's impressive and varied household, the exception being the larger-than-life character of Mrs. Belmont herself. The scene where immigrant workers are invited to talk at an event hosted by Mrs. Belmont is inspired by a real-life occasion co-organized by Anne Morgan (daughter of John Pierpont Morgan), which took place at the Colony Club, an exclusive women's social club on Madison Avenue.

Christina Baker Kline's story "The Runaway," about a girl slated to board a so-called orphan train who ends up instead in the women's suffrage parade, is fictional, though the trains were real. For seventy-five years, between 1854 and 1929, they carried more than 250,000 orphaned, abandoned, and runaway children from the East Coast to the Midwest in a labor program. Kline's novel *Orphan Train* is about this little-known but significant piece of American history.

In Jamie Ford's story "Boundless, We Ride," the characters Mabel Lee and Paul Soong were rivals in real life. As a student leader, Lee tirelessly pushed for co-ed education, and in 1922 became the first female PhD at Columbia University, graduating with a degree in economics. As a Chinese woman, she was still unable to vote until 1943.

In "American Womanhood" Dolen Perkins-Valdez fictionalizes Ida B. Wells-Barnett's day on October 15, 1915. Black women suffragists were conspicuously absent from the New York City parade, so this piece glimpses the work Wells-Barnett was doing in Chicago at the time. She'd founded the Alpha Suffrage Club, and its mobilization of black women voters was helping to shape municipal elections. The story also includes a flashback to the Washington, DC, parade held on March 3, 1913, in which black women suffragists were present. Parade organizers, led by Alice Paul and Lucy Burns, insisted that black women march at the back of the procession, but Ida refused. Ida's confrontation with the Illinois delegation was captured by a reporter for the *Chicago Tribune*, and this story re-creates that scene from the reporter's account.

In Alyson Richman's "A Woman in Movement," the story of Ida Sedgwick Proper, a painter who used her ties to the New York City artistic world to solicit work for *The Woman Voter*, is based on fact. Proper also organized a suffrage poster contest in New York to support the Nineteenth Amendment, with a generous fifty-dollar prize that helped draw entries from the most talented artists from around the city.

In Chris Bohjalian's story "Just Politics," the unnamed Armenian writer from Constantinople who visits Ani in Adana after the massacre is based on Zabel Yessayan. Yessayan journeyed to Adana in 1909 after the slaughter, and her book *In the Ruins* chronicles what she saw there.

The character of Alva Belmont in Fiona Davis's story was a real person. Belmont was a prominent socialite and active supporter of the suffrage movement.

Acknowledgments

The idea for *Stories from Suffragette City* was launched during a flight home from Literature Lovers' Night Out in Minneapolis, where we had both been invited to speak, so thanks to bookseller extraordinaire Pamela Klinger-Horn for bringing us together, and for everything you do to connect authors and readers.

We are so grateful to James Melia and Amy Einhorn at Holt for your early enthusiasm for the project and sage guidance. Also to Stefanie Lieberman and Dan Conaway for juggling the logistical aspects of an anthology with consummate skill and grace. Thank you to the entire team at Holt, including Maggie Richards, Declan Taintor, and Caitlin O'Shaughnessy.

To the authors whose work appears in these pages: we are so lucky to have you on board and grateful for your splendid and thoughtful contributions.

We are indebted to Meredith Bergmann, whose suffrage sculpture for New York's Central Park inspired this idea, and to historians and authors Johanna Neuman, Robert Cooney, and Antonia Petrash, whose help was invaluable.

Personally, from Fiona:

Thanks to Brian and Dilys Davis and the rest of the Davis clan, and Greg Wands for your support and love.

And from M. J.:

Thanks to all the strong women in my life who have taught by example, especially Mara Nathan. To Jordan Kulick, whose passion for our future and planet continues to give me hope. And, of course, thanks always to my family for their love, and to Doug Scofield for . . . well, for everything.

About the Authors

Steve Berry is the *New York Times* and #1 internationally bestselling author of twenty novels. His books have been translated into forty languages with over 25 million copies in fifty-one countries and consistently appear in the top echelon of *The New York Times*, *USA Today*, and indie bestseller lists. His honors include the Royden B. Davis Distinguished Author Award, the Barnes & Noble Writers for Writers Award, and the Anne Frank Human Writes Award. He is an emeritus member of the Smithsonian Libraries Advisory Board.

Chris Bohjalian is the #1 *New York Times* bestselling author of twenty-one books including *Midwives*, *The Red Lotus*, and *The Sandcastle Girls*. His work has been translated into thirty-five languages and three have become movies. He is also a playwright and screenwriter, and his novel *The Flight Attendant* is now an HBO Max limited series starring Kaley Cuoco.

Megan Chance is the nationally bestselling, critically acclaimed author of several novels. She's won over fifteen awards for her work. Her novel *Bone River* was an Amazon Book of the Month, *The Spiritualist* was chosen as one of Borders Original Voices, and *An Inconvenient Wife* was a Book Sense pick. She has been translated into more than a dozen languages.

Katherine J. Chen is the author of *Mary B*. Her work has been published in Lit Hub and *Los Angeles Review of Books*. She has a forthcoming novel on Joan of Arc (Random House).

Fiona Davis is the nationally bestselling author of historical fiction set in iconic New York City buildings, including *The Lions of Fifth Avenue*, *The Chelsea Girls*, and *The Address*. Her books have appeared on the Indie Next List, been *LibraryReads* Picks and *theSkimm* Reads Pick of the Week, and have been translated into more than a dozen languages.

Jamie Ford's debut novel, *Hotel on the Corner of Bitter and Sweet*, spent two years on the *New York Times* bestseller list and went on to win the Asian/Pacific American Award for Literature. His second book, *Songs of Willow Frost*, was also a national bestseller. His work has been translated into thirty-five languages (he's still holding out for Klingon, because that's when you know you've made it). His latest novel is *Love and Other Consolation Prizes*.

Kristin Hannah is the #1 *New York Times* bestselling author of more than twenty books including *The Nightingale*, which has been published in forty-three languages and is currently in movie production at TriStar Pictures. It was voted the best historical novel of the year by the People's Choice Awards and Goodreads. Her latest novel, *The Great Alone*, debuted at #1 on the *New York Times* bestseller list and is in development for a major motion picture at TriStar. Her novel *Firefly Lane* is in production at Netflix for a limited series.

Christina Baker Kline is the #1 *New York Times* bestselling author of seven novels including *Orphan Train*, which spent more than two years on the *New York Times* bestseller list and was published in forty countries. Hundreds of communities, schools, and universities have chosen it as a One Book, One Read selection. Her recent novel, *A Piece of the World*, an instant *New York Times* bestseller, was awarded the 2018 New England Prize for Fiction and the 2018 Maine Literary Award.

Paula McLain is the author of the *New York Times* bestselling novels *The Paris Wife*, *Circling the Sun*, and *Love and Ruin*. Her work has been published in thirty-four countries. McLain has been credited with revitalizing the historical novel through *The Paris Wife*, which has more than 1.5 million copies in print. McLain has been awarded fellowships from Yaddo, the MacDowell Colony, and the National Endowment for the Arts. She is also the author of two collections of poetry and a memoir.

Alyson Richman is the #1 international bestselling author of seven novels including *The Velvet Hours*, *The Garden of Letters*, and *The Lost Wife*, which is currently in development for a major motion picture. Her books have been translated into twenty languages and have reached the bestseller charts in several countries. Alyson has met with more than a hundred book clubs, and her novels are consistently chosen by the Jewish Book Council.

M. J. Rose is the *New York Times* and *USA Today* bestselling author of more than twenty novels including *The Book of Lost Fragrances* and *Cartier's Hope*. Her last eleven novels have all appeared on the Indie Next List. The Fox television series *Past Life* was based on M. J.'s novel *The Reincarnationist*. Her books have been translated into more than thirty languages. She is also the founder of AuthorBuzz.com and the cofounder of 1001DarkNights.com and Blue Box Press.

Dolen Perkins-Valdez is the author of the *New York Times* bestselling novel *Wench*. In 2011, she was a finalist for two NAACP Image Awards and the Hurston-Wright Legacy Award for fiction. In 2017, HarperCollins released *Wench* as one of eight Olive Titles, limited-edition modern classics that included books by Edward P. Jones, Louise Erdrich, and Zora Neale Hurston. Dolen received a DC Commission on the Arts grant for her second novel, *Balm*, which was published by HarperCollins in 2015. Dolen is a 2020 nominee for a United States Artists Fellowship. Dolen serves on the board of the PEN/Faulkner Foundation. She is currently an associate professor in the Literature Department at American University.

Lisa Wingate is the *New York Times* bestselling author of more than thirty books including *Before We Were Yours*, her most recent, which has been on the *New York Times* bestseller list for two years and counting. She's the recipient of the 2018 SIBA Southern Book Prize, the 2017 Goodreads Choice Award for Historical Fiction, the LORIES Best Fiction Award, the Carol Award, the Christy Award, and the RT Booklover's Reviewers' Choice Award. *Before We Were Yours* was a 2018 National Book Festival selection.